Would you like

Go to my Author Website (below) to download your FREE copy of *Skins Game, and other short fiction*

A baker's dozen of Phil Truman's short stories in a range of genres from humor to horror. Guaranteed to deliver a laugh and make you shed a tear.

A no-obligation, absolutely FREE offer.

http://www.philtrumanink.com

In the last years of the tough and woolly land called Indian Territory, and the first of the new state of Oklahoma, the outlaw Henry Starr rides roughshod through the midst of it. A native son of "The Nations" he's more Scotch-Irish than Cherokee, but is scorned by both. He never really wanted to journey west of the law, yet fate seems to insist. He's falsely accused and arrested for horse-thieving at age sixteen, then sentenced to hang at nineteen by Judge Isaac Parker for the dubious killing of a deputy U.S. marshal, but he escapes the gallows on a technicality. Given that opportunity, the charming, handsome, mild-mannered Henry Starr spends the rest of his life becoming the most prolific bank robber the West has ever known.

"Author Phil Truman captured a slice of Indian Territory history and has woven it into an interesting period novel. Anyone who loves the history of the West will enjoy *Red Lands Outlaw: the Ballad of Henry Starr*." -- Tammy Hinton, author and winner of the Will Rogers Medallion Award for *Unbridled*

"*Red Lands Outlaw: The Ballad of Henry Starr* is a well-conceived yarn about one of the last of Oklahoma's horseback-riding outlaws. A good read." -- Dusty Richards, a Spur and Wrangler Award winning author

Red Lands Outlaw
The Ballad of Henry Starr

Phil Truman

PTI

Publishing

PTI Publishing
Broken Arrow, OK 74012

Visit the author's website and blog at:
http://philtrumanink.com/
http://philtruman.blogspot.com/

Author's Note

This book is largely a work of fiction. It's termed a historical novel, because it's set in the turn of the 20th Century land known as the Indian Territory and young state of Oklahoma. Henry Starr actually lived and breathed as a son of those places and times. He was a Cherokee, a cowboy, a fugitive, a lover, a husband, a father, a movie star, a thief, and a notorious outlaw. Most of the events in this story happened on a macro level—the armed robberies, the wanderings, the prison stays, the movie-making, some of the relationships. All the details in between, and many of the characters—or, at least, their conversations—I made up. For example, I don't know if Henry ever met and dined in the Star House with the great Comanche leader Quanah Parker, but it's not out of the realm of possibilities. They were contemporaries in the same land, and it suited my theme to have them encounter one another and interact. And respected non-fiction writing historians corroborate that the famous lawman Bill Tilghman had dealings with our hero. He also made a silent movie about some of the law-breakers with whom he dealt. So there you go.

I felt, and still do feel, Henry Starr was kind of a poetic figure, a tragi-comedic man, stranded between two worlds and left there as an anachronism.

Phil Truman
March, 2012

To my brothers and sisters, in the order of their appearance:
Patricia Joyce, Donald Lavelle, Gary Duane, Lynn Michele

Chapter One

Late Winter, 1915
Northeastern Oklahoma

As usual, Henry didn't have a clue; only a bold idea.

"Now . . . why you wanting to do this, Henry?" Lige Higgins asked him.

"Because it ain't never been done, Lige."

"Way I hear it, it has," Bud Maxfield said. He paused to lean leftward, spit out a stream of tobacco juice toward a spittoon nestled in the saloon floor sawdust. Wiped his lips with the back of his hand, then passed that residue onto the right leg of his jeans before continuing. "Old Bob Dalton and his boys tried it up in Coffeyville back in '92, only it didn't work out so well for them."

"How's that?" Lige asked. He looked anxiously to Bud, then Henry. Twenty-year-old Lige's birth had come three years past 1892.

"Him and two of his brothers and a couple others got shot through the head," Bud said. "Town knew what they was gonna do, and ambushed 'em before they could get out." He leaned left, and punctuated the end of his story with another brown spit.

"Like I say," Henry said. He paused to reach forward, scooping in the two cards he had asked the dealer to send his way. He held a pair of eights with the ace of spades kicker, and when he inserted the drawn cards into the middle of the others splayed in his hand, he saw he had gotten the ace of clubs and the jack of hearts. That gave him two pair, aces and eights, all black . . . dead man's hand. Henry raised his right eyebrow slightly, and then finished his sentence to Lige Higgins and the rest of the group gathered around the table. "It ain't been done."

"Still, it don't make no sense to me." Higgins persisted, "Why you want to rob two banks at the same time, Henry?"

Henry sighed, and grabbed a blue chip from his stash "Because that's where they keep the money, Lige." Henry tossed the chip onto the pot.

"Bet a dollar," he said.

* * *

The gang of men rode up to a stream two miles east of town, and stopped to let the horses drink. Henry stood in his stirrups and looked around. He knew the spot, because he'd located it back in February when he first came to Stroud to check out the banks. "Let's camp here," he said to the group.

The swarming sky had a gun barrel color, and a thick, cold wind sliced forcefully out of the northwest cutting through their clothing like a blade of ice, and trying to yank their hats from their heads. Lige Higgins wasn't happy about their situation. He didn't much like camping out in the cold, and Henry hadn't convinced him a simultaneous double bank hold-up was such a good idea.

Henry and Lewis Estes rode off early the next morning to check things out one final time. Henry had already cased the banks several months back, but said he wanted to make sure no added lawmen had showed up. As they rode, Henry got a germ of an idea. He thought it'd be sorta funny if he stopped by the post office there in Stroud to mail postcards to the banks letting them know in advance they were going to be robbed. He decided it was a good idea, but they probably wouldn't be delivered in time. It was typical of Henry Starr—more audacity than good sense.

* * *

When Henry Starr's gang arrived at the Stroud stockyards, Bud Maxfield stayed with the horses, as planned, while the rest split into two groups, and walked to their respective target banks a couple blocks away. Bud was the oldest member of the gang, an odd choice for lookout. He could not see nor hear all that well. On the other hand, Henry had thought Old Bud might be more of a liability if a shootout should occur. It was six of one and half a dozen of the other.

Starr led one group; Lewis Estes, the other. Once they reached their objectives on Main Street, a block apart, Starr signaled Estes and the others. They all entered the banks at the same time.

Inside the Stroud State Bank, Starr pulled a scatter gun from under his long coat, leveled it to a spot between the one teller on duty, a customer at that window, and a wool-suited rotund fellow sitting at a desk to his left, behind a waist-high oak railing. Henry said in a calm voice, "This here's a hold-up. I'd be obliged if you'd hand over your cash drawer to my friends here, and open that safe."

The teller took a step back and put his hands above his head. The bank customer did the same, backing toward the side wall of the lobby. The man at the desk stood up halfway, raising both his hands, too. Lige Higgins and Claude Sawyer, Starr's two cohorts, stood apart on either side of Henry, their pistols drawn.

"Come on, now," Henry said, waving his shotgun back and forth between the teller and the bank officer; he spoke without animosity to any of the three fear-frozen men. "Just do as I say, and won't nobody get hurt here."

"I'm Henry Starr," he added, as if having his victims know this would reassure and calm them. In all his robberies, he had never shot anybody.

The teller moved to his drawer and quickly started emptying cash into the bag Lige Higgins held open through the window. Henry swung the barrel of the shotgun from the suited man to the safe door in a motion to indicate the banker should open it.

The bank officer, sweat appearing on his bald head, started to speak, hesitated, then tried again. "Uh, I'm afraid I can't open the safe, Mister Starr."

"Beg pardon?" Henry asked with some irritation in his voice.

"It's time-locked. I can't open it 'til this afternoon at closing time," the man explained.

Henry stared hard at the man for several seconds, sighed before he spoke again. "What's your name, mister?" he asked.

"It's Patrick, Samuel Patrick," the man responded still holding his hands above his head. "I'm, uh, the vice president of this bank."

"Well, Sam, let me tell you something. I ain't never shot a man during all my bank robbering, but there's always a first time. So, unless you want your widow to read in tomorrow's paper about your head being blowed off, I suggest you get on to opening that safe." Henry cocked one of the hammers back on his shotgun, pointed it at the man's jaw, and smiled at him.

Patrick paled and dropped his hands onto his desktop. "Mister Starr, believe me I don't want to die, but there ain't nothing I can do. That safe and its time lock are designed for . . . situations just like this. We open it first thing in the morning to get out our operating cash, and then again at the end of the day to put everything away. There's just no way I can get around it . . . until four this afternoon."

"Stupid banker's hours," Clyde Sawyer offered.

Henry rubbed his chin with his left hand. He looked over at the safe door, then back at Patrick. Still keeping the shotgun trained on the banker, he walked over to the safe door and looked it over, squinting at the time mechanisms protruding from it. He tried the handle and pulled on it to no avail. "Well, hell," he said.

"How much cash you got in that bag, Lige?" Henry asked.

Higgins looked inside the bag. "It ain't all that much, Henry. No more 'n 'bout five 'r six hunnert I'd say."

Henry turned again to Patrick and pointed the cocked shotgun at the banker's chin. "Is there more 'operating cash' out here somewheres?"

"You got all the bills. There's some coins sacked up under the counter," the teller said.

"Pull 'em out," Henry ordered.

The teller did as told, placing two bags onto the counter with a heavy clunk, then did the same with two more bags. Lige tied two of the bags together and slung them over his shoulder. Henry grabbed the other two with his free hand, but one slipped out of his grip and crashed to the floor, splitting open and spilling its contents of quarters.

"Well, hell," Henry said. He tossed the other bag to Sawyer.

The bank door creaked open causing Lige and Sawyer to swing their pistols in that direction. A small girl in a bonnet and a wool coat walked in. She looked over the scene but didn't say anything.

"Get that door," Henry said with some vexation. Sawyer leapt over and slammed it behind the girl causing her to jump and move further into the bank. Her eyes spread wide with surprise and alarm. She appeared to be about eight or nine.

"Why'd you come in here?" Starr asked her in a gruff voice.

The girl looked frightened, tears forming in her eyes. Startled at his tone, she said with a sniff, "Looking for my daddy."

"Is one of these men your daddy?" Henry asked. He softened his voice a bit.

The girl shook her head negatively, then started sucking in air for sobs.

Henry walked over and knelt in front of her. "Now hold on, darlin'," he said in as kindly a voice as he could. "There ain't no need to cry. Ain't nobody going to hurt you. What's your name?"

"Lorrie," she said with a quiver in her voice. She sniffed again, but didn't stop her crying.

"Well, look here, Lorrie. Me and these other men are going to leave by that side door over there. Now what I'd like for you to do is sit right here in this chair," he guided her to a captain's chair against the far wall. "You can do that, can't you, Lorrie?"

The girl nodded, her crying then reduced to just sniffling.

"That's a good girl. Now I want you to stay sitting right here until your daddy comes to get you. Okay? Don't go outside, no matter what you hear. Can you do that for me, Lorrie?"

The girl looked up at Henry and gave him a small nod, brushing her tears away with the back of her hand. Henry smiled warmly at her and patted her on the shoulder. Then he turned to the others.

"Sawyer, you and Lige hang on to them bags of money. Let's go out that alley door with these fellas in front of us in case there's anybody waiting."

They all moved to the door, the robbers behind the other three men, their guns stuck to their hostages' backs. Just before Henry exited the door, as the last to leave the bank, he said to the others, "Hold on, a minute."

He went back to where the bag of quarters had spilled onto the floor, stooped to gather up a handful of coins. He walked over to where little Lorrie still sat obediently.

"Hold out your hands, Lorrie," he said. When she complied he dropped the quarters into them. "Tell your daddy you met Henry Starr today. Tell him I wanted you to have these."

Lorrie looked at the quarters overflowing her held-together palms, then up at Henry. She smiled, nodded, and sniffed.

Henry rejoined the group waiting outside the side door of the bank. "Let's move on out to the street so's Estes can see us," he said, and the group pushed the trio of hostages before them. Once there, Henry waved his free hand above his head in a pre-arranged signal, and shortly thereafter the other group emerged from the First National Bank with their own collection of captives. Both groups started heading back to where old Bud Maxfield waited with their horses at the stock pens.

Shouts arose on the street as citizens began to recognize what was going on. A gun shot popped some fifty yards to the Starr group's left front, and a wad of mud exploded from the street a yard in front of banker Patrick's feet. Another shot sounded to their right, the bullet piercing one of the bags of coins Lige had slung over his shoulder. Dimes began streaming from it like a cascading flow of water. Claude Sawyer and Lige fired their pistols in the general direction of the incoming rounds. Another gunshot exploded somewhere behind them, the bullet almost immediately snapping over their heads. The hostage who'd been the bank customer bolted from the group, running flat out toward the store front to his right.

"Hey!" Sawyer yelled, and fired a shot into the air. "Get back here!"

The man didn't even slow down, crashing through the store's door and disappearing from sight. Sawyer moved next to Lige to share the latter's bank teller shield.

Henry, using Mr. Patrick as his screen, turned in circles to discourage the increasing gunfire coming in around him. Sawyer and Lige began to fire indiscriminately up and down the street, as did those in Estes's group as they made their way closer to their horses.

To Henry's front came a boom, and a big chunk of wood blew away in splinters from a corner post on a building just in front of Henry and his hostage. Starr spun himself and Mr. Patrick toward the sound. A man wearing a vested suit and derby hat, carrying a double-barreled shotgun, stood at the corner of a building thirty yards ahead. Starr caught a glimpse of a tin badge pinned on the man's vest. Henry pushed Patrick aside, knocking him down, and said, "Look out, Sam, I believe that man means to shoot us." Patrick took that as his cue and scurried away on all fours.

The lawman raised the shotgun again and pulled a trigger, but the hammer only clicked against the firing pad. Henry aimed his Peacemaker at the man and fired back. The bullet zinged across the man's wool vest, leaving a six-inch smoking track there, continuing on to blow a quarter sized hole through the back of his coat. The lawman leapt back behind the building. Henry threw his head back and whooped. By that time Lige, Sawyer, and the bank teller had advanced to the corner leading to the stock yard, and their getaway, well ahead of Henry.

Across the street to Henry's left, and slightly behind him, a rifle shot cracked and almost simultaneously a blow, something like a mule kick, hit him in the butt and sent him sprawling sideways. On the ground, Starr found himself stunned and unable to move his legs. He tried to rise at the waist to fire back at his assailant, but when he looked up, a tall skinny adolescent stood over him pointing a short barrel .22 rifle at his nose.

"Drop that pistol, mister!" the kid said to him.

Henry started to bring his pistol around to bear, but stopped. He held it pointed at the sky three feet to the boy's left. He looked quizzically at the teen and said, "Why, hell, you're just a boy."

"That don't mean I won't shoot your ass," the kid said.

Henry grinned, laughed, then winced. "Hell, son," he said. "I believe you already done that. 'Sides, that ain't where you got that hog-shooter pointed."

"I said drop it!" the kid repeated.

Henry threw his pistol away and let his head fall back onto the street. "I believe you've crippled me, boy. I can't get up."

Still keeping the rifle pointed at Henry, the boy moved over to where the pistol lay, and picked it up. He stuck it in his pant waist and headed for the stockyards. By the time he came around the back corner of the land office building, all the outlaws had mounted and started to ride off, except for one. The rider, leading another horse by the reins, came straight to where the boy stood, apparently heading back to Main Street to get his fallen comrade. The boy raised the short-barreled rifle and fired.

The bullet hit Estes in the left collarbone and ricocheted into his neck. The impact flung him backwards almost unseating him, but he recovered. He swung his horse about and spurred him away, dropping the reins of the other horse. Estes had ridden out of sight by the time the boy had opened the rifle's bolt and put in another round.

Back on the street, a small crowd had started to gather around Henry. He still lay in the street, seemingly holding court with the curious mob.

Sam Patrick and his teller returned to their bank a good hour or so after Henry Starr and his gang had first entered the door. They found little Lorrie Hughes still sitting dutifully in the chair Henry had assigned her; however, the dozen or so quarters the outlaw had given her no longer remained in her hands. She'd deposited those well down into the pockets of her coat.

Chapter Two

Bill Tilghman brushed the whisker tips of his mustache over and over with his left thumb and forefinger, moving each from the middle of his upper lip outward, as he stared down at Henry. In all his lawman days, he'd never known so audacious, so brash, so prolific an outlaw as the man lying there in that bed.

Henry floated in and out of a morphine-induced haze while Tilghman stood there looking at him. Lewis Estes, his neck and shoulder and chest wrapped in bandages, in a bed across the room, lay there out cold.

"Henry," Tilghman said in a firm voice. Getting no response, he called out the bank robber's name again, a little louder.

Henry's eyes fluttered open. He blinked several times, squinting to get his eyes and mind focused on the form standing beside his bed.

"Well, hello, Bill," Henry slurred. "What the hell're you doing here?"

Tilghman stopped stroking his mustache, and hooked both his thumbs in his vest's watch pockets. "Come to arrest you, Henry." He turned his head to his right, looked at the other bed. "You and that other fella over there."

Henry raised his head a little, and looked over at the bed where his patched-up colleague lay. "I believe that there is Lewis Estes," he said. "Guess he caught a little lead, too."

Tilghman nodded. "Soon as you boys are able to travel, I'm taking you back to Oklahoma City to await trial. And it's a good thing I come, too. Folks here are callin' to lynch you."

"Why, hell, Bill, I'm crippled," Henry responded.

"Yeah, you are that," Tilghman said. "But Doc Hanson said he didn't think it'd be permanent. Boy named Curry shot you in the butt. Bullet broke up your leg bone there, but the doc got the slug out, set the bone back as best he could. He thinks it'll heal awright, but figures you'll probably have something of a limp from here on out."

Henry took Tilghman's prognosis in with a solemn expression. "First time I ever been shot," he said. "And by a damn kid to boot."

"He's used to shooting living things," said Tilghman. "Butcher's kid, I hear. Shot your partner over there, too. Some pretty fair shootin', considerin' what he had to shoot with."

Henry considered all this, scrunching his eyebrows in a look of puzzlement. "I thought you'd quit marshalling, Bill. Ain't you a politician, or something, now?"

"State senator," Tilghman said. "But I'm also Chief of Police over in Oklahoma City. Town marshal here is an old friend of mine, so he called me. What you and your boys did was a federal crime, so you'll have to stand trial in a federal court."

Henry nodded. "Yeah, I reckon so," he said.

Tilghman snorted and shook his head. "I swear, Henry. You just about beat anything I ever seen in an outlaw."

"Why, thank ya, Bill." A pleased smile creased Starr's face. Coming from as renowned a lawman as Bill Tilghman, Henry considered the man's comment a supreme compliment.

"I didn't mean that as a tribute, Henry. I meant you've had several chances to straighten yourself out. When I arrested you down in New Mexico back in oh-eight, you promised me you'd never rob another bank. But in the year since you got out of Canon City Prison, there's been a whole passel here in Oklahoma with your brand on 'em. And now you pull this double dutch." Tilghman shook his head and laughed quietly. "I hear you were a model prisoner in Canon City. Warden even made you a trustee; sent you out as a walkin' boss on the road gangs. But you just keep reverting back to your old ways. How many times have you been in prison? Two? Three times? This here'll make one more."

Henry stiffened a little. "I reckon I've robbed more banks than ever anyone did," he said with pride.

"Yeah, I suppose that's true," Tilghman said. He pulled a chair out from the wall and sat down on it, crossing his legs. He removed his derby and wiped the sweat from the inside headband. "The question is why? You sure ain't got nothing to show from it. And look at you now; your future prospects ain't too bright."

Henry stared back at Tilghman, but he didn't have a good response. The lawman had pretty much nailed it. A reason existed as to why Henry kept on committing bank robbery after bank robbery, but he didn't exactly know what it was, didn't know how to express it. All he knew, he couldn't stop doing it. He had quite a few acquaintances and relatives who drank alcohol, and the more they drank, the more they wanted. Finally, they just couldn't do without it. Henry didn't drink; didn't smoke, either, but like the effect of alcohol on some of his red brothers, that's exactly what bank robbing had done to him.

Setting his hat on the foot of Henry's bed, Tilghman fetched a short thin cigar from the breast pocket of his suit coat, lit it up. "If you took a hard look at it, Henry, I 'spect you'd see it wasn't so much the money you want as the act of robbing itself."

The lawman blew a cloud of blue smoke toward the ceiling. "How long you been outlawin' now?" he asked.

Henry tried to shift his position, but the pain in his hip and leg stopped him. "Hell, I don't know, Bill. A few years now." Since he'd decided to make outlawing his career back in '92, Henry thought he'd done about two dozen armed robberies, mostly banks, since then. "I'd be obliged," Henry said. "It you'd call in the doc to give me some more of that painkiller."

"Why, sure, Henry. I'll do that," Tilghman said as he casually flicked the cigar ash onto the floor. "But I was just curious as to how much you got away with. According to what I know, it ain't been all that much."

With the exception of that bank in Bentonville, Arkansas, Henry and those with him never netted more than about $2,500, and usually less than a thousand. Once he'd gotten no more than $180.

"I think I done awright," Henry said. He knew Tilghman was trying to get him to admit to his recent activity. Why in the past five months alone he, and the bunch that attended Henry's robberies, had accounted for fourteen holdups, two in one day back in October, and five alone that past January. And now, even though he and Estes didn't make it out, his gang had pulled off the never-before-accomplished double bank hold-up; something even the Dalton Gang hadn't been able to pull off. The fact that most of Henry's outfit made off with the money, made it so. By any standard, the quantity, if not the quality, made for a remarkable record, which most newspapers in the Indian Territory, and now the young state of Oklahoma, had reported with relish. Several speculated that the members of the Henry Starr Gang were the culprits, basing their conjecture on other reports where witnesses told of Henry announcing himself before he robbed them.

During the latter part of the Nineteenth Century, the northeastern and eastern parts of the Indian Territory—more or less governed by the semi-sovereign Cherokee and Choctaw tribes—were conducive to outlawry. Men, and on occasion a few women, could range into the neighboring states, commit crimes, and retreat back into The Nations without much fear of reprisal. Judge Isaac Parker, the federal judge in Fort Smith, Arkansas, whose jurisdiction included the Indian Territory, would often send U.S. Marshals, themselves not much more than common thugs, into the woolly land to chase down felons. But the tribes, with their own governing bodies, courts, and police forces, seemed reluctant to allow any extradition, and usually refused at the point of a gun. That was especially so if the party or parties in question had Indian lineage.

This became the land into which Henry Starr was born, some three-eighths Cherokee, in 1873. At the age of eighteen, he had his second run-in with the law, and his first meeting with Judge Parker on trumped-up charges of horse-thieving. Despite his innocence, he never made that court date, but instead jumped bail and decided to dedicate his life to crime, specializing in robbing banks.

Henry was a good looking man, dark and handsome. Despite his native blood being less than half, he "showed his Indin," as they said, and considered himself totally Cherokee. He also had a good wit with a fair amount of charm. Kind to women, children, and dogs, people mostly liked him, even some of the jailers and lawmen he'd come to know over the years. The famous Bill Tilghman being one of those.

Henry tried to start out his life on a lawful track. In his early teen years he thought he'd become a rancher, marry his sweetheart, and live out a normal life in the Cherokee Nation part of the I.T. But fate, bigotry, and politics conspired against him.

When Henry was sixteen, the long-running blood feud between two Cherokee political factions crossed his path, a path upon which some of Henry's ancestors had played a prominent role.

A rift existed in the Cherokee Nation dating back to the signing of the Treaty of New Echota in 1835. The treaty involved the cession of sovereign Cherokee land—then in the young American south—to the United States government, and the subsequent removal of the Cherokee people west into the Indian Territory. The split in the nation came between those who'd signed the treaty, led by John Ridge, and those who strongly opposed it, led by John Ross. Each side, the Ridge men and the Ross men, hated the other, and spent much time killing one another. Henry's grandfather, Tom Starr, created so much havoc in his vendetta against Ross men, for the killing of his own father during this tribal civil war, that it became known as the Tom Starr War.

Many legends arose about Tom. One says he killed a hundred men. Another says he once rode more than a hundred miles to kill one of his father's murderers. Hardly a Cherokee family remained untouched by Tom Starr's bloody retribution. And the family name Starr, in the generations that followed, became greatly feared and hated within the two largest tribes in the eastern Indian Territory—the Cherokee and the Choctaw.

Henry's course toward law-breaking began with a frame-up. One day the sixteen-year-old ranch hand was stopped on the road by two tribal marshals. He was on a return trip into town where he'd been sent with a wagon to get supplies. Henry knew the men, although he didn't much like them. They were both Ross men—Ben Turtle and Stand Whitehawk.

The big one, Whitehawk, held a rifle with its butt resting on his right thigh, the barrel pointed skyward. He came right to the point. "We was told you got some whiskey on your wagon, Starr."

"This here's Mister Roberts's wagon," Henry said. "I's in Nowata getting some supplies for him. Ain't no whiskey in it."

"Uh-huh," Whitehawk responded. "Well, I 'spect we oughta take a look."

Deputy Turtle had already dismounted and gone to the wagon. He pulled back a corner of a tarp at the front of the wagon bed revealing a small keg of whiskey. Turtle held it up.

"Ain't no law agin bein' a liar, Starr, but it looks like we got ya on haulin' spirits," Whitehawk said, grinning.

"I didn't know that was there," Henry said, rising from the wagon seat. "I told you, this is a borrowed wagon."

"Well, alls I know is you're travelin' down a territory road with whiskey, and we got to bring you in for that. 'Sides, Roberts is a teetotaler, so I doubt you can lay it on him." Whitehawk lowered his rifle barrel resting it on his left forearm, the muzzle pointing at Henry's chest. "You can sort out what you know and don't know with Judge Glory over in Muskogee. You bein' a Starr and all, I reckon he'll go easy on ya." Deputy Turtle laughed loudly, and Deputy Whitehawk joined him.

The judge Henry would be hauled before at the Whiskey Court in Muskogee was Joshua Glory, the son of Ethan Glory, one of the men Henry's grandfather, Tom, is said to have killed.

Although he maintained his innocence, Henry got a little jail time and was fined one hundred dollars. Still, it was a message of things to come for the sixteen-year-old grandson of Tom Starr.

Not two months later Henry got accused of horse-thieving. It turned out to be a misunderstanding; a curious misunderstanding between Henry and a prominent rancher, who just so happened to be a Ross man. Henry was arraigned in Judge Parker's court and bound over for trial, but the judge had a rare soft spot for the teenager and let him out on bail. Henry's cousin

Kale Starr, a well-respected landowner who promised Parker he'd return the boy for trial, posted his bail, but Henry ran off and hid, failing to appear.

Judge Parker sent two deputy U.S. Marshals into the Territory to bring the boy back to Fort Smith. The deputies found nineteen-year-old Henry on a road outside the settlement of Lenapah, and one of the marshals, Floyd Wilson, tried to shoot him. Unfortunately for Wilson, he missed. A deadeye shooter, Henry shot back and sent a .45 slug through Wilson's heart.

Henry knew Wilson by reputation, as did most in the Nations. He was a vicious and cruel man, who'd killed two Cherokees in cold blood, one a thirteen-year-old boy. But he'd been acquitted of those murders by an all-white jury in Fort Smith. There'd been another time when he'd brutally raped and beaten a Choctaw woman, but no charges were ever brought against him, despite eye witnesses. No being in heaven or on earth, white or red, was sorry to see Floyd Wilson shot dead, but when an Indian killed a white man in 1892, no matter how despicable the victim, and even in self-defense, it was still considered a crime.

Wilson was the first man Henry had shot and killed, and as it would turn out the only one ever, but it cemented his life in crime. Henry decided that if everybody around him wanted him to be an outlaw, then, by God, that's what he'd be. He sealed that bargain with the Devil by shortly thereafter robbing a train depot in Nowata, and the general stores in two other towns.

Less than a year after his killing of Deputy Wilson, Henry got into a running gun battle with some Indian police in the town of Bartlesville. They'd gone after Henry mainly because he was a Starr. His recent robberies had only given the Ross men a legitimate excuse to chase him down and kill him, like the son of a dog they considered him. It didn't much matter to them that Henry was wanted for killing a white man, even the vile Floyd Wilson; but they'd take the reward for bringing him in, just the same. He escaped their treachery, though, and robbed his way south into more politically-friendly territory.

Henry didn't discriminate between his red brothers and white men, though. He distrusted them both with equal and balanced enmity.

Chapter Three

Spring, 1893
Indian Territory

Henry didn't quite know what to make of the boy. He stood there in the street strapped with six-shooters, his brown leather hat thrown back onto his shoulder blades, held there by its drawstring around his neck. He wore a faded blue cotton shirt and well-worn jeans tucked into plain cowhide boots, but he didn't appear to be a farm or cow hand. His stance, the tight leather gloves he wore, and his surly attitude made him look like a range tough, a gunslinger wanabe. Henry himself was only nineteen, but he judged this youth to be no more than about fourteen or fifteen. He had a boy's face, pocked with pimples, and no whiskers. He was a white kid, and a fair-haired one at that. The late afternoon sun almost gleamed off his thin blond hair, and he stared back at Henry with a look of insolence.

The boy had called out to Henry as he and Frank started up the wooden steps leading to the general store. "Henry Starr?" he'd yelled from twenty feet away. That annoyed Henry because he and Frank were going to rob the store they were about to enter, and it drew attention to him. The name Henry Starr had gained some notoriety in that part of the country, especially amongst the mercantile, several of whom had recently been robbed by him and his partner Frank.

Henry stood with one foot on the top step looking back at the youth. On the one hand he was pleased that the kid knew who he was; on the other, calling out his name on the town street of Inola at that particular moment was downright inconvenient and annoying. From the looks of it, the boy appeared to be calling him out for a gunfight, but Henry couldn't be sure. He turned on the steps and walked back the twenty feet between him and the adolescent. Henry didn't know if the kid would draw on him or not, but his irritation prevented him from figuring the risk.

When he stood two feet from the boy, he looked him in the eye and asked him, "How'd you know my name?"

Although three inches shorter than Henry, the lad didn't appear intimidated.

"Didn't really," the youngster said with a smirk. "I's looking for a Indin about your description, and when I saw you making for that store, I thought I'd ask. A Indin named Henry Starr is said to be fond of robbing stores in these parts."

Henry placed his right hand on the butt of his holstered pistol. His partner, standing to one side of the boy, did the same. "You after the reward money, son. Is that it?"

"Aw, hell no," said the boy, still smirking. "Can't make no money on rewards. I want to join up with you."

Henry relaxed his hold on his pistol grip. "You picked a heluva time to come looking for a job. What makes you think I'm hiring?"

The lad shrugged, then spit to the side. He looked coolly over at Frank. "Sooner or later you're going to need more help. Figured you could use someone good with a gun."

Henry looked at Frank and they both laughed. The boy lost his smirk and got steely-eyed. "How old are you, son?" Henry asked.

"Don't see that it matters," he said. He looked back and forth from Henry to Frank. His expression had quickly become cold; his eyes danced with fury. "You want to try me?"

Henry looked at the ground and let out another small laugh. He leaned in closer to the boy and spoke to him in a lower voice. "Look, kid, we ain't looking for a fight. We got a job to do right now. It's kind of a small job, but it's only because we need to outfit ourselves for something bigger . . . Tell you what, you want to join us on this job, I'll give you a try. If I like what I see we'll consider letting you join up with us."

The boy nodded.

"What's your name?" Henry asked him.

"Wilson."

"That your first name or your last?"

"Last," the boy said. "First name's John. Most folks just call me Wilson."

Henry leaned in closer to the boy, and spoke in an amicable tone. "Now, c'mon, tell me how old you are."

"Eighteen," the boy said.

Henry knew it was a lie. He smiled and nodded back. "Well, I already know enough Johns. Think I'll call you, Kid . . . Kid Wilson. That okay with you?"

A small grin cracked the boy's stony glare, he returned a slight nod.

"Awright, then," Henry turned to his partner Frank, looked up at the door of the mercantile. "Let's do this," he said.

Just before he grabbed the store's doorknob, the door swung opened to the inside, and a heavy-set woman came out. Henry stepped back and to the side, grabbing the rim of his hat in a tipping gesture to the woman. She nodded and smiled, moving on across the wooden sidewalk and down the steps. Watching the woman cross the street, Henry turned back to the boy behind him. "One other thing, Kid. Don't shoot nobody," he said.

* * *

No one followed them after they rode out of Inola, so they proceeded across the prairie at a leisurely lope heading for Frank's cabin down near the town of Wagoner. Henry and Frank, the backs of their horses laden with gunny sacks full of merchandise, rode in silence. The Kid, carrying his share of the loot, chattered on like a dog-treed squirrel.

Henry and Frank were bone-tired. It'd been a long, hard week. Six days earlier they'd gone up to Caney, Kansas where they'd robbed a bank. A posse had doggedly pursued them nearly ninety miles into the Territory before the two finally lost them in the Osage Hills. They'd ridden fairly hard all night and by dawn couldn't detect the men chasing them. It was Henry's first bank robbery, and he discovered he liked it. He liked it so much, he decided those would be the main thrust of his criminal activities. The store robbery in Inola, as well as those other two or three in the past few days, they'd done more out of necessity than for fun.

Henry had another bank in mind, and robbed the stores in order to provision up. They took mainly guns and ammunition from those, enough for ten men. They took the till money, too, but that never amounted to much, maybe a hundred dollars at the most. Henry thought they could use that to buy food. It never occurred to him that they could steal it from the stores. He felt only low-life outlaws would steal food. He had a higher calling.

"Shut up, Kid," Frank said, finally.

It worked. Kid Wilson pouted quietly the rest of the ride to Frank's.

Henry was glad for just the rhythmic sounds of the hoof beats, as it allowed him to mull things over. The Kid confronting him on the street in Inola seemed sort of providential. It started the wheels turning, and now his thoughts began to galvanize into a real plan. If he was going to pull off the job he was thinking about, he already knew he'd need more hands, preferably gun hands. That's why he'd started stockpiling guns and ammo. But he didn't want a bunch of ragtag yahoos. He wanted to enlist who he wanted, men he thought he could trust, and train them. His gang, The Henry Starr Gang, would be more efficient and skillful than anyone who'd ever ridden on the wrong side of the white man's law, and they'd rob more banks than anyone ever had. This kid showing up when he did was a good omen. He might be his first recruit.

Frank poured some coffee he'd set to boil after they'd arrived at his cabin. Henry slouched on one of the bunks; the boy sat at the table, a tin cup of steaming coffee in front of him.

"Where you from, boy?" Henry asked. He was half-reclined, his back against the cabin wall.

"Missouri," Wilson said. He still wore sort of a pout. "Been here in the Territory for about two weeks, looking for work."

"You got family?"

"Not here. My folks and my brother died of the cholera when I was five. Had an uncle back in Joplin I lived with after that, my ma's kin. Got some other people back in Missouri, but don't know 'em very well."

"Why'd you leave your uncle's place?"

"I shot the sumbitch. Got tired of his beatings, so I shot the sumbitch and left. Come on over here to the Territory. He may still be alive, I dunno; don't care, neither."

Henry nodded, but didn't say anything. He thought of his own stepfather, and the beatings he'd dished out to Henry. He'd left that home at about this boy's age, too.

"You did okay today, Kid." He said after a bit. "You kept your cool; didn't shoot nobody. I think we'll let you join up with us."

Henry looked over at his partner who leaned against the rough fireplace mantel, drinking his coffee. "That okay with you, Frank?"

"Reckon so," Frank said.

"I got me in mind another bank," Henry said to the both of them. "A bigger bank than that one in Caney. Bigger town, too. We're going to need about four or five more men for the job."

Frank and the Kid remained quiet, waiting for Henry to elaborate.

"Can you really shoot them pig irons you got on?" Henry asked the Kid.

"Damn right I can," Wilson replied.

"How'd you come by them?" Henry asked.

"They were my uncle's. I took 'em, and then I shot the sumbitch with 'em."

"Well, in the morning you can show me what you can do."

* * *

Henry stood next to Kid Wilson as they faced the morning sun. It'd risen just above the low hills east of Frank's place and cast a red glow on their faces. Henry had wedged dollar-sized flat rocks into the tops of four fence posts in Frank's corral, and walked back to where the Kid waited. The two of them, with Frank watching, stood fifty feet away looking at the fence posts and into the sun.

"I'll go first, Kid," Henry said and drew his revolver. He sighted down the barrel with a squint, and fired after about a five second aim. The stone on the left most post exploded in a cloud of white dust. Henry aimed at the rock on the next post and fired again. A small puff of rock dust came off the edge of the stone, but it stayed wedged in the post. Henry fired again and the rock disappeared. He re-holstered his gun.

"Not bad," the Kid said.

He drew both his guns and aimed with the right, firing with only a moment's hesitation. The first rock became a small cloud. He fired with the left, and the fence post splintered an inch to the right of the stone about two inches below the top, but the stone kept its perch. He fired again with the left, sending wood fragments flying off the top left of the post; he fired almost immediately with the right again, and blew the rock to bits.

"Shit!" Wilson said.

"Don't be too hard on yourself, Kid," Henry said. "Pretty dang good shooting with the right, and not too bad with the left. All's you need is a little more practice, which is what I aim to give you. You'll do."

Kid Wilson holstered his guns, but his face remained clouded with anger. He sulked.

Henry decided to offer a little more counsel. "Any good shooter could hit them rocks shooting with the sun behind 'em. It takes a fair skilled hand to hit a target that small with the sun in their eyes. That's why I set it up that way. You got talent, Kid. But talent don't mean nothin' without skills. Just keep practicing."

The Kid nodded, kept looking at the ground.

"Well, I got to go look for a feller," Henry said to the Kid. "You stay here with Frank and help him around the place." He looked over at Frank. "The two of you might ought to go into town and stock up on some grub," he said. "I expect we'll be feeding a few more hands here before long. Be back in a day or so."

His partner Frank nodded.

* * *

Henry had known Link Cumpelin and a fella named Watt for a couple of years. He'd cowboyed with them on the Roberts Ranch near Nowata. During the long, dusty trails of pushing cattle, he'd listened to them talk about how they'd get rich someday, and that it wouldn't be by punching cows. Well, he listened to Link, anyway. Watt never said much.

"How you figure to do that, Link?" Henry had asked.

"Hell, boy, there's plenty of rich men out there ripe for the pluckin'. You just need a proper plan, and the guts to carry it through."

Link was an older man, somewhere in his thirties, Henry thought. He knew him as a tough man, a hard worker. Most of his talk had been just that, though. The man never had followed through with his bold talk, but Henry thought he could depend on him. All's Link needed was someone to get things planned and lead the way.

Watt, the only name he ever gave anybody, was about the same age as Link. He didn't talk as much as Link, but he rode just as raw and hard. He had keen blue eyes and a fierce look. Henry wanted him to join his group because sitting in a saddle, Watt could shoot the head off a rattlesnake from thirty paces. Henry had seen him do it more than once. And, although he was skinny and only about five-and-a-half feet tall with his hat on, Henry had also witnessed Watt beat the crap out of a man twice his size in a fist fight.

Henry rode along the eastern fence line of Robert's land in Nowata County. Earlier he'd spotted a group of cows some men were working, and rode toward them. Loping in from the right rear of the small herd, he recognized Boone Tyler, another cowhand he'd known while working for Roberts. He angled his mare to approach the man from behind.

"Howdy, Boone," Henry said.

The man, thick at the waist and narrow at the shoulders, turned in his saddle. Hearing another man's voice coming out of the yellow-gray dust cloud and the mewling of the cattle startled him a little. He immediately recognized Starr.

"Well, howdy, Henry," he said. Besides being fat and short, Boone Tyler wore a five-day-old growth of whiskers, and had gapped teeth stained brown by chewing tobacco. "Sure never expected to see you out here. Mister Roberts know you're here?"

It was Robert's wagon Henry had been driving when he'd been caught with the whiskey. That'd been a couple years back, but Roberts had told Henry never to set foot on his land again.

"No, don't reckon so," Henry said. "Just passing through. I's looking for Link and Watt. They still around?"

"Yeah, they're around. I expect you'll find 'em fixing fences up east of here. Why's it you're looking for them two?" Tyler hadn't seen Henry since Roberts had run him off, but he knew of his exploits. Henry had become somewhat of a celebrity in the two years since Tyler had last talked to him.

"I got some work needs done," Henry said. "Wanted to see if them boys wanted to join up with me."

"What kind of work?" Tyler asked.

"Well, it ain't cow work, Boone. More of a business venture." He rode alongside the cowboy, keeping pace with Boone's bay. Henry looked straight ahead, grinning slightly.

Boone leaned to his left to spit tobacco juice. "Figured as much," he said. He wiped the residual drool with the heel of his left-hand glove. "I been hearing about your bidness ventures."

Boone spat again, and asked, "How many men you figure you'll be taking on?"

"Already got two besides me," Henry answered. "Frank Cheney and a fella called Kid Wilson. Link and Watt'd make five, if they sign on. I figure one or two more ought to round it out."

"Frank Cheney," Boone said. He scratched under his chin, and seemed to give that name some thought. "That the Frank Cheney down around Wagoner?"

"Yep."

"I believe I know him," Boone said. After a few seconds he added, "I been thinking of getting out of cowboying, myself. Always seem to get stuck here riding drag, and I tell you what, I'm plenty dang sick of it."

Henry, still looking ahead, nodded. "Yeah I could see where that'd start to wear thin," he said into the dust cloud around them. Riding drag on a cow herd ranked as probably the worst job in cowboying—always at the back eating dust, rounding up strays, busting cattle out of hard places to reach, and generally doing all the jobs no one else wanted to do. It was the lowest position in the wranglers' pecking order, and generally reserved for the youngest or slowest-witted hand in the bunch.

"You reckon I could sign on for your business venture, Henry?"

"I don't know, Boone. It's kind of dangerous work." Henry liked Tyler, but he wasn't sure he could keep up, mentally or physically.

"Couldn't be no worse than facing down a pissed off steer cornered in a wash," Boone countered.

Henry laughed. "Naw, I s'pose not," he said. He would need someone to stay with the horses during a job; he figured drag-ridin' Boone Tyler could do that just fine. Henry believed he could depend on him to do what he told him to do.

"Tell you what, Boone, you ride over to Frank Cheney's place. Tell Frank I sent you. Tell him I thought you'd fit in. If he says it's awright with him, you can stay on."

"I reckon I could head out tomorrow," Boone said.

"Tomorrow?" Henry said. "What's keeping you from leaving out now?"

"Well, I need to tell Mister Roberts I'm leaving, and pick up my wages. Need to get my cat, too."

"Whoa, whoa, wait a minute," Henry reached out and grabbed the reins of Boone's horse. "Now you don't need to be telling Mister Roberts about any of this or where you're going."

"Well," Boone said and then he thought for a minute. "I reckon I wouldn't do that, but I would like to get my wages . . . and my cat."

"How much wages you figure you've got coming?" Henry asked.

"Well, this here's the twenty-eighth; I reckon I'm due most of a month's pay."

"How much do you make a month, Boone?"

"Ten dollars," Boone said.

Henry stood in his stirrups and pulled a fold of bills out of his jeans pocket. He counted out a few. "Here's twelve, Boone. Now if you want to ride with me, you head on over to Frank Cheney's."

Tyler looked at the proffered bills, then reached out and took them. "Wull, what about my cat?" he asked.

"Go get your damn cat, Boone, but don't stop and talk to Roberts or nobody else. Okay?"

Boone nodded thoughtfully. "You reckon I ought to tell Dooley I'm leaving?"

"Who's Dooley?"

"He's the foreman. He'll want to know ain't nobody riding drag."

"Don't worry about that, Boone. He'll figure it out sooner or later."

* * *

The trio rode up to Frank's barn and corral at about eight that evening. Henry had found Link and Watt working on the eastern fence where Boone had told him. When Henry made his proposal, still sitting in his saddle, the two men looked at one another, then at Henry; and without saying a word, dropped their tools and mounted their horses. They rode on toward Frank Cheney's mostly in silence; Henry and Watt, that is. Link talked a fair amount, about what he'd heard concerning Henry's doings, about his own ideas on robbing banks and such, about what he aimed to do with his future earnings. Henry didn't say much, only an occasional grunt to acknowledge whatever Link said at the time. Watt didn't talk at all, not even a grunt.

When they finally reached Frank's, he came out onto the porch, hearing them ride up. "Did Tyler make it in?" Henry asked his partner as he dismounted.

"Who?" Frank asked.

"Boone Tyler. He's supposed to join us."

Although Henry couldn't see it in the gathering gloom of the spring evening, Frank furrowed his brow in disapproval. "You asked Boone Tyler to join us?"

"Boone'll do okay. He said you two knew each other."

"Yeah, I know Boone. He's an idjit."

"Don't disagree that he's probably that," Henry said as he undid the cinch to his saddle, and pulled it off his horse's back. "But I figure we can trust him. He'll pretty much do whatever we tell him to."

Frank sighed, but he didn't say anything more on the subject.

"This here is Link Cumpelin and Watt," Henry said. The two men nodded to Frank, and he nodded back.

"You boys hungry?" Frank asked.

"I could eat," Link said. Watt nodded again.

* * *

The next morning Kid Wilson and his new companions stood in the barnyard shooting at rocks on the corral fence posts, when Watt spotted two riders about a mile away on the road to the northeast of them.

"Riders coming," he said to the other two. They holstered their guns and waited.

Link yelled over his shoulder toward the outhouse, "Starr!"

Henry came out of the privy, walked over to wait with the others. Frank came out of the small barn, stood next to the barn door. The horsemen had ridden close enough for Henry to see one of them was Boone Tyler. The head of a yellow cat stuck out of one of Boone's saddlebags. He didn't recognize the other man; bigger than Boone, but not as round. The two men trotted their horses into the yard and reined up.

"Howdy, Henry," Boone said. He looked toward the barn, spotted Frank. Spat to his right. "Howdy, Frank," he added. The cat wriggled out of the saddlebag, jumped to the ground. It stretched fore and aft, looked around, ambled toward the barn.

"Boone," Henry said in greeting; Frank nodded, watching the cat approach him.

The group of standing men looked over Boone's companion; the two newcomers remained in their saddles. The stranger was a square man, burly looking. Henry thought him to be in his later twenties, but the diagonal scar running from the right side of his forehead, across the bridge of his nose, down to the bottom of his left cheek, made him look older. His thick arms looked powerful, his left displayed a blue-black writhing dragon breathing red fire. Despite the severe look given by the scar across his face, he grinned merrily at the group below him.

"Who's your friend?" Henry asked Boone.

"Name's Happy Jack," the man said before Tyler could introduce him. He spoke kind of funny with an accent Henry couldn't identify.

"Got a last name?" Henry asked.

"Not since me mum dropped me off at an orphanage when I was four. Nuns just called me Jack, that is, when they weren't strappin' me." He said all this still wearing his grin.

"What makes you so damn happy, then?" Link asked.

Happy Jack looked at Link with black eyes and a bigger grin, "It's freedom, mate. No one shackles old Jack."

"Where you from?" Henry asked.

"Lately out of Frisco; before that shippin' on the seas. I run away from that orphanage when I was fourteen, and signed on with a whaler. That was down in Australia. I think I was born there. There was a Chinaman on a freighter I worked on out of Singapore started calling me 'Happy Jack.' I liked it, so's I kept it." He held up his left forearm displaying his tattoo. "He's the one give me this beauty."

The group of men stood digesting the stranger's comments when Boone spoke up. "I couldn't make it here yes'dee before dark, Henry, so I set up camp. Happy Jack here come up on my camp and we shared supper. As we got to talkin' I told him about you, and that I's comin' to join up with ya. He allowed as how he'd like to get in on some of this, too; so I brung him along to see if you could use him."

"Kind of curious how you got all the way out here to the Territory from Frisco," Henry said to Jack.

Jack laughed and swung his head around looking at the countryside. "Had to get out of there, mate. I killed a man was the First Mate on the whaler I last shipped on. I heard a man didn't have to worry much about the law out here in Indian Territory."

The group nodded in unison, seeming to accept the man's story, and assessment of local law enforcement. Henry looked at Happy Jack. "Can you handle a gun?"

"Aye, mate, but I better prefers me knives."

"Knifes?" Link asked with a sneer. "Whut kinda knifes?"

Happy Jack looked over at Link and with a dark grin said, "These kind, mate." He reached behind his neck and in one swift move threw a knife which stuck firmly in the ground between Link's feet. Before anyone could respond, he reached to the side of his right boot, and with an underhand flip, sent another blade solidly into the barn door beside Frank's head.

Frank looked at the knife still vibrating in the wood six inches from his left ear, then reached up and pulled it out.

"Pretty impressive," Henry said. He scratched the back of his head, pushing the front rim of his hat forward. "Onliest problem I see with that is, once you throw them, you'll most likely want to retrieve them. I ain't so sure we'll have time for that on our jobs. Thing about guns is we don't have to retrieve bullets."

"To be sure," Happy Jack said. "Like I say, I can handle a gun. Just prefers me knives."

At lunch Henry addressed the group.

"I got some jobs in mind. Several small ones and one big one. We'll pull the small ones to get tuned up for the big one. And before we do the small ones, we're going to train up on shooting, and riding, and tactics.

"We might could be a pretty good gang here, but right now we're just a bunch of individuals. We've got to coordinate our actions and learn some discipline."

Henry paused to let all that sink in. He spooned up and swallowed three bites of Frank's squirrel stew, downed a gulp of water from a clay mug. Wiped his mouth with the back of his hand before he continued. "Most important, you boys also got to learn who's in charge here."

Henry stood, walked over an open window in the small cabin. Put both hands on the sill and leaned forward, looking out. "First thing we're going to do is rob a train," he said. "One comes in every day over at Pryor Creek at about ten in the morning. It'll be good practice."

Chapter Four

A mile from the Pryor Creek Station, Henry rode up beside the huffing black and brass train engine, and swung from his saddle into the cab. The engineer, still in his seat, leaning out, looking forward down the track, hadn't seen Henry come onboard, but his fireman did.

The big black man, shining with grease and sweat, had just thrown a shovel full of coal into the open firebox. Had turned to get another scoop full when Henry entered the cab behind the engineer. At first, the fireman looked surprised at Henry's appearance, but seeing the drawn six-shooter, he realized what was up. Drew back and swung the huge shovel at Henry, intent on knocking him off the steam engine.

Still oblivious to Henry's entrance, the engineer pulled the whistle cord to announce the train's arrival to the small crowd standing on the station's platform. The whistle emitted two short screams and one long one, not loud enough to drown out the gunshot two feet behind the engineer. He turned to see his fireman stagger backwards and heard the man right behind him holler, "Drop that damn thing!"

Henry saw the shovel scoop heading toward his head, pulled the trigger and blew a half-dollar sized hole through the heart of it. The bullet's impact slowed the shovel's forward swing and changed its angle of attack, but the scoop still clipped the end of the gun's barrel. Henry dodged backwards stumbling toward the opening where he'd entered the engine's cab. Could feel himself falling back into space, and flailed his arms in a frantic attempt to gain control of his balance. His feet and legs moved in a frenzied dance as his boots slipped on the coal dust covered steel floor. In a momentary insight of terror and odd resignation, Henry could see himself falling backward and head-first onto the moving gravel rail bed behind him. His right hand banged into the vertical brass hand bar at the cab's rear, he fought to grab it. That hold prevented his outward fall, but as he put his foot on the metal step below the cab entrance, his ankle turned and all his weight came down on twisted bones and flesh and tendons. He swore loud at the pain. The fireman started to advance again, Henry quickly cocked his pistol, pointed it to a spot between the black man's wide open eyes, from a half crouch hollered at the fireman to drop the shovel.

The engineer swung out of his seat holding a long pipe wrench. "Git off my train!" he hollered.

"Shut up!" Henry yelled back at him, as he swung his cocked pistol toward the engineer. "Unless you want to get dead, you just get back in your seat and pull into that station like nothing's wrong."

Henry grimaced from the intense hurt shooting up his right leg. The engineer, a nasty-looking old codger, held his ground. Henry fired another round into the steel ceiling above the man's head, the bullet whanged twice in its ricochet. Henry eared back the pistol's hammer, hollered, "Next one's going between your eyes, mister!" Reluctantly, the man lowered the wrench and slid back into his seat.

Henry hopped back into the engine's cab with moans and curses, holding his right leg up stork-like. Pointing his gun at the fireman, he yelled, "Git!"

The fireman looked uncertainly back at Henry, Henry waved the barrel of his gun toward the open back of the cab. "Jump," he said to the fireman. "Get off the train!"

Without much hesitation, the fireman complied.

At the time Henry entered the locomotive's cab, Happy Jack came out of the brush beside the track and ran alongside the rear passenger car of the train. Grabbed the vertical handrail, and jumped up onto the steps and rear platform of the car. He adjusted his hat, pulled his pistol from its holster before opening the door. Once inside the car, he reached down and pulled his eight-inch knife from inside his boot with his left hand.

None of the five people in the last train car—a matronly woman, an adolescent girl, and three men—had noticed Happy Jack's arrival.

"What the hell is he doing?" one of the men near the front of the car said. Out a window on his right a cowboy was running alongside the train.

"Did you see that?" the lone woman sitting on the left side shouted. She pointed out her window at a large black man tumbling along the roadway, and down its sloping embankment.

"See what?" the man across the aisle from her asked. He stood slightly and looked where she looked.

"Someone must've fallen off the train," she said, bringing her fingertips to her lips.

The rest of the passengers moved to her side of the car looking out the windows, still paying no attention to Happy Jack standing near the back door holding a gun in one hand and a knife in the other.

Happy Jack cleared his throat to announce himself. "Oy!" he shouted. The passengers turned to look at him. "That'd be yer engineer, I'd say." He cocked his pistol, keeping it pointed to the ceiling.

"You might be interested to know you're about to be robbed by the 'enry Starr Gang," Happy Jack told the small group. "All you men keep your 'ands where I can see 'em.

"You there," Jack said, pointing his pistol at the nearest man. "Take out your piece, and slide it on the floor toward me." The man did as told.

"Now you other two do the same," Jack instructed. One obeyed; the other held out his suit coat to reveal his waist. "I ain't armed," he said.

"Everyone relax," said Jack. "When we pulls into the station, get off the train keepin' your 'ands up."

One of the men at the back of the group, opened the door behind him and jumped from the train.

"Oy!" Jack hollered. When he saw the man moving past him on the other side of the window, he fired his pistol at him, but he missed, and the man leapt into the woods beside the tracks. Jack turned and went back out the door behind him. He stood on the rear platform of the car, firing his gun again and again into the woods where the man had disappeared.

The train started to creak and groan and squeal as it slowed, pulling into Pryor Creek Station. The four people remaining in the car, still with their hands in the air, watched Happy Jack standing with his back to them outside the door at the other end of the car shooting into the woods over and over. They looked at one another and, as if a single animal, quickly turned and exited the front door of the passenger car, jumped to the ground, and ran toward the town.

Happy Jack turned again to the inside of the car just in time to see one of the men helping the woman off the last step, and the both of them hightailing it with the girl, the other man ten yards ahead of them.

"Oooy!" he screamed. He leaned off the back platform of the train car and fired his pistol into the air, but none of the fleeing passengers slowed. "OY, DAMN YOU!" he yelled and pulled the trigger again, it clicked into the back of a spent cartridge. "'oly bleedin' 'ell," he said and started pulling bullets out of his belt and reloading.

Earlier, when he saw Happy Jack mount the rear platform of the last car, Link broke from his hiding place near the tracks, and ran to the back steps of the first passenger car as it passed by. He reached out to grab the handrail, it stayed just beyond his reach. Tried to run faster, but the loose gravel of the railroad bed slipped beneath his boots, hampering his pursuit. He ran on, desperately trying to catch up to the rear steps of the passenger car. For a while he stayed even with the train, but not close enough to grab the handrail; the train began to inch away as he tired and fell back. He kept running; ran on and on, but lost ground with each painful pound of his heart. Just as he was about to give up, the train began to slow. He had no kick left, but he staggered on, finally grabbing the handrail as it came back to him. He pulled himself up onto the car's platform and slammed against the door. His chest heaved, and he sucked in ragged gulps of air, exhaling only fast enough to grab more air. His right side stitched up into a painful knot almost doubling him over. Drawing his pistol, he crashed through the door. The seven people sitting in the car—three men, three women and a boy—jumped and turned toward him.

"Don't. . . ," Link started, his laboring lungs wouldn't allow him enough breath for more words. Held up his left hand index finger up, gesturing to his audience to give him a second. After a few, he summoned the strength to continue, ". . . nobody . . . move!" His legs began to quiver uncontrollably, and he plopped himself down onto a seat, still panting raggedly. "And hand . . . over . . . your valuables." He pointed his gun in their general direction, its barrel bounced around as his hand shook.

One of the men started to reach inside his suit coat. Link pointed the pistol above the man's head, pulled the trigger. The big Colt boomed and sent the bullet into the car's ceiling above the passenger's head. A woman screamed, the others cringed.

"I said . . . don't move," Link reprimanded. The man returned his hands above his head. "Gimme your valuables, I said," Link reminded them.

The passengers looked at one another. The man who'd started to reach into his suit coat said, "Mister, can't none of us give you nothing if we can't move."

"Well . . . " Link said. Had to think about that for a minute, while he continued to catch his breath. Put his forehead on the seat back in front of him, and pressed the gun barrel into the spot in his side that continued to stab him with pain.

The train slowed and lurched as it came to a halt at the station platform. "C'mon," one of the men whispered to the others, and led the way hastily out the door and off the train.

Link heard them exiting and raised his head. "Hey!" he said, but they ignored him. He started to raise his gun, but let his forearm fall onto the seatback when he saw it would do no good. "Well, shit," he said to no one.

Gunfire greeted the passengers from Link's car when they stepped onto the station's platform; a small crowd already huddled there. Frank, with Henry's horse in tow, and Kid Wilson, flanked the platform firing into the air, keeping the herd of passengers and train greeters bunched together. Henry, his arm around the engineer's shoulders using him for support, his pistol in the man's ribs, hopped back toward the platform. Arriving at the front of the small crowd, he said to the engineer and the station master standing there, "Help me up onto this thing," indicating a wheeled baggage cart. The two men helped Henry onto the cart, he yelped and groaned in discomfort. Stood on one leg to face the crowd.

"Folks," he addressed the group. "I'm Henry Starr, and these here men is my gang. Won't nobody get hurt if you just hand over your valuables."

Link and Happy Jack started to move through the crowd holding out gunny sacks. The people obediently deposited their belongings into the sacks. Frank and The Kid, still on either side of the station platform, stayed mounted with their guns drawn. Watt, who'd been stationed on the far side of the train, came riding up and dismounted. He walked up onto the platform to assist in the crowd control.

Henry, still standing unsteadily atop the flat baggage cart, spoke to his colleague. "Hey, Watt, I sprung my ankle. Flip that tongue up here so's I can lean on it." Henry, using his pistol as a pointer, indicated the cart's tongue laying on the platform deck. Watt picked up the tongue and bent it on its hinge toward Henry's waiting hand; walked around to the back side of the cart and leaned against it.

Left hand on the handle of the cart tongue, weight shifted to his left leg, pistol held up in his right hand, Henry spoke to the crowd again. "Now, folks, this ain't. . . ." He paused as he felt movement. The cart, nudged by Watt's leaning, had started to roll. It moved slowly at first, but picked up speed as it headed for the edge of the platform.

Henry tried to steer the rolling cart with the tongue, placing both his hands on it. "Whoa, dammit!" he said to the unresponsive cart. Watt tried to grab the tailgate of the cart as it moved away, stumbling him forward. His boot toe stubbed against a warped board sticking up from the platform, causing him to dance sideways into a stack of canvas mail bags, losing his grip on the cart.

Henry managed to turn the cart slightly left and into Link, who had his back to Henry while collecting valuables. Link had turned somewhat when he heard his boss holler, but not enough to avoid the collision, or the left front wheel running over his foot. It veered right again towards the edge of the platform. Went nose-over the three foot drop sending Henry flying face-first into the butt end of Kid Wilson's horse. The mare whinnied with surprise, started bucking away from the scene, the Kid holding on tight and cussing anxiously.

The small crowd had broken into gales of laughter, still standing with their hands raised high, some bending at the waist in their mirth. Even Frank Cheney's firing a couple more pistol rounds into the air didn't seem to stop them, only spooking the Kid's horse more. Happy Jack, still standing amongst the crowd, couldn't contain his own amusement, and joined in the laughter.

Henry, his dignity in flames, got to his one good foot, and with his pistol still in hand, shot out two panes in one of the station's windows, then the glass of the tall gas lamp on the platform, showering the laughing crowd below it with shattered pieces.

That sobered the crowd and shut them up. Henry glared at the bunch, pointing his gun at them. They waited for him to speak.

After a few seconds, Henry said to his gang, "Mount up." Frank, still with the reins of Henry's horse in his hand, led the animal up across the platform and down the other side to where Henry stood waiting. Henry holstered his gun, grabbed the saddle horn. He leapt up, trying to stick his left boot toe into the stirrup, but the horse stepped sideways and Henry missed. He tried again with the same result. More titters came from the crowd, until he glared back at them.

"Come give me a hand, Watt," Henry said, and the silent cowboy turned outlaw, ambled over to help his boss.

Once mounted, Henry reined his horse around to face the crowd. He looked as if he wanted to address them again; the crowd, still hands up, waited quietly but with a few smirks. Henry looked at them for a bit, then looked at Frank and said, "Let's go." With that he turned and spurred his horse to head back along the railroad track.

Boone Tyler lay stretched out in Frank's wagon waiting for the gang to return. He'd been assigned as the supply wagon driver. Henry had decided to use it to carry their extra ammunition and gear, and to help haul their booty back to their hideout. He'd stationed Boone several miles from their objective, and Boone had pulled the wagon off the road into a spot in the woods. There he found ample cover from curious passersby, as well as shade for his intended nap.

The sound of multiple hoof beats approaching roused Boone. He lifted his hat off his face and sat up. Frank was the first to ride up, followed by Henry and the others. Boone could tell something wasn't right with the boss.

"Help me get Henry off'n his horse, Boone," Frank said as he dismounted.

Boone rolled to his knees and looked at the riders. "You get shot, Henry?" he asked.

"No," Henry said, his face twisted in pain. "I sprang my ankle."

"Sprang your ankle," Boone echoed. "Well, how'd you do that?"

"It don't matter, Boone," Frank said with some irritation. "Just help me get him down and onto the wagon."

Once they got Henry off his horse and onto the wagon bed, Boone scratched his head and looked at Henry's booted foot. "How you know it ain't broke?" Boone asked.

"It ain't broke," Henry answered. "Help me get my boot off."

Boone continued without responding to Henry. "'Cause I knew this cowboy onest got bucked off high and come down on a pile of rocks. He come up limping around and claimed he sprung his ankle. It didn't get no better for a month or so, so he went to a doc who told him he had broke it and the bones had set up crooked. Last time I seen him he still walked with a limp."

"Just shut up and help me with my boot," Henry said.

"Well, you don't have to get so all danged hateful," said Boone. He grabbed the toe and heel of Henry's boot and yanked causing Henry to scream in pain.

"Did that hurt?" Boone asked.

"Hell yes, it hurt, you idiot."

"She's on there pretty tight. I 'spect your ankle's all swole up. We might have to cut this here boot off."

"You ain't cutting nothing, Boone," Henry said. "These are the best pair of boots I ever stole. Just let me catch my breath, and you can try again." Henry looked over at his silent partner. "Frank, you come over here and help him."

Frank and Boone manned the boot. "Now, don't yank it," Henry instructed. "Just pull slow and steady."

The two men did as told, while Henry filled the woods with his shrieks. By the time Boone and Frank had worked the boot backward, and Henry's foot popped free, he'd passed out.

Chapter Five

Henry sat back on the bunk with his right foot propped atop two pillows. The others stood around the table as Frank sorted the loot on the tabletop.

"Looks like we come away with eight pocket watches, three gold rings, and thirty-eight dollars and seventy-five cents in cash money," Frank said once he'd completed his accounting.

"One bloke had this on 'im," Happy Jack announced. He pulled a small black cloth bag out of his shirt pocket, and threw it onto the pile. Frank loosened the sack's drawstrings and emptied the contents onto the table.

"What the hell are those?" Kid Wilson asked.

"They're diamonds, lad," Happy Jack replied.

Kid looked up at Jack and nodded; looked back at the rocks on the table. "What are diamonds?" he asked.

"Why, gemstones, boy," said Jack. "The jewels of kings and princes. Could be worth a good bit."

The Kid looked doubtfully at the twenty or so scattered cloudy gray stones. "Them?"

"Aye," Jack said. "These here are uncut. A right diamond cutter could make 'em valuable."

"Ain't no diamond cutters I know of here abouts," Frank said. "Prob'ly have to go to Kansas City or Saint Louie for such as them."

"I know a feller in Tulsey Town," Henry interjected. The group at the table turned to look at him. "Soon as I can ride, I'll take those to him; see what he'll give us."

Within a week Henry could put his boot back on . . . as well as take it off without too much pain; and put enough weight on his right foot to walk . . . with a limp. On the morning of the seventh day he saddled up the gray, and headed northwest towards Tulsey Town. Rode off alone.

Henry felt disquiet in the pit of his stomach, an uneasiness bordering on anxiety. The Pryor Creek train robbery had been a disappointment, a disaster, and it wasn't just about the quantity of the haul. He didn't think the gang he'd assembled would be a crack unit this soon, like he wanted, but after this first job, they were much worse than he expected. Despite the fact they were well outfitted, and had good mounts, they looked more like a bunch of rodeo clowns. And he felt like he'd looked the fool, himself, with all his stumbling and falling. The people he held up didn't fear him; they'd laughed at him. It all added anger to his mood and depressed him.

The further he rode, the more he thought about Megan. That green-eyed Irish beauty he'd called his sweetheart for the past three years. She'd always been there for him even when he got in trouble. The first time he got arrested on that phony horse-thieving charge, Meg had been the only one who'd believed in his innocence. Even later, when he wasn't so innocent, she stuck with him, constantly telling him he was a good person and didn't have to behave the way he did.

Megan had been fifteen when they'd first met; Henry sixteen. She'd moved into the Territory with her folks four years past, where her old man had set up a livery and black smithy business in Nowata. Henry could still remember the first day she came into the schoolhouse. She stood there like a shining angel—Irish red hair and green eyes. She was the most beautiful white girl he'd ever seen, and fell instantly in love with her. Had to fight Stanley Poppingbird and Willie Watson in order to get her attention away from them and onto him. It cost him some loose teeth, a busted nose, and damn near a broken leg when Willie hit him with a stick of firewood, but he'd take it all again in a heartbeat. She was worth that much and more to him.

In his reverie, Henry didn't notice that he'd angled his horse more in a northerly direction than northwest. It surprised him a little to find himself on a small rise looking down on his old hometown of Nowata. He reined back on the gray to bring her to a stop, and studied the little row of frame and brick buildings surrounded by the scattering of houses. He picked out the livery stable on the north end of Main Street, and the small schoolhouse at the south end. Meg would be there, in the schoolhouse.

He couldn't just ride into town. Meg was probably the only friend he had there. He'd robbed the depot once, and had been arrested on the street for his alleged horse-thieving a few years back. Even though his home-town, most there knew his reputation, and not many wanted him around. Most likely any citizen would shoot him on sight, especially Meg's pa—a brawny, hard-muscled Irishman—who'd warned Henry more than once to stay away from his daughter, or risk serious injury.

Henry looked at the sun, figured about an hour before it set. He decided to wait before heading down to the school.

As usual, Megan Morrisey stayed in the schoolhouse well past the time she dismissed the children for the day. She'd do all the housekeeping chores then, and look over her students' daily work. With the lengthening days, she could stay longer. So focused on grading the writing assignments on her desk, it surprised her when she looked up at the window, seeing only half a red sun above the hill a mile away.

She gathered the papers into a neat stack at one corner of her desk, placed the horseshoe she used as a paperweight atop them. She stood and looked about the room to make sure all was in order before she left.

"Hello, Meg," a man said behind her, and she whirled toward the voice, letting out a short terrified screech. The man stepped out of the gloom and into the room's dimming light. Meg's terrified expression turned to anger. She took two steps toward the man, and slapped him.

"Henry Starr, don't you ever do that to me again! You scared me half out of my wits."

Henry rubbed the side of his face where it stung, laughed softly. "Sort of thought that's the kind of welcome I'd get in this town, but didn't expect it'd come from you."

Meg threw her arms around Henry's neck and kissed him hard. The two stayed embraced and lip-locked for several seconds, until Meg pushed back and slapped Henry again. "You think you can show up after a year and just start kissing me like that?" she said.

"Now just a dang minute," Henry said. "Believe you's the one started kissing me. There ain't a day gone by in the last year I ain't wanted to see you. 'Sides your pa said he'd stomp a mud hole in my gut if I ever come around you again, so I had to pick my time, hopin' maybe he'd forgot about that."

"Oh, shut up," Meg said and flung herself onto Henry again.

The passion grew in their kissing, their bodies pressed hard against one another. Henry slipped his hands to caress forbidden places, and Meg pushed against his chest, resisting. "Henry, don't," she breathed, but there didn't seem to be much conviction in her words, so Henry pressed on, bending her back toward her desktop. "No, Henry, stop," she pleaded as she relaxed into his reclining embrace. Henry relentlessly fumbled with buttons and belts and bloomers.

Meg once again pushed forcefully against her suitor's chest holding him at arm's length away from her. "We can't," she insisted between gasps. "The door's unlocked. What if someone came in; one of the children?"

Henry continued kissing her neck, shoulder, ear. He whispered to her, "It's a schoolhouse, ain't it? Maybe they'd learn something."

Absorbing his fervent kissing, Meg sighed, "At least take your boots off."

Henry looked down at her sympathetically, "I can get one off, but t'othern ain't coming off without some work. I got a sprung ankle. I'd need some help, but I ain't really in the mood for that right now. Are you?"

Meg sighed and arched her back into his body, and he gently, without haste, took her.

* * *

"I better get going," Meg said. She pushed at her hair and rubbed her hands across her face to remove the drowsiness. The twilight had almost dissolved into blackness, and the diamond brightness of Venus hung above the horizon out the west window. "Ma's going to be wondering about me."

"I ain't staying," Henry said.

Meg stood and continued to adjust her hair, her clothing. "Didn't expect you would. I just hope you haven't got me pregnant."

Henry remained sitting, his back against the wall, watching her. No words passed between them, until Meg headed for the door. "I want you to marry me, Meg," Henry said.

Meg stopped, kept her back to him. "No you don't," she said. "Besides, why would I want to do that? You think I want an outlaw husband? You think I want to raise a child on my own with you off in jail, or worse yet, me being a widow?"

"I'm going to quit outlawin', Meg. We could go off somewhere, where I ain't known. Start a whole new life. Something respectable."

"Like what?" Meg asked. She turned halfway back toward him.

"I's thinking about getting a little cattle ranch going. Been thinking about Colorado. Some Cherokee people have carved out an area. Hear prospects is pretty good out there. And you could still school marm."

"Colorado?" Meg stayed half turned to Henry, looking at the floor. "That's a long way off. Anyway, if I married you, Pa would have a fit."

"I ain't planned on asking your pa. Figure doing that would make you a widow before we even got married." Henry grinned at Meg, and she giggled.

"I got one more thing to do," he continued. "Then I'm coming back for you."

"What thing?"

"Promised some boys I'd help 'em with something. And I got to get a grub stake for that ranch in Colorado."

Even in the darkness, Henry could see the anger flash in Meg's eyes. "Is that how you're going to quit being an outlaw?" She turned toward the door again, but stopped after she opened it. "If you don't get killed and manage to come back, Henry, I'll be waiting for you." She paused for a few seconds, then added, "But not forever."

* * *

"I'll give you five hundred for the lot." The small man removed the jeweler's loupe from the front of his right eye, and looked at Henry.

"Hell, Feingold, them rocks is worth more than that, and you know it."

The jeweler stuck out his lower lip and shrugged. "Perhaps, but they're uncut. If you'd brought them to me cut, I might offer you more."

"I could take them to Kansas City and get twice, three times as much. Dammit, man, you're robbing me."

Feingold chuckled as he gathered the diamonds and returned them to the sack. "So I'm robbing you, am I? Now that's rich." He reached up offering the bag back to Henry. "Here, then, you take your uncut stones up to Kansas City."

Henry looked at the proffered bag, walked small circles with his thumbs hooked in his belt. He stopped to face the jeweler again. "What about them watches and gold rings I brung?"

"Like I said, five hundred for the lot." Feingold dropped the bag of diamonds onto his counter next to the watches and rings.

Henry rubbed his chin and walked in another small circle. "How 'bout you give me six?" he asked.

The jeweler sighed. "This is a business, Starr. Certain parts of it are a risk, like doing business with fellas like you. You calculate your risks in your business; I calculate mine. But I like you, Henry, so I'll give you five-fifty. It's my final offer."

Henry made a disgusted noise and nodded quickly. Feingold reached under the counter and pulled out a tin box, removed a stack of bills and started counting them out. Henry watched him intently and when the merchant finished, he folded the money and put it in his pocket.

"You're a dang thief, Feingold," Henry said. "You're lucky I don't just take all that money in that box, and give you a knock on the head to boot."

"Yes, yes." Feingold smiled at Henry. "I'm a thief. But who else would you go to with all your watches and diamonds? I could easier get the reward for you than sell all the watches you bring me."

Henry smiled and nodded. "Yeah, I reckon that's true enough." Something in the display case caught his eye, he bent to take a closer look. "How much you want for that there ring?" he asked.

The jeweler opened the case from the back side and took out the ring. "Ah, this is a beautiful diamond, Henry. It's a half carat Marquis."

"How much?"

"I'd sell it to you for eight hundred."

"I'll give you five."

"I'll take six."

Henry pulled out the bills he'd put in his pocket, then extracted the other fifty from the other pocket. "I wish you could ride a horse and shoot," he said as he handed the money to the little man in the black vest and small skullcap. Feingold placed the ring in a small box and handed it to his customer. Henry touched his hat and said, "I'll see you on another day, Mr. Feingold."

"Good day, Mr. Starr. Always a pleasure doing business with you."

Chapter Six

Happy Jack pulled a knife from his right boot and flung it. It gave out a sharp ring when the tip stuck an inch into the window frame. Link Cumplin let out a long string of angry oaths, and Watt spit into the fireplace. Kid Wilson glared at Henry, his hand on the butt of his holstered revolver, his thumb rubbing the back of its hammer. Boone Tyler scratched an armpit.

"You spent all of it?" Frank asked Henry.

"Hell, it weren't that much," Henry said. He looked sheepish, and a little anxious, at the men in the cabin.

"On what?" Link asked.

"Something personal," Henry said. He stood and faced the group with a look of defiance. "Now look here, the haul we got from that train didn't amount to a hill of beans. All we got out of that job was practice, and from how we done, it appears we dang sure needed it.

"Ever blame one of you has got a place to sleep and plenty to eat. I got a job planned that will bring us all a good haul."

"Then let's get to it," Kid Wilson said. "I'm tired of hanging around here shooting rocks." He looked at the others, they nodded and muttered agreement.

"Yeah, I know," Henry said. "But if we just jump into it we're likely to get shot, judging from that train deal. We got to get ready. We got to do some training."

Link kicked the back of a table chair, sending it on a spinning crash to the floor. "I don't need no damn trainin', Starr. That ain't what I come down here for."

Link walked over to the others. The men, except for Frank, formed up into a loose group behind Link, each looking darkly back at Henry. Frank walked over and righted the chair Link had kicked. He stood beside Henry, but didn't say a word, only looked at the floor.

Henry surveyed the gang, and looked at Frank. "That the way all of you feel?" he asked. No one spoke, their expressions seemed to indicate that's exactly how they felt . . . except for Frank. Henry sat in one of the table chairs facing the group. He removed his pistol and laid it on the tabletop in front of him, then pushed the front of his hat upward, off his forehead.

"Aw right, then," he said. With his right palm on the table inches from the butt of his Peacemaker, he pointed at the cabin entrance with his left index finger. "There's the dang door. Any of you wants to leave, is welcome. No hard feelings."

The men all looked at one another. "Frank, we got any money left in that stash of yours?" Henry asked.

"They's a bit," his partner answered. He looked back at the group, too; his hand resting on the butt of his holstered gun.

"Enough to give all these boys fifty dollars?"

Frank didn't say anything for a few seconds, shifting on his feet. "Yeah, I reckon . . . maybe," he said.

"Okay, then. I'll give any of you yayhoos fifty dollars for your trouble, and you can walk on out of here. But if you do, I don't never want to see your hide again. We'll be through ridin' together."

More looks were exchanged among the group, waiting for someone to make the first move. Link took a step toward Henry. Watt and Happy Jack stepped in behind him.

"Course if you decide to stay," Henry said. "We'll take that fifty bucks I promised you to buy supplies and ammo. We'll do some training and practicing for a couple of weeks, then we'll ride to a town where I know a big fat bank is ripe to be robbed. I figure each of us stands to make at least a hundred times that fifty dollars." He looked up at the trio standing in front of him. "It'd be a bigger split, if some of you decide to leave."

"How do we know this ain't another bust, Henry?" Link asked with a sneer.

"I already checked it out, before I come and got you boys. It's in a big town, and they got some company payrolls held there."

"Why don't we just get on over there today and get it done?" Kid Wilson wanted to know. Link looked at the Kid and nodded; the others muttered agreement.

Henry sighed and looked up at the Kid, then Link. "Cause if we went into that bank like we went into that train, most of us would get our butts shot off, or we'd likely end up in jail. That's why we need to practice, boys. I got the layout of the town and the bank. We'll practice every move we're going to make, start to finish, so's we'll know what we're doing and where we're supposed to go and there won't be no surprises."

Link shuffled his feet and looked at the others. Henry, seeing their wavering, added, "Ain't no easy way to success, boys; just hard work."

"Well . . . mebbe I'll stick, then," Link said. Watt and Happy Jack nodded. "I ain't never been a stranger to hard work," Link added.

Frank stood at the corral leaning forward at the waist, his chin on his forearms folded on the top rail, his foot propped on the bottom rail. Watched the others at one end of the corral shoot rocks off post tops at the other end, when Henry came up beside him.

"You didn't have enough to cover all that leavin' money, did you?" Henry asked Frank.

"Nope," Frank answered. He watched in silence as the Kid shattered three post-top rocks in quick succession. "What was you going to do if all of 'em decided to walk?"

"That's why I put my gun on the table," Henry answered. "Wanted to send them all a little message. Plus, I knew you'd help me out."

"Did ya now? Two against five? That ain't too powerful a message."

"Well, it was a calculated risk, Frank. Besides, with Boone it was more like two to four."

Frank snorted, then spit to the ground away from Henry. He rubbed his whiskered chin and looked at the setting sun. "I sure hope that bank's all you say it is," he said. "And I sure hope that little gal is worth all the welchin' you done to these boys."

"I ain't welched on nobody, Frank. I'm giving them an opportunity they wouldn't had if they didn't stick with me. Look at 'em: three broken down cowboys, a no-count pirate, and a farm boy on his way to getting shot through the heart by someone he shouldn't uh picked a fight with. They're a raggedy bunch, but they do what I say, and in a couple weeks they'll all be walking in tall cotton."

"Yeah," Frank said. "Either that or git their necks stretched." He yawned large, turned to head back to the house. "I best get supper started."

* * *

"Fellas," Henry addressed the group in the cool of the bright June morning. They'd gathered beneath the large white oak behind Frank's cabin. Some stood, others squatted on the ground, all in the shade of the tree. Henry stood in full sunlight facing them; held a three-foot piece of windfall in his right hand which came to a jagged point at one end. Their first day of training for the coming job, and he had their full attention. ". . . we're going to ride about a day east and north to the town of Bentonville in Arkansas. That's where we'll go to work.

"I been there and looked this place over, and I picked it for a couple reasons. First, because of the haul. Like I told you, the bank holds some payrolls, in addition to the normal stuff. I figure we can come out with a hunnert thousand, easy."

The group stirred and murmured.

"Second," Henry continued. ". . . it ain't far from the Territory line. We'll need to get in and out of there quick, and get back into the Territory before they can form up a posse. Once we're back over here, they won't come after us. It don't look like they got much law in town, so I don't figure we'll get much trouble. We'll hit 'em before they know what happened."

Henry looked down to his right where he'd laid out a model of the operation on the ground. "This," he pointed his stick at a six-inch-wide rock on the ground, "is the Peoples State Bank. These here," he indicated two ruts intersecting at a right angle on one corner of the rock, ". . . are the streets next to the bank. As you can see, it sits on a corner.

"We ain't going to ride into town all at once, and we ain't going to be armed, so's we won't draw no suspicion. Me and Boone will drive a wagon into town from this direction, and pull up near the rear of the bank. There's a big elm back there we'll stop under and wait for the rest of you." He drew a little circle in the dirt to indicate the position of the tree. "All your rifles and pistols will be covered in the back of the wagon.

"Each of you will ride into town alone and from different directions. Frank, you and Link come in from the south here, about a minute apart. Happy Jack will swing up north and come in that way, Kid you go around to the east side and come in, Watt you'll follow us from the west." Henry moved the stick about, pointing out each man's movement. "We'll all meet here at this elm to pick up our hardware. Jack and Watt will take a position near the front corner, where the two streets meet. Link, you'll go to the front of the bank to keep anyone from coming in; me, Frank, and the Kid will go in through the back door. If everything goes according to plan, we should be in and out of there in less than five minutes."

Henry paused a few seconds to let all this information sink in. "Any questions?" he asked.

"Wull, what is it you want me to do, Henry?" Boone Tyler asked.

Henry tapped the stick on the top of the rock, and rubbed his chin. "You stay with the horses, Boone."

"You gonna drive that wagon outa there?" Frank wanted to know.

"Good question," Henry responded. "I reckon we'll have to tow in our riding horses. We'll leave the wagon when we're done."

Henry pointed the stick toward the open field to his left. "I got things set up out here in this field sorta like the bank and town. That stack of wood will be the bank; that pile of rocks behind it yonder will be the elm tree. Let's mount up and run through this a few times, just so we're clear on what to do."

* * *

Boone reined up the horse pulling the wagon, stopping in the full shade of the elm. Henry pulled out his pocket watch and looked at it—half past two. Thirty seconds later Frank came around the corner, his horse at a slow trot toward them. At various intervals, the rest arrived at the rendezvous point. All of them pulled their pistol belts from under the tarp in the wagon bed, strapped them on, grabbed their rifles. Watt and Happy Jack took their positions at the side of the bank. Link stood next to them and watched as Henry, Kid Wilson, and Frank headed toward the back door of the bank. Link counted to ten and went around the corner to station himself at the front door. Boone gathered the seven horses and held them under the elm.

Henry, his left shoulder against the back door, his hand on the knob, his shotgun cradled in his right arm, looked back at the Kid and Frank. He nodded to them; they nodded back. Henry twisted the knob and pushed hard with his left shoulder. The door didn't open. He tried again, with more force. Still, the heavy wooden door wouldn't budge.

"Gimme a hand," Henry said to Frank. His partner put his boot on the door above the knob. "On three," Henry said. He paused and counted. Both men applied as much force as they could, but the door stayed closed.

"Damn," Henry said, and backed away from the door. "Must be barred from the inside." He sighed, and thought for a second. "We'll have to go in the front."

When Henry and his group passed a confused Watt and Jack, he said in passing, "Door wouldn't open," and moved on.

Link paced in front of the door, stopped when he saw Henry and the others come around the corner. "We're going to have to go in this way," Henry said to Link, and the three pushed past him and through the bank door.

Link took the change of plans in stride and continued his pacing. Almost immediately he noticed a small man with a satchel under one arm stopped on the street ten feet away. The man stood watching as the armed men entered the bank. His mouth hung open, his eyes wide with surprise. He looked up at Link without changing his expression.

Link lowered his rifle and pointed it at the man. "Git on outta here," he said with menace. The man broke out of his frozen stare and bolted, diving through the door of a dry goods store catty-corner from the bank.

Henry confronted six men inside the bank—three customers, a teller, and two bank officers. "Awright, this here's a holdup!" Henry yelled. All in the bank turned to look curiously at the gun drawn trio. "Git yer hands where I can see 'em!" Henry instructed.

Frank went straight to the vault, grabbing the closest bank officer to take with him. Kid Wilson entered the teller's cage, shoved out the teller, and began filling his bag with cash.

"Now I want all you boys to come over here and line up against this wall," Henry instructed. The bank customers and employees, hands high, complied. A distant shot popped outside and almost immediately there came the thud of a slug against the door. Those inside the bank could hear the explosion of Link's rifle as he fired back. More shots came with whacks and slaps as the slugs peppered the front of the bank. Window glass shattered and slugs ripped up pieces of wood from the floor and bank fixtures; one whanged off the potbellied stove in the center of the lobby. Link could be heard swearing, returning fire as rapidly as he could.

"Hurry it up, Frank!" Henry yelled. "Let's go!"

Frank emerged from the vault with his hostage in front of him. "Ain't as much in here as we thought," he informed Henry.

"Whadda ya mean?" Henry asked.

"Vault's near empty," Frank answered.

Henry raised his shotgun, pointed it at the bank officer's nose. "I know you keep payrolls in here. Where's them payrolls?"

"You're a day late," the sweating banker said. "Payday was yesterday."

"Shit!" All Henry could think to say. The Kid exited the cage with his bags full, came to stand beside Henry and Frank. The gunfire increased outside, they could still hear Link shouting cuss words and firing back.

"Awright, you men line up here in front of us. You're gonna be our shields when we go out the door." The hostages looked at one another, visibly frightened. "C'mon, now," Henry said with a wave of his shotgun, the group moved slowly toward the door. Gathered there, Henry said to the Kid, "Open it."

When the door opened, the gunfire slackened off, except for Link's. He continued to blast away. "Hold it, Link!" Henry shouted. "We're coming out now with these boys in front of us," he yelled to the unseen mob. "I reckon you'd shoot them before you'd shoot us!"

Henry, Frank, and the Kid prodded the group forward. "Link, get over here behind us," Henry said. "Damn," a hostages gasped when Link shuffled toward them. His face a splotch of blood and his left eye gone, his left arm hung limp, blood oozing out of two holes in his shirtsleeve. Another hole in his right pant leg had a ragged halo of deep red at mid-thigh. He'd dropped his rifle, but he still held his pistol in his good right hand.

"Gimme your pistol, Henry," he said. "I can't reload." Henry, a little aghast himself, handed Link his six-shooter butt-first.

The group moved into the street with the robbers huddled behind the hostages, firearms at the ready. Not three feet outside the bank door, a shot rang out from the mercantile window, the slug whizzing past Henry's ear. Several other shots followed. "Damn!" said one of the bankers and took off running. The other hostages followed suit and scattered to the four winds, leaving the gang of outlaws fully exposed. A heavier barrage opened up from the citizens.

Frank took one to the shoulder; the heel of Kid Wilson's left boot flew off knocking him down; he got right back up, firing. Watt and Happy Jack moved up from their positions to cover their colleagues in retreat, the Kid and Henry supporting a bloody Link, his mangled face further twisted in pain. Watt and

Happy Jack peppered the windows of the mercantile where most of the gunfire seemed to emanate; then they fell back as the others covered their own retreat. Boone brought the horses to them and they all mounted, galloping headlong out of the town.

Chapter Seven

"Eleven thousand two hunnert thirty-eight dollars and fifty cents," Frank told the group.

Henry looked distraught, as did his men. "Count it again," he said.

"Henry, I already counted it again. Another time ain't going to make it any more," Frank said.

Frank's right shoulder bulged where Billy Crow Hat had placed a slippery elm poultice and a bandage to cover it. On the way back to Frank's cabin, Henry sent Boone to Wagoner to fetch the Cherokee medicine man. "Check the saloons first," Henry told Boone. "That's where you're likely to find him."

Frank had been lucky. The bullet had gone straight through the inside of his shoulder, breaking no bones nor hitting a major vessel. Crow Hat had an easy cure for that; Link wasn't so lucky.

"Your arm's broke," Billy told Link during his examination. "Left eye is shot out. Got medicine for those. Legs not bleeding bad; no break, but the bullet's still in there. Going to have to dig it out so's there won't be so much poison in your leg. I can probably save it, but you'll be laid up a spell."

Link, who'd already consumed half the quart of moonshine whiskey he held, slurred a string of cuss words at no one in particular, and passed out.

* * *

After Crow Hat did his work and packed up to leave, Henry gave him two twenty dollar gold pieces. "Billy, I reckon you won't tell nobody where you been or what you done this evening." The little man nodded and left. It was then Henry told Frank to tally up the haul.

"Divide 'er up seven ways, then," Henry said to Frank. His partner, with some difficulty and discomfort, took a pencil out of his left shirt pocket with his right hand, and started ciphering on the tabletop. The other men, except for Link, gathered around Frank to look over his back.

After a two-minute calculation, Frank laid the pencil aside and said, "It figgers out to about sixteen hunnert and five dollars apiece."

Most of the men looked at the floor or the wall, none said anything. Boone decided to speak for the group. "Well, it beats a stick in the eye." He looked at the faces around the table and half grinned, but no one in the group shared his humor.

"What the hell, Boone," Watt said. "You reckon Link would feel that way?"

Everyone looked at the drunk and semi-conscious cowboy with the bandage over his left eye. Boone Tyler looked at the floor, embarrassed.

"Boys, I know you're disappointed," Henry said after a few more seconds of silence. "I am, too. Y'all done a good job. I'm proud of the way you executed the plan, and except for my fool mistake, we'd've made off with plenty. It's my fault we didn't." He looked over at Link lying on the bed all bound up with Billy Crow Hat's poultices and bandages. "I let you down." He stopped talking, his voice choked with emotion on the last word. No one looked at Henry during the awkward silence that followed.

Henry cleared his throat, and continued. "If any of you wanted to move on, I wouldn't blame you a bit. In fact, I'm thinking seriously about getting out of outlawin' myself."

"Wull, how come, Henry?" Boone asked. "Whatcha gonna do?"

Henry scratched the side of his face. He walked to a front window and looked out. "Gonna get married, Boone. Gal wants me to settle down. Think I'll head on out to Colorado, maybe get me a small ranch."

"Believe I'll head down to New Orleans," Happy Jack said. "I heard some profits could be made there in privateering."

"What's that?" Kid Wilson asked.

"Piratin', Kid. Piratin'. I ain't much good on land. I'd be better off at sea."

"What about Link?" Watt wanted to know. He looked at Henry, expecting him to answer.

"What about him?" Henry returned.

"I'm taking off. He can't ride," Watt answered. After some further thought, he added, "He's my pard." He looked at Henry, nodded once as if satisfied his few words explain what he was trying to say.

"Well, I reckon he can bunk here with Frank 'til he's back on his feet." Henry looked at Frank for confirmation. Frank nodded.

With that Watt headed for the door. "I'll go get my gear, and saddle up," he said. "Pick up my share when I come back in?" Frank nodded again, and started counting out the bills placing them in individual stacks.

"I got a cousin lives down in the Ouachitas," Boone said. "Reckon I could ride with you that far, Happy Jack?"

"Aye, mate."

Without turning from his gaze out the window, Henry asked, "What about you, Kid?"

"I heard about Colorado," he said. "Thinking maybe I could travel along with you. I'd like to see Colorado and them mountains."

"I reckon that'd be okay," Henry said. He turned back to the room. "Kid, you and Boone and Jack go on out to the barn with Watt and get your stuff. We might as well divvy up and get on out of here.

"Boone, I'd appreciate it if you'd saddle up my horse. I need to talk to Frank for a minute before we go."

After the three men had exited the cabin, Henry sat down in one of the chairs at the table, watched Frank count and stack the money.

"You about got it all divided up?" Henry asked.

"'Bout," Frank answered, still counting and building the last stack. When he finished, he started aligning the bills in neat stacks at their spots on the table.

Henry grabbed the closest stack. "This here mine?" he asked.

"Good as any," Frank answered.

Henry started counting out some bills, stopping at two hundred dollars. "Put this here in Link's stack. Don't tell the others."

Frank looked up at Henry, but didn't say anything. He took the bills Henry held out, gathered up the stack designated as Link's, folding the bills, and shoved them into his shirt pocket. "I'll make sure he gets this," he said.

The two men sat in silence, Henry drumming the tabletop with his fingers, Frank still fiddling some with the stacks of money. Both men felt something needed to be said, but neither knew where to start.

Henry had known Frank only a little over three years, but it seemed longer, like half a lifetime. Frank had befriended him back on Roberts' ranch. Frank was maybe ten years older than Henry, but he didn't know for sure. When Henry came to the Roberts bunkhouse the first time, he was only sixteen. Most of the hands ignored Henry at best, harassed him at worst. He was a kid and a greenhorn . . . and an Indian. Some tried their level best to kill new guys, or at least send them packing. In the tough, hardworking and dangerous world of the cowhand, new men had to earn respect, and acceptance. It was even harder for teenagers . . . boys, especially boys they called "breeds."

But Frank wasn't quite like the other men. Oh, he did his share of teasing, but he didn't leave Henry out on a precarious limb so much. Frank would let Henry learn a lesson the hard way, even a dangerous way, but he never abandoned him. And he never set Henry up in some devious trap that would leave the boy looking guilty of some wrong doing.

Once, a burly cowboy named Krause—the biggest bully of the bunch, in size as well as attitude—had accused Henry of stealing some of his things. Everyone avoided any confrontation with the big German, but he clearly had it in for Henry. Immediately following the angry accusation, Krause had tossed Henry out of the bunkhouse and followed for further thrashing. Several blows and kicks into the beating, Frank drew his pistol, came up behind Krause, and whacked him across his right ear with the gun barrel. Krause fell like an oak from the force of the blow; when he rolled over to see who'd delivered it, found himself looking up the bore of the big Colt, just as Frank cocked back the hammer.

"You best lay off that boy, Krause," Frank had said to him with calm menace. "I seen you put them things of yours in his footlocker, so you know and I know he didn't steal 'em. Now if you put a hand on him again, I'll damn well shoot you."

Krause's demeanor darkened around Frank, didn't bother Henry *or* Frank after that, nor did any of the other hands. Henry stayed close to Frank, and their friendship increased. Both gained an appreciation for the other's abilities as time went on. The two of them thought the bogus horse thievery pinned on Henry a few months later, and which sent him off to face Judge Parker, was engineered by Kraus, but they never could prove it.

"Whadda you reckon you'll do, Frank?" Henry asked eventually. "You want to go to Colorado with us?"

Frank remained quiet for a few seconds. Then he spoke, in his usual slow manner, not looking up at Henry. "Naw, I seen Colorado. Don't need to see it again, I reckon." He rubbed his chin and looked out the window. "Got me this place here, but I expect the law will be tracking me down soon enough. They's a fella named Case in Wagoner once told me he'd like to buy this land if I ever wanted to sell. Think I'll find out if he's still interested. Then I might take off for Texas."

Henry didn't say anything for a while, just nodded. "Texas is big," he said at last. "Fella could likely find plenty to do down there."

Frank smiled and nodded back in agreement.

* * *

"Meg, this here's Kid Wilson. He's going to be traveling with us out to Colorado."

Meg had told herself not to expect Henry to show up at all, so she'd be pleasantly surprised if and when he did. But she hadn't told herself to suppose he'd bring along a scruffy, surly teenager with double mounted six-shooters on his hips. If they were going to run off and get married, she didn't see how this boy figured into the wedding party, and that's exactly what she would tell Henry.

"Nice to meet you," Meg said to the Kid with as sincere a smile as she could muster. He tipped his hat, blushed, and looked at the ground where he described a circle in the dirt with his boot toe. He looked like one of her male charges in the schoolhouse, all of whom had a crush on her.

Meg grabbed Henry by the forearm and pulled him along with her. "Would you excuse us for a minute?" she said politely to Wilson. With Henry in tow, she entered the back of the school and closed the door behind them. "Why'd you bring him?" she demanded.

"He's just a kid," Henry answered, not at all certain why she seemed so angry.

"That's not what I asked you. We're supposed to be going off to get married. Why is he coming with us?"

"Well, he said he'd never seen Colorado and would like to. I didn't see how him riding along would be a problem. He's a good kid."

"Well, it is a problem for me. I swear, Henry, sometimes you can be so . . . so . . . obtuse.

Henry screwed up his brow, and looked out the window to where the Kid stood with the horses. He didn't have any idea what *obtuse* meant, but figured it wasn't a compliment.

* * *

The man had a round body; his pink moon face made him look childish, but Henry didn't figure him to be no child. Had a mustache of sorts, a sparse one. The guy'd tried to let it grow long like maybe the length of the whiskers would make up for the lack in numbers. The vest of his brown wool suit puckered at the buttons from the expanse beneath it, and when he'd remove his derby to mop his brow—something he did frequently— pomade plastered down his thin head hair which had a part in the middle. The front ends of the parts formed flat curls which laid on both sides of his forehead like little horns.

He sat next to the Kid on the train seat facing Henry and Meg; Meg at the window, him opposite Henry at the aisle. Sat down with them before the train left the Coffeyville Station, and struck up a conversation. Introduced himself as Audubon Henderson, offering Henry his hand. "Folks call me Audie," he added, smiling at Meg and tipping his derby. Settling into his seat he looked at the Kid, his stare lingering, a wicked smile on his lips. Turning back to Henry his smile faded some. "Who might you folks be?" he asked.

"Name's Jackson," Henry answered. "This here's my missus. Believe that feller next to you goes by the name of Charlie Smith."

Audie nodded to the couple across from him, directed his look at Kid Wilson again, leaned closer and offered his hand. "Pleased to meet ya." He turned to look at Meg. Lowering his eyes to her ankles which she had exposed with her legs crossed, he frowned disapprovingly. Henry watched all this—the man's attraction to the Kid, his disdain for Meg. He decided he didn't like the guy.

The fat little man looked studiously at Henry, twisting one end of his scrawny mustache with some fingers. "Seems like I know you, Mister Jackson. You ever been in Bentonville, Arkansas?"

Henry glanced over at Wilson, who shifted in his seat, stared out the window. "I had me some bidness there some time back. Only there onest," Henry said.

"Were you in the bank?"

"Don't reckon," Henry answered. "Sold a man some pigs; cash money. Believe I ate some supper at a hotel. Like I said, been a while back."

"Well, you sure look familiar." Audie looked at the kid again. "We had us a bank hold-up there a few weeks back. You hear of it?"

"Can't say I did. We come from Missouri."

Audie nodded as if accepting the explanation. "Yeah, quite a deal. Gang of about ten or twelve come riding into town in broad daylight, shootin' and hollerin'. Walked right into the bank and took every last cent. Town people and the lawmen waiting for them when they came out, though. Shot and killed about four or five of 'em, but the others still got away. Bank had some big payrolls at the time. I heard they made off with a couple hundred thousand dollars. Rode off into the Territory, and disappeared into the sticks. Stupid marshals are afraid to go in there after 'em. They say the leader's an Indin by the name of Henry Starr. Kin to Belle Starr. As fierce and bloodthirsty as they come."

Audie lifted his derby, dabbed his forehead while looking steadily at Henry. "Yessir, quite a deal," he said again.

Henry and Wilson traded looks. "Well, by the way you tell it, it sure musta been," he said. "I heard of Henry Starr. Don't believe he was kin to Belle Starr, though."

"Well, I wasn't actually there. Just heard tell of it. Some of them shot weren't all outlaws neither. A few was citizens."

Henry furrowed his brow with real concern and asked, "Did any of them die?"

"Not by gunshots," Audie said. "One old man named Feathershed was sitting in front of the dry goods store across the street from the bank when all the commotion started. They found him still sitting there later, deader'n a doornail, but no bullet holes in him. Several holes in the store front, but none through the old man. Doc said it was likely from a stroke brought on by all the excitement. He was close to eighty, old war veteran."

Henry shook his head sadly and said, "Durn shame."

"Well, I expect they'll catch up with Starr sooner or later," Audie said.

"What makes you think so?" Henry asked.

"Likes to rob places, especially banks. Gets a little bolder after every one. Also, when you ride with a bunch of brigands, there's always at least one who'll get drunk and start braggin' about what him and his friends have done. Pretty soon, a man like Starr, thinking he's better than the law, will make a mistake which'll get him caught . . . or shot."

Meg leaned closer to Henry and put her arm under his, looking at him with alarm. Henry patted her hand on his forearm, smiling at her. Audie watched the exchange, smiling back at them.

"What line of work you in, Mister Henderson?" Henry asked. "You sort of talk like a lawman."

Audie chuckled. "Naw, I'm in debt collections. I get hired to find people who don't pay their debts, and see if I can't work something out for my clients."

"Seems like that could get a little dangerous."

"Not if you do things right," Audie said with a grin. He looked at the Kid again. "But it does have its moments."

The two men fell silent for several minutes, looking out the window at the passing Kansas prairie.

"So where you folks headed?" Audie said, breaking the silence.

Henry hesitated for several seconds before he answered. "West," he said. "Then getting on a ship in San Francisco. We're missionaries. Going to China to save some of them heathens over there. What about you, Mister Henderson?"

"Nothing that exciting. Getting off at Garden City. There's a debtor there I need to see."

Meg spoke up for the first time. "The Lord tells us we need to forgive our debtors just as He forgives us for our debts."

"Yes, indeed," Audie said. "But that don't pay the bills, Miz Jackson."

Chapter Eight

July, 1893
Colorado Springs

Henry had a difficult time understanding how a dress could cost seventy-five dollars, especially one which weren't likely to be worn more than once, but that's the one Meg wanted to get married in, so that's what he bought her, and another one for after the wedding . . . with a hat. On top of that, she thought he needed to be outfitted better for the occasion, too, so they went to a haberdasher, fitted him up in a dark wool suit, a navy blue one with blue pinstripes running through it. Then a new hat to match. New boots; not range boots, boots like a city man would wear. Still, it wasn't like they got hitched in a church or anything; just him and her and Wilson and the justice of peace and his wife in the man's cluttered little office. They made a handsome couple, the justice's wife had told them.

The wedding night had started out well enough, even if it didn't end so. First they convinced Wilson he needed to go find his own entertainment for the night, then the two of them went to dinner at the fanciest restaurant in Colorado Springs. It was the big dining room at the Antlers Hotel where they were staying. A place with chandeliers, where the waiters dressed fancy, and a collection of fiddle players over in one corner played soft music the whole time. Fancy prices, too. Their waiter had introduced himself as "Onray."

"You a Frenchman?" Henry asked him.

The man stood straight, grabbed the bottom hem of his vest pulling it down with a jerk. "Non, monsieur," he answered in a haughty, superior tone. "I am Canadien."

Besides their steak dinners, they also ordered some champagne, at Meg's suggestion, to toast the occasion. After their waiter presented the bill and then stood discreetly off to the side, Henry examined it closely. When he got to the next to the last line, he furrowed his brow and frowned. The word looked French, and it had a price of four dollars assigned to it. The total at the bottom read $19.50.

"Onray?" Henry signaled to the waiter while still looking at the bill. When the man approached, he bent slightly toward Henry and asked in a half-whisper, "Oui, monsieur?"

"Uh, what's this?" Henry whispered in return, pointing to the line in question.

The waiter turned his head slightly, placing his lips closer to Henry's ear. "That is the gratuity, monsieur."

Henry kept looking at the word on the bill, slowly shook his head side to side. "Well, Onray, I just don't recall ordering no gratuity."

The waiter straightened, closed his eyes, and sighed. Still talking in a lowered voice, he said, "Non, monsieur. It is what I believe you Americans refer to as a teep."

"A teep?"

"Oui, monsieur. For my services."

"Ah. I see." Henry smiled and nodded. Reaching for his wallet in the pocket inside his new suit coat he said, "I sure could've used a man like you in my former business; however, me and this lady has just got married and I'm going to buy me a ranch."

He took twenty-five dollars out of the wallet and handed the bills to the waiter. "You done a fine job tonight, Onray. You keep whatever is left over there."

Onray bowed graciously and said in his heavy French Canadian accent, "Merci, monsieur. I wish you and your beautiful new wife the best of fortune in your marriage."

When they entered the expansive hotel lobby, still giddy and tipsy from the champagne, Henry and Meg, laughing and arm-in-arm, didn't at first notice the round little man wearing a brown suit and derby approaching them.

"Mr. Jackson?" the man said loudly from the couple's left and slightly behind them.

Henry, a mirthful grin still spread across his face, stopped and looked back at the inquisitor. He studied the man's face a few seconds. "Why if it ain't Mister. . . " Henry hesitated trying to recall the man's name.

"Henderson," the fellow said. "Audie Henderson."

Henry nodded, still grinning. "Yeah. I thought you was in Garden City."

"Nope. I'm right here in Colorado Springs."

Henry broke his grin, and swiveled his head to look about the nearly empty lobby. He noticed two uniformed policemen, who'd been leaning against wooden pillars, start to approach them, too. "You got some debtors you're looking for around here?"

"Believe I do, sir. Believe I do." Henderson snapped his fingers and made a "come here" motion with his right hand. A third gentleman rose from a lobby chair and walked to Henderson's side.

"Take your time, Mister Feurstine. Is this him?"

The man next to Henderson, perspiring some and looking nervous, nodded. "Yes. Yes, this's Henry Starr."

"Awright, arrest him, boys," he said to the two policemen.

Henry looked at the man called Feurstine. "Who the hell are you?" he asked him.

"He's from Bentonville, Arkansas," Henderson answered for the man. "One of the people you lined up in front of you when you and your boys shot your way out of that bank. Just sort of your bad luck he was here in Colorado Springs on business and spotted you. Good luck for me he went to the police and told them who you were. I was already on your tail though. His identifying you only made this business go quicker."

"Why, hell, Audie, you told me you wasn't a lawman," Henry said as one of the policemen put him in cuffs.

"I'm not, Mister Starr. I'm a Pinkerton detective. I work for the railroad you robbed a few months back. You stole some diamonds off a passenger who is the brother-in-law of that railroad's president. That's all my client wants you for. Of course, I intend to collect the reward on you for the Bentonville bank holdup, too. That and the one on your head for murdering a deputy U.S. marshal. So, I'm taking you and your associate back to Fort Smith so's you can stand trial for all those crimes, and I can collect the rewards."

"Well, if it's just the rewards you're after, Audie, maybe we can work out a deal. Save us all a lot of time and inconvenience."

Henderson leaned in close to Henry, looking at him eye-to-eye. "You and your associate are a debtor, Mr. Starr. I'm of the conviction that all debts need to be paid. Bribes won't work with me."

"What associate?"

"Why that young boy, Wilson."

"I doubt you'll find Wilson. He lit out the day we got here."

"He's already in custody. Found him in a bawdy house caught. . . " Henderson hesitated glancing at Meg. ". . . totally unawares."

"What about Meg here? You ain't going to arrest her, are you? She ain't done nothing."

Meg had taken a couple steps back from the group of men when the policeman had handcuffed Henry; her fingers covering her lips, her eyes wide in disbelief.

Henderson looked at Meg, frowning. "Other than her ill-advised association with you, I have no argument with her." He tipped his hat to Meg. "We're going to need to search your room and belongings for any stolen money, but after that you're free to go, ma'am."

"Now hold on," Henry sprung toward Henderson, but the policemen pulled him back. "We just got married. I can't just leave her here unaccompanied. She ain't got no wherewithal."

Henderson looked at Henry then back at Meg with displeasure. He reached inside his prisoner's coat pocket and pulled out the wallet. Opening it, he extracted a fifty dollar bill, handing it to Meg. "Here you go, Missus Starr. This won't leave you destitute, and should allow you to purchase a train ticket back to wherever you came from."

Meg, starting to cry, looked at the offered bill then Henry.

"Damn you, Henderson," Henry said, lunging again toward him. "There's more than that in that billfold. Give her all of it!"

"I expect this money is all ill-gotten, Starr. Giving her any is only on account of my kind-heartedness. Fifty should be plenty for her needs. Besides, these two boys here are off-duty. I'm thinking they'll be wanting a gratuity."

* * *

The train trip back across Kansas didn't have the enthusiastic expectancy as did the trip out. Henderson had allowed Henry and Meg to sit together, after Meg pleaded for it and convinced Audie it would do no harm, but he sat opposite them the whole time and Henry remained in shackles. Audie had enlisted a deputy U.S. marshal to help him take the two outlaws back to Arkansas. The deputy and the Kid took seats across the aisle.

At around midnight that first day of the trip, Henderson could no longer stay awake, so he clasped Henry to the seat and moved a row back on the empty bench there to try to sleep. He and the deputy would trade off watching their prisoners. As Audie stretched out on the seat bench, he pulled his revolver from his shoulder holster, laying it across his chest, his trigger finger inside the trigger guard. He looked seriously at Meg and said, "Don't try nothing stupid."

When she heard Audie start to snore, Meg said quietly, "Henry, what are we going to do?"

Henry, himself nodding some, came fully awake and looked at Meg. She looked back broken-hearted, awaiting his answer. He looked across the aisle at the deputy and his charge. Wilson was fast asleep, snoring and drooling with his head up against the window; the deputy stared back at Henry with a sleepy, yet stern expression. "Well, darlin'," Henry said. He lifted his left arm, cuffed at the wrist and chained to a restraint around his waist. "I can't see that there's much we can do at the present time, except try to get some sleep."

"I mean about your coming trial." Meg said. "They'll hang you if you're found guilty of murder. You said you killed that man in self-defense."

"Well, I did, Meg. Only he was a deputy marshal." Henry looked at the deputy looking back at him. He continued talking in a lowered voice so that the man couldn't hear him over the clatter of the train. "Even though most of Judge Parker's marshals is thievin' murderers themselves, he usually takes sides with the prosecutin' lawyer in such cases." He patted her right knee. "It don't look real promising."

Meg started crying again. She'd done a fair amount of that at the beginning of the ordeal, when Henry had first been arrested, but she'd stopped and sobered up when Henderson said she could ride back with them on the train and sit next to her husband. Now she opened up again in earnest.

"I reckon you're sorry you married me, aintcha Meg?" Henry said.

Meg dabbed her eyes and blew her nose. "Yes, somewhat," she said. "I knew in my heart marrying you was a fool idea." She made some more adjustments to her cheeks, eyes, and lips, sighing hard.

"But I did," she continued more in control. "And I'm going to stick with you. I don't know why, Henry, but I love you. I think I have since the day we met. I believe you told me the truth when you said you'd quit outlawing. Now we need to see if we can get you out of this mess. We need to find you a good lawyer. I expect you'll go to prison, but I don't want to see you hanged."

"Lawyers cost money, darlin', even bad ones. Henderson got all our money."

"No he didn't," Meg whispered.

Henry looked quickly at the deputy, who'd dropped his chin dozing, then back to Meg. "What do you mean? I thought he searched our room and bags."

"He did, and he got all that you put in the carpetbag. But he didn't search my bustle."

Henry grinned at her. "How much you got?"

Meg tried to smile, whispering close to Henry's ear. "I'm sitting on about two thousand dollars."

Henry nodded and scratched the side of his face. "That ought to get me a pretty good lawyer. My cousin Kale over in Tahlequah got me a good one when I went to jail for horse-thieving." He look quickly at Meg. "Another crime I never done." With her nod, he continued. "Man's name was Birdsong. He got me freed on that. I expect Birdsong could get me off that murder charge, too. There was witnesses; old Albert Dodge who I worked for as a cowhand, and another man who was with the deputy I shot. Don't reckon they'd lie under oath."

Suddenly another thought struck him, his expression turned cold and fearful. "What about your pa?" he asked.

"Don't worry about my pa," she said. "What you need to worry about is your life."

"I reckon I am," he said

* * *

"Mister Foreman, have the gentlemen of the jury reached a verdict?" Judge Parker asked the man standing in the jury box.

"Yes, your honor."

"The defendant will rise," Parker instructed. Once Henry got to his feet, the judge turned back to the jury foreman.

"What say you, then?"

"On the charge of first degree murder for the killin' of Deputy U.S. Marshal Floyd Wilson on December 13, 1892, we find the defendant, Henry Starr, guilty."

Meg let out a short wail, followed by sobs, and there was a flurry in the courtroom; half in jubilation, half in outrage, most from those with money down on the verdict.

Judge Parker slammed his gavel three times; calmly, but firmly, demanding order. Once the crowd settled down, he looked severely at the defendant and addressed him.

"Henry Starr," Judge Parker began. "This isn't the first time you've been before my court, but it will be your last. Time and time again, I see your kind come before me charged with scurrilous misdeeds against society. Even though you're a young man, it is evident you are an Indian man, and there doesn't seem to be any hope for reformation or redemption in you. I believe you were born hostile, and that it is your sworn vow to do harm to all white people as long as you live. There are other charges against you for which you need to be tried, but considering today's verdict, I don't see where we need to waste this court's—"

Henry slammed the chains of his wrist shackles onto the table top in front of him. "Judge, I have been found guilty of something I ain't guilty of! But I don't believe I need to stand here and listen to you jaw-jack. Now I'd appreciate it if you'd tell me my sentence and just be done with it!"

The courtroom became crypt quiet. The Hanging Judge himself was stunned into silence. Never in his long history on the bench had anyone ever interrupted him in such a manner. He cleared his throat. He opened a ledger on his bench and leafed through several pages, finally stopping and studying one of the pages for a few seconds.

"Henry Starr, I sentence you to be hanged by the neck until dead right outside on that gallows there," Parker pointed the gavel in his hand toward a side window in the courtroom. ". . . four months from today at noon on February 20, 1894." He looked again at Henry, paused to see if the condemned had anything else to say. "Bailiff, remove the prisoner. Court is adjourned for lunch," he said, slamming down his gavel one last time. "We'll reconvene at one-thirty to proceed with the next case."

Standing outside Henry's jail cell, Claude Birdsong, Esq. addressed his client. "Henry, there were some prejudicial issues in your trial, and I believe I can get it overturned. I'm going to petition the Supreme Court for a mistrial. I believe I can get your sentence overturned."

Henry sat on his cot, dejected. He said nothing.

Meg, standing behind Birdsong, came up to the bars of the cell door and spoke, her voice hushed, raspy from crying. "Henry?"

Henry looked up at Meg, and came to the cell door. He kissed her through the bars, and her tears bubbled out some more. Reached out through the bars to touch the sides of her face, her hair.

"I'm so sorry, Meg. I wish I'd never got you mixed up with me. I wish you'd took up with Stanley Poppingbird or Willie Watson back when we was school kids. You'd best find someone else now, and stay clean away from me."

Hot tears of anger mixed with those of her anguish. "You shut up! You're the one I love, Henry, and I can't change that. I'll always stay with you. Mister Birdsong believes he can get you another trial. We can't give up. You stay strong."

Henry nodded and smiled at her. He kissed her once more. The jailer came up behind them and said brusquely, "You folks gotta go now."

Chapter Nine

Through the cell window Henry watched men working on the gallows replacing the ropes and nooses. Apparently, the old ropes had been stretched beyond their usefulness, so it appeared he would get a new one at his appointed time in two days. Lawyer Birdsong had been working frantically to get a stay of execution, but it didn't look like he was going to be successful. Henry hadn't heard from him in three days.

"Dang it," Henry said. His cellmate, Dangerous Bob Lawson, rolled over in his bunk to face the wall. He wasn't interested in Henry's comment, only in blocking out the cold with his broad back and the thin blanket that partially covered it. Their cell was on the east side of the jailhouse, but the north wind still cut around the corner and knifed through the small open window. Heat from the potbellied stove in the aisle between the rows of cells did little to offset the permeating cold, even when Turnkey Pogue remembered to stoke it.

Henry's oath was more for his regrets than his misery from the cold. He had a few. He regretted not seeing his sisters more, or his ma. He regretted not putting a bullet through the brain of the green-eyed reprobate of a stepfather when he'd had the chance. He regretted the decision to rob that depot in Nowata when he was sixteen, which set him on the path to his current state. He regretted he wouldn't live to see his twenty-first birthday. But his biggest regret was Meg. He regretted making her love him, because she did, and now he was going to fill the one love of his life with a great sorrow. For that, he wished he'd never met her.

Keys rattled in the lock of the wooden door at the front of the cell block and it swung open. "Starr! Your lawyer's here," Turnkey Pogue hollered. Birdsong rushed through.

"Henry! They granted your stay!"

"What?" Henry clung to the cell bars. "What does that mean?"

"It means you won't hang. Not this week, anyway. It means the Supreme Court has decided to review your appeal. We'll probably get a new trial!"

"How soon will we know?" Henry asked.

Lawyer Birdsong's excitement abated some. "Well, these things take time in the high court. Maybe late spring, early summer."

* * *

July 1895

Turnkey Pogue moved a checker piece forward, then back, forward, then back. He took his finger off the piece and studied the board some more.

"Come on, Lester," Henry said with exasperation. "You're going to get jumped no matter which move you make."

Pogue had moved the small wooden table and his chair close to the bars of Henry's cell so they could play, something he'd done most afternoons for the past year.

"Well, I know," Pogue said, scratching the scruffy stubble on his face. "I just can't decide which move would get me jumped the least, that's all." He sighed and moved the piece again, this time removing his finger to finalize the move.

Henry jumped three of Pogue's checkers right into a royal square. "King me," he said, collecting the jumped pieces.

Pogue placed a black checker atop the new king. "When're you s'posed to get your new trial?" he asked Henry.

"No word yet. Don't expect old Judge Parker's too keen on trying me again. I think he's still upset the high court threw out my last one."

Pogue moved a checker piece and Henry performed another double jump. Pogue shook his head and stood up. "Well, I better go start passing out supper," he said.

Henry lay back on his cot and dozed in the hot, still air of his cell. He'd had the cell all to himself since the day they'd hung Dangerous Bob, some six months prior. While cellmates, Henry didn't think Bob was all that dangerous, or how he come by the name. Dangerous Bob had only been convicted of horse-stealing, along with aggravated assault for shooting his arresting marshal in the foot. But Bob rode with old Blue Duck who, still at large, was a known killer of women and children. It was said he was the same Blue Duck who lived with Belle Starr during her final days, and may have been the one who killed her. Nah, it seemed poor old Bob got hung more for guilt by association than anything else.

A loud war whoop and a gunshot brought Henry awake and upright in his bunk. Others in the cell block stirred, too.

"What the hell?" asked Sammy Broder grasping his cell bars and looking out.

"Sounded like it come from downstairs," answered Jake Dempsey from the cell next to Sammy's.

Two more gunshots rang out from two different guns, then a third from still another gun. A floorboard in the aisle between the rows of cells splintered upward. Another war whoop followed from below.

"Must be a jailbreak going on," Jake said, backing further away from the bullet hole in the floor.

A deputy, gun in hand, came crashing through the cellblock door at one end and headed for the door at the back end. He opened the door a crack, peering down the back stairs cautiously, pistol at the ready.

"What's going on?" Henry asked him.

"Cherokee Bill's got a gun, and he has shot Lester Pogue," he rasped.

"Is he dead? Henry asked.

"Bill's got a gun?" Sammy asked enviously.

"Yeah, he's dead awright," the deputy answered. "Ain't no doubt about that. Shot in the head."

"How'd Bill get a gun?" Sammy asked.

"Good question," the deputy said. "Could've been one of his brothers tossed it in through his cell winder."

Another two shots exploded and the deputy flinched, ducking involuntarily. Someone downstairs screamed, "Eeeeyi! Yie! Yie! Yie!"

"That's gotta be Cherokee Bill," Sammy said.

"Has to be," Jake agreed.

More shots fired, more savage whoops. "How come Bill ain't left yet?" Jake wondered.

"Lester unlocked Bill's cell door to take him his food," said the deputy. "If he hadn't shot Lester, Bill probably could've left, but now we got him pinned in his cell. If I figured right, he's shot five times; only has one bullet left. Onest he's emptied that gun, we'll get him."

"You going to kill him?" Henry asked.

"I 'spect so," the deputy said, still looking down the stairs through the partially opened door. "Hell, he's set for hangin' in a couple days, anyhow."

Another shot. "That's it," the deputy said and stepped through the door leaving it ajar. He descended the staircase slowly, stealthily, his pistol pointed forward. After a quarter of a minute he disappeared from Henry's view.

Another half minute, Henry and his fellow inmates heard the deputy shout, "Throw the gun out, Bill. You do that and we won't shoot ya."

There immediately followed two shots in rapid succession, the deputy grunted, then swore. The upstairs inmate trio could hear him clomping unsteadily back up the stairs. He crashed through the door. "The crazy sumbitch got me," the deputy said with pain in his voice. Blood seeped through his fingers where he had them clasped around his upper arm. He no longer held his pistol in his hand. Another red splotch spread out on the right side of the man's shirt just above his belt.

"Someone musta throwed in some extra ammo for Bill along with that gun," Sammy said. His tone was matter of fact; his lips twisted into a tight smirk.

"Think my arm's busted," said the deputy; although, none of the inmates had asked after the lawman's well-being. It appeared he wasn't aware of his other wound. He staggered to the other door in the cellblock and went down the stairs without saying another word.

Halfway through the third hour of the standoff, with intermittent exchanges of gunfire, Captain Jed Pride, the head jailer, entered the frontward door of the upstairs cellblock. He came straight to Henry's cell, stood looking into it.

"Starr," he spoke into the near dark of the cell.

Henry, like the others, had moved as far away from the front of his cell as he could. He sat on his bunk, feet off the floor, knees to his chin. "You might get your ass shot off standing there, Cap'n," Henry responded.

Pride ignored the warning and got right to the point. "We want you to talk to Cherokee Bill, Starr. See if you can't calm him down and have him give up this nonsense. He ain't got no way out of this . . . not alive, anyways."

"Maybe he's figured that out, Cap'n. Maybe that's why he keeps shooting."

"I got two deputies wounded and a jailer dead. Cherokee Bill's going to die one way or the other, but I don't want no more of my men killed or hurt. We need you to talk to him."

Henry stayed on his bunk. "Why me? Why don't you talk to him?"

"I tried, but all I got was shot at. You're an Indin, aintcha? We thought he'd listen to reason with another Indin."

"Reason?" In a mocking voice, Henry said. "Bill, why don't you quit shooting at these white men? Now put down your gun and stop all this, so's they can go ahead and hang you in a few days.

"That the reason you're talking about? Don't think I'm interested, Cap'n."

"We could make your life easier in here, Starr. If you do this, mebbe I could do something for you."

Henry got up off his bunk and went to the cell door. "Tell you what I want, Cap'n Pride. I want my new trial to start. I want out of this hell hole. It's been over a year since the Supreme Court threw my last trial out, now I want Judge Parker to give me that new trial like I'm s'pose to get, and I want it pronto."

"I'll talk to the Judge," said the Captain.

"You do that. You come back with a set date in writing and signed by the Judge . . . and I'll go down and talk to Bill." Henry paused to let his proposal sink in. Then he thought to add, "I know Bill." He hesitated before offering the next bit of information. "We even rode together some time back. Don't believe Bill would shoot another Cherokee."

Captain Pride scoured the inside of his cheeks and lips with his tongue, as he thought. "I'll be back," he said at last, turning to go back downstairs.

"I 'spect I'll be here, Cap'n," Henry said.

* * *

"Hey, Bill, it's Henry Starr!" Henry remained concealed at the base of the back stairs. He could see the shot deputy's pistol on the floor where he'd dropped it. It lay halfway between where he stood and the open door to Cherokee Bill's cell.

After a few seconds, Bill answered. "Henry? I thought they hung you."

"Not yet, Bill. I got me another trial first. Maybe they won't."

Bill laughed. "You really believe that, Henry? Hell, it'd spoil their sport not to hang another Indin."

"I'm going to do my best to keep that from happening. My lawyer says they rarely convict on a retrial."

"Izzat right?" Bill said. But it was more derision than a question. "Well, you do your way, I'll do mine. I wish you luck, Henry." Bill fired off another shot toward the hunkered deputies at the front of the cellblock.

"Bill, don't shoot. I'm going to come over there to your cell so's we can talk."

"Talk about what, Henry? They send you down here to talk me into givin' up? 'Cause I ain't givin' up." He fired another round in the direction of the deputies, then gobbled like a turkey.

"Now come on, Bill. You keep doing that, you're going to shoot me. Don't believe you'd shoot a brother, would you?"

"I might. I just might."

"Why hell, Bill, we rode together."

There was studied silence from Bill's corner for several seconds. "Awright, you come on in here, Henry, but I'm tellin' you right now I ain't givin' up." Then he said to the men bunched behind walls and crates at the other end of the building, "Any you bastards try anythin', I'll kill ya."

"Okay, Bill. I'm coming over there," Henry said. He stepped around the corner with his hands raised. "I'm unarmed," he added. He walked into Bill's cell looking down the barrel of a .44 pointed at his nose.

"Howdy, Henry," Bill said without lowering the gun. "It's been awhile."

Henry glanced down at the lifeless body of Lester Pogue sprawled on the cell floor. "It surely has, Bill. It surely has." He stood five feet away from Bill, his arms still raised. "Why don't you aim that pistol somewheres else. Makes me a little uncomfortable you pointing it at me."

Bill smiled and lowered the gun. "Sorry, Henry. Just wanted to make sure you knowed I'uz serious about maybe shootin' you."

"Well, I knew that, Bill. I'm much obliged you ain't yet."

Cherokee Bill threw back his head and laughed.

"What's this all about, anyway?" Henry asked.

Bill sat down on one corner of his bunk, leaning left to peer back toward the front area where his adversaries hid from his line of sight. Satisfied that none of them were advancing, he spoke to Henry.

"I'm bustin' out of here. Little brother Luther's waitin' outside with horses."

"He the one brought you that pistol?" Henry asked. He'd moved to the back of the cell so he'd be out of the line of fire, too.

Bill nodded. "Yeah, we aim to head back to the Territory where it'll be safe."

"Well, Bill, normally I'd say that was a good plan," said Henry. He stood leaning against the back wall his arms folded across his chest. He'd raised up on his toes to look out the small barred window, then settled back down on his heels. "But I can see maybe twenty armed men outside this jailhouse waiting for you to come out. Most of 'em got Winchesters."

Bill looked back at him belligerently. "I ain't dyin' in here. I ain't bein' hung. A man who don't fight for his freedom, ain't a man."

Henry nodded. "I can see your point, Bill. But what about your little brother? You want him to die for your transgressions, too?"

Bill, though still looking defiant, appeared to think about it, so Henry continued. "Now you could maybe make it out of the jailhouse here. I doubt it, but it's possible. You could even maybe make it to Luther and your horse, but I seriously doubt you'd get much beyond that. And don't think any of them men and deputies out there would hesitate to shoot you, Luther, and your horses to stop you from getting away. You wouldn't want that boy to die today, would you? His blood would be on your hands."

Henry stopped again to let Bill think about all this. He stretched up to look out the window again. "Just how old a boy is Luther, Bill?" Henry asked.

"Believe he's fourteen . . . mebbe fifteen." Bill stared at the floor, the gun held loosely between his legs. "When I's his age, he was a little tyke. I'd take off to go huntin' . . . deer, wild hogs, bear, didn't matter . . . little Luther'd come runnin' after me wantin' to go along. I'd fuss at him, but he'd just run along beside my horse, lookin' up at me with them big sad eyes. So I'd take him along. He'd ride to the front of me on that saddle holdin' the reins. Truth is, I kind of liked havin' him with me. We was pretty close back then. Most things I done, he'd be right there with me."

"Well, there you go then. Even if they didn't shoot Luther today, they'd arrest him. Now that you've kilt Lester, Luther getting you that gun makes him an accomplice. That could get him a hanging sentence from old Parker. You hand over that gun to me, and we call this whole thing off, we won't mention Luther or his part. Once he sees you're not busting out, he'll probably head on back home."

Cherokee Bill looked up at Henry. "You think you could get word to him, Henry? I figure he'll want to hang around for a few days to see if there's anythin' else he can do to get me out. I'd like to tell him to get the hell on outta here."

"I think so, Bill. You know, Trustee Heller's wife comes in here all the time to read us Bible verses. I bet if we explain the situation to her, she'd let Luther know."

Henry held out his hand, palm up, gesturing for Bill to give him the gun. Bill slapped the barrel of the pistol onto the palm of his own left hand over and over, trying to decide what to do. After the sixth or seventh slap, he closed his left fingers around the barrel and handed it butt first to Henry.

* * *

September 15, 1895
U.S. Court in Fort Smith, Arkansas

"Have you reached a verdict?"

"We have, your honor."

"What say you?"

"For the murder of Deputy U.S. Marshal Floyd Wilson, we find the defendant, Henry Starr, still guilty."

The usual hubbub surged through the courtroom. Judge Parker whacked his gavel and demanded order, as usual. "Henry Starr," the Judge said, looking smugly at the convicted. "Again, I sentence you to hang by the neck until dead three months from today. Do you have anything you want to say?"

Henry looking stunned, sat back down heavily in his chair. Lawyer Birdsong patted his shoulder and assured him he'd appeal the case again.

"Court's adjourned," Judge Parker said with one last gavel whack.

* * *

Meg sat across the table from Henry in the jail's visitor's room. She held a kerchief to her nose more to hold off the stench of the jailhouse than to suppress any nose drip caused by her tears.

"Meg, I've been in here over two years now," Henry said speaking low. He held her hands, his head bowed almost to his chest. "Don't know how much longer it's going to be now. Wouldn't blame you a bit if you wanted to divorce me."

"What do you mean, divorce you?" she sniffed. "Our marriage hasn't even gotten started."

"We ain't had much of a marriage."

"Well, we will. Mister Birdsong got you that third trial. They won't convict you a third time."

"Don't be too sure about that. I'm pretty sure Parker means to hang me. Now more than ever. Besides, I don't expect he's in any hurry to bring me to trial again. The Supreme Court overturning his court twice has to be dang humiliating to him. He's a proud man.

"You should get on with your life, Meg. You're a young woman, and pretty. You deserve a lot better than me."

"Henry, I'm not leaving you, so stop talking that way. I love you."

* * *

Lawyer Birdsong sat his satchel on the table, then himself in the chair opposite Henry. He sighed, then spoke. "Henry, Parker is willing to try you as many times as it takes to get you hung. I don't think I can take your case to the Supreme Court for the same conviction three times, and more than likely that's what you'll get at this next trial. There won't be a fourth trial."

"Hell, Birdsong, I don't really care no more. It has been almost five years I've been in this damn hell hole. I had what the doc called distentery, I had food poisoning, I had pneumonia, I got fleas and lice, I been ratbit I don't know how many times, these big sores are all over me," Henry held his forearm up for his lawyer to see. "Why look at me," then he stood. "I've probably lost thirty pounds. Truth be known, I think I'd prefer to hang. Keeping me in here is Parker's way of punishing me. It's worser than hanging."

"I know, I know." Birdsong looked around at the guard, then reached over to grab Henry's shirt sleeve to pull him back down into the chair. "Calm down."

The lawyer continued. "I can get you out of this place, Henry, but here's what we got to do. I'm going to see if I can work a deal to get your murder charge reduced to manslaughter. You plead guilty to that and I believe maybe Parker won't hang you."

Henry slumped back in his chair and rubbed his eyes. "Plead guilty?" he asked. His lawyer nodded.

"Aw right, Birdsong," he said after a bit. But if I plead guilty, you tell Parker I want this thing done quick so's I can get the hell out of here."

* * *

When Henry came into the visitor's room, Lawyer Birdsong stood opposite the table with a big grin on his face.

"You got some good news, Birdsong?" Henry asked.

"Parker's dead," the lawyer said.

Henry hesitated before sitting. "Is that a fact?" he asked, a little stunned.

"Yes. Yes, it is, Henry. He succumbed this morning."

Henry grinned at his lawyer, then the guard. "Well, damn," he said. "That *is* good news."

"I believe we'll have a better chance of getting that plea bargain worked out when his replacement gets here."

Henry's grin faded. "You mean saying that I done manslaughter?"

"Well, yes, Henry. That's what we talked about. The Supreme Court Justices recommended that charge for the new trial."

"But I figure with a new judge, I'll be found innocent of murder."

Birdsong sat down and looked Henry in the eye. "No, Henry. I don't believe that's going to happen. Best chance we got is copping this plea."

"Well, what will it mean?"

"It'll mean you won't hang, Henry. But you will do some prison time. Not here, though. Probably in a federal penitentiary somewhere back east."

"For how long?"

"Hard to say. Could be as little as two years or as long as twenty. Whatever it is, I think I can get it reduced for time served."

"Okay, Birdsong. But I hope it's soon. I'm tired of being rat and flea food."

November 15, 1898

The Honorable John R. Rogers placed his glasses on his nose and looked at the paper he held in his hand. Henry stood below him in front of the judge's bench, shackled at the wrists and feet.

"Alright, Starr, your guilty plea for the charge of manslaughter in the first degree has been entered. The court sentences you to eight years."

Birdsong cleared his throat and said, "Your Honor—" but the judge held up his hand to silence him, and continued reading the sentence.

"The term of that sentence will be reduced to three years for the time you've already served here." Rogers lowered the paper and looked at Henry. "The deed you did to disarm one Crawford Goldsby back in ninety-five." Judge Rogers again consulted the paper he held. "Also known as Cherokee Bill. . . " He read a few more lines silently before adding, "rest his renegade soul . . . that deed did not go unnoticed by this court. I've read Captain Pride's report of the incident, and have taken that into consideration in pronouncing sentence." Henry nodded, so the judge proceeded.

"On the counts of armed robbery in Indian Territory, as well as that train robbery at Pryor Creek in Indian Territory, you are sentenced to seven and five years, respectively, which brings your total sentence to fifteen years. This court will remand you to the federal penitentiary at Columbus, Ohio to serve out these sentences." The judge set the paper down and looked at Henry. "Is there anything you'd like to say, before I adjourn this court?"

Henry looked at his feet, then up at the judge. "Well . . . onliest thing I can say is, I appreciate you not hanging me. I surely do, Judge."

Chapter Ten

Standing on the prison grounds with fifteen other men in chains, Henry gazed up at the walls rising a vertical thirty feet above the frozen dirt. It was difficult to tell where the dull gray limestone blocks left off and the sullen sky began. Pellets of snow and sleet blew in a confused swirl around the men giving no true direction of the wind. All they knew for sure was that the frozen spits came from the hostile, leaden clouds gathered above them.

Three guards had shoved the new prisoners into two loose lines facing a door in the stone wall, told them to keep quiet. They waited, silently, in the biting cold and stinging sleet. After ten minutes, a small man in a wool overcoat came out, and stood on the raised porch in front of the door. He wore thick leather gloves; a fur hat covered his head and ears. He waited in silence while the guards prodded the standing men, demanding that they pay attention to what was about to be said.

"My name is Coggin," the man began. "If any of you ever has occasion, you will address me as Warden Coggin, or Warden. You men have entered the Ohio Penitentiary where you will remain as prisoners for either the remainder of your life, or until your sentence expires, whichever comes first." Coggin paused to let his last sentence sink in.

"All of you have been convicted of crimes against humanity, and for those your incarceration will be served here. Your punishment will include hard labor. We have rules here. Obey those rules and your stay will be unremarkable. Disobey them, and we'll make you wish you had. None of you will escape. If you try you will be shot in the attempt, or tied to that post in the yard over there," he pointed to the seven foot pine pole sticking out of the ground to their left and behind them; they all turned to look at it, ". . . and flogged."

With no further word, the warden turned and went back through the door in the wall.

When Henry entered his cell, he found it already occupied by a tall skinny man with dirty blond hair and rheumy blue eyes. He lay on his bunk, looked at Henry impassively.

"Howdy," Henry said. He threw the draw sting bag, containing the clothes and linens he'd been issued, onto the unoccupied upper bunk. Extended his open hand toward the man. "Name's Henry Starr."

The man waited an uncomfortable ten seconds before he responded. "Bodeker," he said taking Henry's hand in a weak grip. "Most around here call me Dutch."

Henry released Bodeker's hand and said, "Well, Dutch, looks like you and me are going to get to know one another. What brought you here?"

"Killed a man," Bodeker said. "He took something from me. What about you?"

"Well, I killed a man, too. But only because he tried to kill me first. Jury didn't see it that way, though, and called it murder; then I got a re-trial and got manslaughter. But that's only part of it. I robbed some banks and such, too.

Bodeker, still lying on is back with his hands clasped behind his head, gave a small nod.

"What did that man you kilt steal from you?" Henry asked.

"My wife. Shot her, too, but she didn't die. Got convicted of aggravated assault for that; which was true enough, as I's plenty damn aggravated when I shot her. Found both of them lying together naked in my own bed."

Henry stood leaning against his bunk, shaking his head. "Well, yes sir, I could see where you'd be upset."

February 21, 1899
Dear Meg,

I have been here a little over a month now and am settling in. This is a much bigger place than the Ft. Smith jail, and not near as rat infested. I believe there is about 500 men in this prison. Most is white men, but there seems to be a fair amount of Negros. I do not see many men of Indian blood. I suspect most of that nature have already been hung, or put in a separate place. As to why I'm here and not in that other condition is only by the good luck of Judge Parker dying, and Judge Rogers' kindness.

It is very cold here. More colder than the Territory. It appears to me some of the boys I come up here with will not survive this cold country.

I hope this letter finds you in good health.

Your loving husband,

Henry

March 13, 1899

My dearest Henry,

I was most pleased to receive your letter, and to hear that you are adapting to your new surroundings. Although it is colder there in Ohio, I believe your conditions will be much improved over those of the Fort Smith jail. And spring is just around the corner.

News here is that my father died late last month due to an accident. He was kicked in the head while shoeing a mule. He lingered unconscious for five days before he passed on. My mother is greatly grieved, and I suppose I'm saddened, too. Father was never an affectionate man and was prone to bouts of anger. When I remember him, it's mostly about his meanness to my mother and me. I don't recall him ever telling either of us he loved us. But he was my father.

Please stay out of trouble, Henry. If you show yourself to be a model prisoner it's possible they may shorten your sentence. Mr. Birdsong told me that, and he wants me to tell you he is working to gain your pardon.

I will always love you, Henry. I believe you are a good man at heart.

With affection,

Megan

Warden Coggin frowned at the papers as he read them. Henry didn't feel good about being called to see the warden. In his experience, such interviews didn't bode well for those summoned. He waited silently while the warden read and frowned, ignoring Henry's presence. The only sound in the room came from the slap of a billy club into Boss Tucker's open left palm. Henry glanced nervously over his left shoulder to see the guard rhythmically slapping club-to-palm as he rocked flat-footed to the balls of his feet and back. His smile back at Henry had no kindness.

"You killed a man, Starr." The warden looked up at Henry with cold eyes. "A law enforcement officer."

Boss Tucker's club-slapping stopped. Henry glanced quickly back at the guard again seeing the mean smile replaced with a look of pure hatred. Henry swallowed, and addressed the warden. "Yes sir, Warden Coggin, sir . . . But it was in self-defense. He shot at me before—"

"Shut up!" Boss Tucker shouted, jabbing the end of the billy club sharply into Henry's ribs. Henry winced and shut up.

Coggin continued giving Henry that cold look for several seconds, before consulting the papers once again. "It says here in your file that you are not to be assigned hard labor." He looked at Henry again. "Men sent to this prison are all sentenced to hard labor. Why shouldn't you be? You seem to be worse than most. After all, you killed a lawman."

Henry started to speak, but quickly remembered Boss Tucker's billy club. He only shook his head, and tried to look contrite.

The warden laid the paper back in the open folder, then closed it. "Fortunately for you, Prisoner Starr, I know Judge Rogers. We served together in Congress. And if John Rogers said you're not to have hard labor as part of your sentence, then I must assume he had good reason.

"So you will not be assigned hard labor at this time. But let me just say that if there is the slightest infraction by you of any of the prison rules, I will slap you on the chain gang. Do you understand?"

Henry opened his mouth to speak, but looked back at Boss Tucker before he did so.

"The prisoner may speak," Coggin said, as much to the guard as to Henry.

"You won't get no trouble out of me, Warden. I swear that on my dear mother's grave. Thank you, sir."

The warden waved his hand, palm down, in a gesture of dismissal, and Boss Tucker jerked and prodded Henry out of the office none too gently.

* * *

May 23, 1899
Dear Meg,

I am sorry to hear about your Pa. I know he never liked me much, but like you said, he were your pa. I hope you can find some peace in his passing.

Prison life ain't so bad now that warmer weather has come. I am doing as you said and keeping my nose clean. The warden is not too hard a man. When we arrived he told us all that if we followed the rules and didn't cause no trouble life would be a lot easier for us here and I vowed that I would do that. Birdsong said the last time I saw him that I could probably come up for parole in a year or two if I did so.

They have put me into the bakery to learn bread making. It ain't hard work and I think it will be a good trade to learn for when I get out. Judge Rogers put in my sentence that I did not have to do hard labor. The warden said he would honor that as long as I obeyed the rules which I aim to do, as I said.

I hope this letter finds you in good health.
Your loving husband,
    Henry

July 25, 1899
Dearest Henry,

High summer has come here to the Territory. The days are very hot and the nights warm and sultry. We have not seen a rain storm in several weeks, and dust and flies abound.

Mother and I have been quite busy with the canning. We had a bountiful garden this year. Mother had not much interest in planting in the spring after Father died, and I could not do it on my own, although I tried as I was quite anxious that we should have something put up for the winter. Mr. Thomas McGuinness, a gentleman farmer in the area, noticed my poor efforts at plowing and planting our small garden, and determined to lend his helping hand. With that, and the spring rains, our harvest became most generous.

We sold Father's livery and smithy business to a man named Ridge Watie for a sum less than we'd hoped. The man could see two women in straits for income, and took full advantage of the situation, choosing miserliness over compassion. The amount will see us through a year, perhaps a little more, but even with my teaching wages we will have to pinch every penny.

It is pleasing to hear you are learning a good trade. I have not heard from Mr. Birdsong on the progress of your pardon.

I remain,

Affectionately yours,

Megan

Nobody in the prison population was sorry to hear that Ironhead Crutchfield had died, or Miner Hadley, or Eustus Reiner. No men were hated or feared more than those gangsters. But the cause of their death caused alarm. One day they were bullying the inmates as usual, the next they were laid up with fever and delirium. And two days after that, they were dead. That kind of fast-spreading disease created more terror than any marauding those three could manufacture.

"I hear there's mebbe a hunnert others got this jail fever," Dutch said. He stood at the bars of their cell looking out.

A wail echoed from somewhere in the cellblock followed by a long incomprehensible babble. It had the sound of a lament, a sorrowful sobbing dirge from the dying. The prison infirmary had long since filled to overflowing; the remaining sick were left in their cells.

"Hard to tell how many's got it," Henry said. "Most likely it ain't as many as you heard.

"Yeah, I guess if you're one of the dead or sick, it don't matter how many others got it," said Dutch.

September 12, 1899

Dear Meg,

I have waited to hear back from you since my last letter of August 15th, but will go ahead with another anyhow. I suspect you was busy getting the canning done with your Ma, and did not have time to pen me a letter. Maybe my last letter did not make delivery.

I do not recall the man you call McGuinness. It could be he arrived around Nowata after I departed. At any rate, I am glad a kind man such as him stepped forward to assist you and your mother with the planting.

As I wrote in my last letter, there was a spread of typhus in the prison this past summer. I did not catch the disease, but many did. Because it is spread by lice and fleas it is thought one of the work gangs sent out to clear a wooded area brought the disease inside. There was about twenty or so fellas that died of it. We have spent a lot of time dusting down our bedding and clothes to get rid of the nasty little bugs, and it appears we have gotten past the worst. There are now many new rules in place for all inmates to have better cleanliness.

I suppose you have started up your new school year by now. It don't seem that long ago when you and I first met as kids in that school house.

I look forward to hearing from you soon.

As always,

Your loving husband,

Henry

September 28, 1899

Dear Henry,

I'm so sorry I haven't written you sooner. I did receive your letter of August 15, but I was pre-occupied with the business of running this household. Mother isn't much skilled in that area, nor much inclined to do so. We had some live stock transactions, plus the matter of Father's livery to settle. But I don't offer that as an excuse. Time just slipped away from me, and I do apologize.

Mr. McGuinness bought the old Turley place south of town, that of about 600 acres near the Verdigris River. He moved there with his family three years ago, using half the land to raise wheat and the rest for a small cattle operation. You wouldn't have known him. He has a seven year old daughter, Emily, who attends my school and a young boy of about four. He's called Tommy, being Thomas Junior. The poor man is now a widower, his wife having died of the cancer about two years ago.

He has been most kind to help with the work around our place. He is such a dear man. I had mentioned to you his help with the garden, and he graciously took up the tasks of fixing some things that needed it around the house and barn. He also lent his expertise to assist me with the aforementioned livestock sales. Also, although the deal had already been struck with Mr. Watie for the livery, Thomas was able to persuade him to append some additional funds to the final price.

I was so distressed to hear about the epidemic of typhus there, but relieved to know you didn't contract it. I hope you stay well through this coming winter.

Affectionately,

Megan

"Dutch, when your wife was cheating on you, did she give any indication what she was doing?" Henry lay on his bunk staring at the ceiling. He held Megan's latest letter in his right hand. When he got no response from his cellmate, he inquired again. "Dutch?"

"What?" came the groggy reply.

"I said, your wife. You know, before you shot her. Did she let you know in any way what she was doing?" There was another extended silence, and Henry decided to drop it, thinking Dutch had drifted back to sleep. He put the letter back in its envelope, then into the tin cigar box where he kept all of Meg's letters. He rolled onto his side and punched his pillow.

"I thought about that a lot," Dutch said in a low voice. "There was times when she'd say things I didn't pay much attention to then, but after, they come back to me. For instance, she'd tell me how a man would flirt with her, how another would even make improper suggestions, but she'd tell it in a laughing manner, like it was nonsense and she didn't pay no mind to any of it.

"Now when I look at it, I think she was telling on herself. And that man with her who I kilt probably wasn't the onliest one she'd bedded down with. Even so, it's still a puzzle why she'd do such a thing. Tell me, that is. Mebbe she felt guilty; mebbe she just wanted to check to see if I'd get jealous; mebbe she figured if she talked about those doin's out in the open with me, I wouldn't get suspicious. Whatever the case, it all made me feel like a damn fool when I did finally figure it out, though.

"But it's a funny thing, now that it's all said and done. In the heat of the moment, I thought shooting her would make me feel better, about being made to feel the fool and all. Truth is, it didn't. Not as much as I'd hoped, anyway."

Henry laid there on his side staring at the cell wall, not caring to respond to Dutch's testimony, his mind a-swim with thoughts. On the one hand, he was fretful and jealous and angry at what he feared he knew; on the other, it was what he'd told Meg she needed to do all along—get on with her life and forget about him. He loved her, but she was too young and pretty to waste her time waiting around for the likes of him. Sounded like that McGuinness was the kind of feller Meg had always hoped Henry would be. It was a good thing, right?

A fist had balled in the pit of his stomach punching at him from the inside. He drew his knees up and bowed his back to try to ease the pain of it, but it didn't help much.

December 28, 1899
Dear Meg,

It appeared we wasn't as much out of the woods as I said on the typhus, as shortly after I last wrote you I come down with it. For the past 6 weeks I have been laid up in the infirmary. It does not appear that I will die from it, though. The doc sent me back to my cell yesterday.

I thought I had rid all the bugs in my bunk and cell, but apparently I was flea bit from one jumping off my cellmate Dutch Bodeker. He come down with the sickness a day before I did. Unfortunately for him, though, he died.

Due to my being laid up so long, I lost my job in the bakery. They have moved me into another shop learning to make gloves.

It sounds as though your acquaintance with Mr. McGuinness came at the right time. You need someone of his station and experience to help you in your hour of need, and I am happy about that. He has done things I could never have did for you. If you've made him aware of our relationship, please convey to him how much obliged I am. I am sorry I weren't that kind of man for you.

It has got cold here already. Winter comes early in these parts. There is already a foot of snow on the ground. I am surely looking forward to the new year and the new century. I can only believe both will bring us better conditions in our lives.

I remain,

Your loving husband,

Henry

April 13, 1900

Dear Henry,

It has been a most difficult winter. We had an abundance of ice and snow, more than we're accustomed to, and the cold seemed to seep into the very marrow of my bones. It appears quite reluctant to loosen its grip on the land. Only in the last week have we started to a gradual warming and signs of spring.

The winter seemed to take its greatest toll on Mother. Since Father's death she had descended into a deep depression, and nothing would draw her out of it. When she caught a cold in January, she could not or would not rid herself of it. It deepened into pneumonia in February, and by early March she was gone. It's almost as if she willed it that way.

Now I have this little house, and what is left of the rest of the estate, all to myself. Even in her gloomy state of mind, Mother was still a companion. I truly miss her.

Thomas has been a welcome friend these past few months, especially through the ordeal of Mother's illness and passing. I don't know how I could have survived without his help. She required a lot of care, especially toward the end, but I could not stay with her and keep my job at the school, so Thomas sent his housekeeper, an Indian woman called Aylisee Smallhawk, to stay with her and help. Both she and Thomas gave kindnesses for which I'm thankful beyond my words to express.

I hope this letter finds you in good health and spirits.

Affectionately,

Megan

May 10, 1900

Dear Meg,

I received your letter just today with the news of your mother. I am very sorry to hear of her passing. I know that must have been a blow to you. You have certainly had your share of hardships in the past few years.

I know the old woman you call Smallhawk. We all called her Grandmother (that is what Ay li see means in Cherokee) when I was a boy. She must be a hundred years old by now. I remember her as a kind and gentle soul, although she was not agin taking a switch to small boys in need of one. I believe your mother was in good hands in her final days.

Meg, I know it must be difficult to live there on your own without no man to support you. And I know that your friend Mr. McGuinness has been especially helpful in looking after you and your ma. It is a difficult thing for me to say this, but if you decided to take up with that man, I would understand. You deserve someone like him, and it will likely be several more years before I get out of this here prison.

I always told you, you need to get on with your life. If you did that with Mr. McGuinness, I would not blame you any.

Sincerely,

Henry

September 22, 1900
Dear Henry,

It is with a heavy heart that I pen this letter to you. It will probably be my last.

As you have surmised, I have come to depend heavily upon Mr. Thomas McGuinness since the passing of my parents. He has become a great friend to me, and I have grown quite fond of him, more so than just as a good friend. Subsequent to this, I have decided you are correct in that I need to get on with my life. Therefore, upon your advice, I have asked Mr. Birdsong to draw up papers of divorce between you and me. I suspect he will be contacting you before long with a set of those papers for you to sign.

Henry, it has never been my intent to hurt you. I have loved you dearly since we were children, and I suppose in some small way I always will. However, I must put away my childish ways. It has been almost ten years that we have been apart, during which I've suffered much hardship and longing.

You will always have a place in my heart, Henry.
Fondly,
Megan

Henry's actions confounded Warden Coggin. He had no doubt the pounding Prisoner Dugan received from Henry was deserved. Dugan had deserved many in the five years he'd been there, although he was mostly the deliverer, not the receiver. Henry's beating of Dugan was as surprising as it was confounding. Dugan was large and mean, always looking for a fight. Henry was about half Dugan's size, smallish, skinny; and easy-going; even passive, you could say. Dugan was the yard bully; Starr was the compliant model prisoner. So the bloody unconscious heap that Henry made of Dugan surprised guards and prisoners alike.

The warden had no choice, of course. Fights between prisoners was a major infraction of the rules. Prisoner Starr would have to do time in the hole. But it confounded Coggin so much, he had to know why Henry did what he did.

"Starr, you confound me." Henry stood before Coggin in shackles as he had almost a year and a half ago during their first meeting. "Up until today, your behavior here has been exemplary. You have been in every way a model prisoner, so you can understand why I'm confused about your fighting with Prisoner Dugan."

Henry stood in silence, his head bowed. After a few seconds, Warden Coggin continued.

"Captain Tucker tells me witnesses say you struck the first blow; that you sought out Dugan and proceeded to beat the hell out of him unprovoked."

Henry remained bowed and unresponsive. Coggin walked around to the back of his desk and seated himself. "Starr, I want you to tell me why you did this," he said.

Henry shrugged and looked at the warden. "I was looking for a fight, Warden. Dugan seemed like the best choice."

Coggin nodded. A package of legal papers from Starr's lawyer in Indian Territory had come through his office for the prisoner to sign, divorce papers, so the warden figured he knew the source of Henry's rage, although he questioned his wisdom on choice of opponent. Still, if he had to pick a fight with someone, he was glad it was Dugan; probably would turn out better for everyone all around. Still, rules were rules.

"Well, Starr, you broke a major rule. I'm going to have to put you in solitary for thirty days. When you get out, we'll reevaluate your status."

Henry said nothing. Coggin motioned for Tucker to take Henry away.

* * *

October 1902

"Warden wants to see you, Starr," Boss Tucker said.

Henry, sitting at his workbench in the glove shop, looked up at the burly guard. He laid the materials in his hands onto the bench and rose to follow. "What's this all about?" he asked Tucker. Except for his setback a year ago, there wasn't a mark on his record. In fact, his bout with Dugan had turned out to be a good thing. Anytime Dugan started to cause trouble, all Henry had to do was show up and Dugan would back off. Henry had become a champion of the prison yard.

But a summons to the warden's office was never a good thing.

Tucker shrugged. "Warden didn't tell me. Just said to go haul your ass over there."

The warden sat at his desk writing when Henry and Boss Tucker entered the office. Coggin glanced up at them and pointed his pen to a captain's chair in front of his desk. "Have a seat, Starr," he said and returned to his writing.

Henry, his brow furrowed with a question, looked at Boss Tucker. The prison guard looked back at him and shrugged.

"If it's all the same to you, Warden, sir, I'd just as soon stand," said Henry.

Coggin stopped writing and looked up. Setting the pen aside, he folded his hands one on top of the other and looked sternly at Henry. Then he almost smiled. "Well, I prefer you to sit." He motioned with one hand towards the chair. "Please," he said.

Henry nodded and complied.

"I'll get right to the point," the warden started. "You've received a pardon from President Roosevelt." He waited for Henry's response, but all he got back from the prisoner was a slack-jawed wide-eyed expression of astonishment and disbelief.

The warden continued. "Don't know when your specific release date will be, but as soon as we get all the paperwork in order, you'll be set free. I expect it will be shortly after the first of the year."

Henry's stunned mind finally allowed his voice to engage. "A Pardon? From the President? Why would he do that?"

Coggin picked up his pen and started writing again. "I have no idea. You'll have to ask him that," he said.

Chapter Eleven

March, 1903
Tulsa, Indian Territory

Henry stepped off the train and looked around. Tulsey Town had grown since he'd last seen it. That had been almost ten years ago when he'd fenced those stolen diamonds to Feingold. He wondered if that old Jew was still in business. If so, Feingold would be the only person in town he knew. The streets had changed, the town had grown, but he thought he could still find the jeweler's place.

The store looked a little more prosperous, the old man behind the counter working on a watch still looked the same.

"Howdy, Feingold, you old skinflint," said Henry.

The old man removed the loupe from his eye, and squinted in Henry's direction. He turned his head slightly to one side then cocked it to the other. "Why, Henry Starr," he said when recognition set in. "I thought you were in prison."

"Was. Roosevelt give me a pardon."

"A pardon? President Roosevelt?"

"Yep. The old Lion Tamer hisself."

The jeweler shook his head and laughed. "Who can figure those damn Republicans."

Henry looked around the jewelry store. "Looks like things are going good for you here in Tulsey Town."

"Boom times," said Feingold. "Town's grown. They call it Tulsa now. Folks got money to spend." He leaned back in his chair and pulled open a drawer, reaching in to put his hand on the butt of a pistol. "Hope you ain't planning to rob me, Henry."

Henry, who'd been examining a big brass eagle underneath a lampshade glowing with electric light, gave Feingold a hurt look. "Well, hell no, Feingold; I been rehabilitated. Aim to be an upstanding citizen now."

"Good," Feingold said. "Glad to hear that." He kept his hand on the pistol. "Last time you were in, you bought an engagement ring. You marry that girl?"

Henry turned back to the brass eagle lamp to study it some more. "She left me for some Irish farmer while I was in prison. I reckon she's still got the ring, though."

"Sorry to hear that, Henry. That was a nice ring. So what brings you in here today?"

"Looking for work. You're the only person I know in Tulsey . . . Tulsa. Figured you could put me on to something. You said it was boom times. What's causing the boom?"

"They struck oil over in Red Fork across the river. Talk is, there's plenty more around here."

"What kind of oil?" Henry asked, then turning his attention to a six-foot grandfather clock encased in mahogany wood.

"Why black oil, petroleum. Just about every kind of machine uses petroleum—trains, saw mills, river boats. There's a new kind of machine called an automobile. They have an engine runs on something made from petroleum."

Henry looked briefly at Feingold, then back at the clock. "Yeah, I seen one of them. Obnoxious thing. Damn glad their ain't more of 'em."

"I don't have work for you, Henry, if you're thinking of that. But I know a fella might could help you out. Name's Bagby. Sells real estate."

"Real estate? You mean land?"

"Well, some of that, I s'pose. Mainly houses and buildings, I think. Lotsa new houses being built."

"Where can I find this Bagby feller?"

* * *

Hiram Bagby said he'd come out from Saint Louis where he'd been in the real estate business. Heard about the oil strike and knew there'd be a growth in Tulsa; thought he could make a killing. As they sat talking, Henry sized the man up. Figured Bagby was as big a thief as he was, only better dressed. The man was a talker, that was evident; near as Henry could tell, about three-fourths of what the man said was bull crap. His smile was big, but his eyes weren't sincere; more snake-like than honest. Yes, Henry thought he'd be able to work with Bagby just fine.

"So what kind of work have you been doing, Henry? You don't mind if I call you Henry, do you?"

"Why, no, Hiram. Okay if I call you Hiram?"

Big smile. "Please do," he said.

"Well, Hiram, the last ten years I've been with the federal government working in security up in Ohio. Before that I was self-employed, financial stuff, travelled a lot."

Bagby's eyebrows shot up, he smiled bigger. Henry wasn't sure Hiram had bought what he was peddling. "No kidding?" Bagby said. "Why'd you leave gummint work? Hear that pays pretty well?"

"Just felt sort of restricted; kind of locked into my position. Like you, I'd heard about the boom going on back here, and wanted to see if I could get in on some of it. Maybe make my fortune."

"Ever done any real estate work?"

"Nope," said Henry. "Don't know a dang thing about it."

"Well, any recommendation from Mort Feingold is good enough for me.

"I can teach you the business. Most of it is convincing people to buy what they don't know they want. I'm pretty good at reading people, and I believe you can sell. It'll be straight commission, but I'll pay you a draw until you get on your feet."

Bagby stood and extended his hand. "When can you start?" he asked Henry.

"Well, thank ya, Hiram. I appreciate you taking me on." Henry stood and took Bagby's hand. "Got some personal business I need to attend to first, so I'll need a couple days."

"Not a problem. Why don't you plan on being here at eight Monday morning?" Bagby led Henry to the front part of the office stopping at the desk of his secretary. "You met my girl when you came in, right?"

Henry looked at the pretty young woman sitting at the desk and smiled. "Yes, we spoke," he said. The girl smiled back and nodded.

"Well, this is Miss Ollie Griffin," Bagby said. "Not only is she the best decoration in the place, she pretty much runs things around here, too. She'll get you started Monday morning."

Henry locked eyes with Miss Griffin and bowed slightly. "Pleased to meet you," he said. When she looked back at him with her big soft brown eyes, Henry felt a small electric charge course down his left ribs.

* * *

As he rode northeast only the slightest spark of pink lined the eastern horizon. Feingold had spotted him ten bucks to get him through the next week, and he'd rented the horse and tack for a buck fifty. He wasn't sure what he was doing, or why, or what he'd find, but he felt it was something he had to do. Nowata was about fifty miles away; the old Turley place a bit closer. He figured he could get there before sundown if he rode steady.

The house was fairly big, a two story structure with a wide porch on all sides. It sat on a flat stretch, maybe five acres, with hills behind it. Wooded land, but a lot of it around the house had been cleared. A large painted barn with a big corral sat off to the west and behind the house some fifty yards. Eight or ten horses milled around in the corral. On the east side, straight rows of trees covered about an acre. From where he sat on the hill a half mile away to the south, Henry couldn't tell if the orchard was apples or peaches. It looked like they were just starting to bud out in the early spring warmth.

A man was going in and out of the barn doing his evening chores, a young girl helped him. That'd be McGuinness, Henry thought, and his daughter. No sign of Meg. He suspected she was inside fixing supper.

He sat watching the scene some fifteen minutes or so. When the big red sun touched the top of the hills behind the barn, Henry gently spurred the horse and started him descending toward the farm house at a slow walk.

He smacked the trail dust off his hat with his left hand, then brushed the shoulders and lapels of his coat to do the same before knocking firmly on the front door, and waited. He could hear voices in the back of the house, then heavy footsteps—a man's—approaching the door. A tall burly fellow in a green plaid flannel shirt, sleeves rolled halfway up, opened the door. He had massive forearms covered with bronze hair and freckles, his face wind-burned, crow's feet etched the corners of his eyes. Short-cropped hair sat in tight red curls atop his large head like a tangle of briars. Looked to be in his mid-forties; regarded Henry, not with malice, but curiosity.

Henry cleared his throat. "Uh, Mister McGuinness?" he asked.

"Yes."

"I'm Henry Starr."

McGuinness pulled his head back slightly and narrowed his eyes. "What do you want?" he asked bluntly.

"McGuinness, I'm not here to cause no trouble. Honest. I just got out of prison a few weeks ago . . . Got a pardon from the President." Henry hesitated, hoped adding that bit would help his case. But it didn't seem to impress McGuinness. "Anyway, I was wondering if I could speak to Meg, just briefly, and then I'll be on my way." He held up his right hand, and added, "As God is my witness, no trouble, I promise."

McGuinness stood blocking the door, looking at Henry for what seemed like a long, long time. Henry, holding his hat in both hands and looking down, shuffled his feet, looked back up at the big Irishman.

Finally, McGuinness spoke. "I'll ask her. It'll be up to her."

"Much obliged," said Henry.

McGuinness shut the door in Henry's face. He waited. He could hear voices in the house, getting louder in the swirl of an argument. He turned and walked to the porch steps, looking out at the darkening woods a few hundred yards away with the dirt road cutting through it. He looked to his right where the top curve of the sun was just dipping below the hills. Watching the sunset, he waited some more, turning the brim of his hat in his hands. Could hear no more voices inside the house. Clouds moved across the sky from the southwest, darkness increased by degrees. Presently he sighed, put on his hat, and started down the steps towards his horse.

"Hello, Henry," a woman's voice said behind him.

Henry turned at the bottom porch step. He could see a woman framed in the doorway, but it was too dark to make out who she was. He didn't recognize the voice, it was husky and low like she had a cold, nor her shape. This woman was greatly pregnant. Enough light remained to tell that for sure.

Henry took one step back up toward the porch. "Meg?" he asked.

"What are you doing here?" the woman responded, still with that husky voice.

"I . . . I don't know. I just thought . . . I just wanted . . . Gosh, Meg, you're gonna have a baby."

"Yes, Henry. I know."

"I mean . . . I didn't think you was going to talk to me, so I was just gonna leave." Henry turned halfway back, looking down, as if that's what he'd do if she wished.

"I didn't either," Meg said. "Think I wanted to talk to you, I mean. I stood behind the door a long time just looking at you."

Henry studied the hat his hands fumbled with, and nodded. The silence between the two grew awkward. Henry put his hat on his head, and without looking directly at Megan said, "Well, I better be heading out." Waited a couple more seconds to give Meg a chance to stop him, turned and walked to his horse.

"I was starving, Henry. I was nearly destitute."

Henry stopped, keeping his back to her. "I'm sorry, Meg."

"Thomas saved me. He's a good man, Henry. An honest, hard-working man."

Henry turned back to face Megan. He looked her square in the face; he couldn't see her eyes in the gathering darkness. "But do you love him, Meg?"

Meg hesitated slightly before she answered. "Yes . . . Yes, I do."

Henry looked up at the house, out at the orchard. "Well, that's good . . . that's good," he said. "You deserve all this. You deserve a good life . . . and a good man."

Another silence grew between them, extending again into awkwardness. "You take care of yourself, Meg," Henry said, turning to his horse and mounting.

"Henry, wait," Meg said with some urgency. He relaxed the reins in his hands and put his palms on the saddle horn, watching her approach him.

"You should have this back," she said, reaching up to him with her right hand.

Henry looked down at the diamond ring held up toward him. Reaching down to take it, he grabbed her hand, held it, squeezed it. She squeezed back hard, jerked her hand away, ran back to the house and inside, slamming the door behind her.

Henry spun the horse towards the dark road, kicked it firmly in the flanks.

* * *

"I'll give you a hundred dollars for it," Feingold said, turning the ring over as he held it between his right thumb and forefinger. "Less the ten bucks you borrowed, of course."

Henry rubbed his hand across his eyes and down over his cheeks and mouth. "Hell, Mordecai, you sold me that ring for six and a half bills."

"Yeah, that I did. But that was over a decade ago. Got plenty of diamond rings for sale now. Don't much need this one."

Henry snatched the ring from the jeweler. "Feingold," he said angrily, "don't ever let nobody tell you, you ain't a thief. Hell, you're a bigger thief than I ever thought about being. Believe I'll just keep this ring."

Feingold looked back at Henry and shrugged.

Chapter Twelve

November 16, 1907
Guthrie, Oklahoma

A brilliant autumn day, an "Indian Summer" day: the sky domed high, deep blue, and cloudless. The bright sun warmed the crisp air, a light breeze barely rustled the spectrum of red and yellow and orange leaves hanging and falling from the scattered maple, oak, and hickory trees. A rare day, a perfect day in the land the United States would now call the State of Oklahoma, this very first governor would be sworn in.

Henry had voted for Haskell, even though the man was a Democrat. The other fella was a carpetbagger, in Henry's estimation, and he wanted no part of that kind. So when Haskell spoke movingly about the new state's duty to the Indian, and gave the Indian Orphan Band a place of honor in the inauguration ceremony, Henry knew he'd made the right choice.

When the governor-elect moved out onto the upper steps of the library, Henry reached for his three-year-old son. "Ollie, hand me Teddy," he said to his wife. "I want him to get a good look at this."

They stood near the front, close to where the new governor would take his oath to the new constitution. Henry hoisted the tyke up onto his shoulders. "Son, I want you to remember this day. This is the beginning of a new state, a state for us Indians. Remember it, and be proud."

Henry felt good, better than he'd felt in years. He'd honestly turned his life around—he'd completely quit outlawing; his business back in Tulsa was prosperous. He'd married a lovely Cherokee girl, who'd given him a perfect son. He named the boy Theodore Roosevelt Starr after the man who'd pardoned him. On that perfect bright autumn day, it seemed to Henry his life couldn't get any better. His future looked bright.

* * *

"Hello, Bagby Real Estate Office," the middle-aged woman said into the fluted mouthpiece of the telephone. She held the stem of the telephone in her left hand, the earpiece pressed onto her ear with her right. She spoke louder than usual.

"Yes," she said. Then furrowing her brow she asked loudly, "Who?" After a few seconds of listening, followed with, "Please wait, I'll tell him you're calling." She sat the phone pieces down on her desktop, and walked to one of the wood partitioned offices behind her.

"Mister Starr, there is a Senator Birdsong on the telephone calling you."

Henry looked quizzically up from his newspaper, quickly grabbed the phone on his desk and removed the earpiece from its cradle. "Birdsong?" he asked loudly into the mouthpiece. He gave the secretary a look which indicated she should leave.

"How you doing, Henry," came a tinny voice from the other end.

"Well, I'm doing fine," Henry continued. "Never expected to hear from you again. I heard you was elected state senator over there in Muskogee. Congratulations."

"Thanks. I guess being a constitutional delegate helped me there."

"So why you calling, Tom?"

"Actually, Henry I've g—ome—ews for—ou." Loud static came on the line and the caller's voice became garbled.

"What's that, Birdsong? I didn't get that last part."

"I—aid, I've got some news fo—you."

"What kind of news?" Henry shouted into the phone.

"The State of Arkansas—" Birdsong's voice began coming in stronger. "—has kept your case open on the Bentonville bank robbery back in ninety-three. As your attorney of record, they sent me notice that they are petitioning Governor Haskell to have you extradited back to Fort Smith to stand trial."

"Stand trial?" Henry yelled. "Why, hell, I already paid my dues in prison for what I done back then." He happened to look out at the secretary who had her ear inclined, listening. Hiram

Bagby had come to the doorway of his own office, stood looking curiously at Henry. He turned his back to them and lowered his voice. "That was over fourteen years ago, Birdsong."

"It doesn't matter, Henry," Birdsong said. "You weren't tried for that charge, and they've re-opened the case. When this was Indian Territory, they couldn't come over here and get you. Now that Oklahoma is a state, they can. It's called extradition. But they have to get the governor's approval first."

"I ain't going back, Birdsong. I ain't going to get convicted and sent to one of them Arkansas convict farms. I'd die there. I got my life straight now. I'm living an honest life."

"Well, I know, Henry. Maybe there's something I can do. I know Haskell pretty well; we worked together at the Constitutional Convention. We're not in the same party, but perhaps I can convince him you're an upstanding citizen now, and get him to turn down Arkansas' request. Just stay put until I can see what I can do. And for God's sake, don't go to Arkansas for anything."

"Okay," Henry said.

"I'll call you when I know something," Birdsong said.

* * *

Henry sat by the phone in his office . . . waiting. He'd come back in after Bagby and Missus Logan had left for the day. It was getting late. Henry pulled his watch out of his vest pocket, held it up to the dim light of the gas lamp on the wall. Almost half past nine. Earlier in the day, a week after his first call, Birdsong had called to tell him he had a meeting with the governor that night at eight, and to wait by the phone. He could not believe he was still wanted for that Bentonville job. The local paper had picked up on the extradition thing in the past few days, now every petty robbery in that half the state—there had been several—had been pinned on him, even though he was completely innocent, wasn't even in the state where three of them took place.

Henry jumped when the phone finally rang. He didn't pick the receiver off its cradle until the fourth ring.

"Hello," Henry said.

"Long distance calling from Guthrie for Mister Henry Starr," the nasal voice of the operator said.

"That'd be me," Henry responded.

"Go ahead, please," the operator said.

"Henry?"

"I'm here, Birdsong. What did he say?"

"He—aid he was—going to g—ant it.

"What?"

"He w—rant it. There'll be—extradition.

"There will be?"

"What? We've got a—ad con—tion—enry. Did you—ear me?"

"You said he granted the extradition?"

"What? I said the go—nor did—grant the—dition."

Henry leaned back in the chair and pushed his thumb and forefinger against his eyes. "Yeah, I think I've got it, Birdsong. Appreciate what you did. Thanks for calling."

"You're welc—Henry. Good—aye.

Well, that was that. He'd been thinking about what he'd do if he got bad news, that the governor would give him up. He'd have to go home and tell Ollie, say goodbye to her . . . and Teddy.

"What's wrong, Henry?" Ollie asked. She'd been sitting in bed reading, waiting for him to get home. She was used to him coming in late, he often did; but that night something about his demeanor alarmed her.

"Something has come up," Henry answered. He sat beside her on the edge of the bed keeping his back to her.

She laid her book on her lap and asked, "What has come up?"

"Ollie, I got some things in my past, things I never told you about," Henry started.

"You mean the prison stuff?"

"No, it's more than that. Back when I was a kid, nineteen or so, I . . . me and a bunch of guys robbed a bank in Arkansas."

"You told me about your criminal days, Henry. Isn't that why you went to prison?"

"It is, Ollie, but this one I never got tried for. It was a long time ago. I thought they'd let it go, but I guess they didn't. And now that Oklahoma is a state, they can come and get me and take me back to stand trial.

"A friend of mine, he was my lawyer back then, he's a state senator now. Anyway, he knows Governor Haskell, and he went and asked him not to allow this exterdition thing. But I guess he is going to allow it. That's where I been tonight, waiting to hear from my friend about it."

His young wife put her hand on Henry's back. "What are you going to do, Henry?"

"Well, I ain't going back to Arkansas to stand trial. I can't. I'm guilty. They got me dead to rights on that, and I'm afraid they'd send me off to one of them convict farms."

Henry got quiet, stayed that way for several minutes, his head bowed. Ollie couldn't see his face, but she thought he was crying. She rubbed his back and waited for him to speak. She didn't know what to say.

"So what are you going to do, Henry?" she asked again.

"I reckon I'd better take off, Ollie. Go on the scout. Figured I'd head out west; get as far away from Arkansas as I can. Maybe in a few months I can get settled in somewhere else, find a job. I'll send for you and Teddy as soon as I can."

"You're just going to take off? Well, how will Teddy and I live?"

"I got some money saved up. I'll take some of it, but I'll leave most of it for you."

"Well, how long will you be gone, Henry?"

"Can't answer that, Ollie. Could be a while. I'll send you some money when I get some. You might talk to Bagby; see if maybe you can't get your old job back. I figure your ma can help you take care of Teddy."

"When are you leaving?"

"Got a couple of things to take care of first, but soon."

* * *

Henry wandered about the parlor looking at the caskets on display, while he waited for the undertaker.

"Henry?" the solemn mortician inquired in as cheerful a voice as he could muster. He offered his hand and a sad smile. "What can I do for you?" He spoke in a sympathetic voice. It was habitual. Most people who came to see him were in a grieving state. To him, Henry looked to be that way, too.

"Abe," Henry started after shaking the mortician's hand. "I'm here to make some arrangements." Henry had sold the man, Abe Morton, the house which was now a funeral parlor. He figured he could take the man into his confidence. Though a young man, the undertaker looked older than his real age. His skeletal pale face and receding hairline aided in that.

Morton looked stricken and grasped Henry's hand with both of his. "Why yes, Henry. I'm so sorry for your loss. Who is it?"

Henry pulled his hand away and snorted. "No, Morton, ain't nobody died . . . not yet. But one of these days you're going to hear about Henry Starr getting killed. When you do, I want you to give me a proper funeral. I don't want to be dumped in no forgotten hole without a marker. I want you to fix me up right, put me in one of these fine caskets, plant me in a respectable cemetery, and get me a headstone."

The undertaker read the newspaper diligently every morning, starting with the obituaries, then spreading to the news stories to see who else had died, or possibly could soon. "Well, of course, Henry. I would be happy to be of service."

"Well, then, you tell me how much all that will likely cost, and we'll settle up. I'm, uh . . . going to have to be away for a while."

"Well, let's see," Morton said rubbing his chin. "There's the casket, the embalming, perhaps some clean-up work." He looked at Henry apologetically before going on, "And, of course, the cemetery plot and headstone. And if you're not here, there may be some transportation costs back to Tulsa. He drummed his long fingers on his cheek while he mentally calculated. "I could probably do it all for around eight hundred dollars."

Henry reached inside his suit pocket and pulled out his wallet. "I'll give you a thousand, in case you run into some unexpected expenses."

Morton took the bills, folded them over once, and discreetly slipped them into his pocket. "Why, yes, we can give you a real nice funeral for that. Would you like to pick out a casket while you're here?"

Henry shook his head. "Don't think so, Abe. You can do that when the time comes. There is one other thing I'd like you to do," he added. Pulled a small sealed package out of his coat pocket. "Instructions are in here. I'd be obliged if you'd not open this until after I'm dead."

Morton took the package and looked at it curiously. "Why, of course, Henry."

* * *

From the top of the rise he saw the glow of a campfire about a mile off in the valley before him. He'd arisen at four that morning, and rode west. Facing the sunset, he figured he'd better find a place to camp. The gathering spring night was crystal clear with a handful of bright stars scattered in the twilight sky. The air was cool and still, remnants of the fading winter still in the air. He could see for miles in the flawless evening, and the campfire appeared to be the only light around, except for the emerging stars. He would ride to the camp , see if he'd be welcomed.

"Hello the camp," he shouted after riding near. A few small oak trees stood at the edge of the flame glow, their leaves just budding out. One figure sat by the fire; a stout man wearing what looked like a buffalo robe. The camper held a Winchester across his lap when Henry called out.

"Who's out there?" the camper shouted back.

"One rider," Henry called. "Would like to share your fire, and some salt pork I got in my bag."

The man at the fire kept his rifle barrel raised in Henry's direction. "Come on in, then," he said.

Henry rode into the firelight and stopped. Still sitting astride his horse, he raised his hands slightly holding the reins loosely in the fingers of his left hand. He gave the nervous camper his friendliest smile. "How you doing, pard?"

The man nodded, but kept his rifle trained on the rider. Henry judged him to be somewhere in his late 50's, early 60's. His face, weather-lined and brown, covered with a short, grizzled beard, his eyes blue and piercing.

Remaining cordial, Henry continued. "I promise, I'm alone. Traveling west. Saw your fire and thought maybe we could share it and some food."

Still a little wary, the man lowered the barrel of the rifle some. "What's your name?" he asked.

"Name's Starr, Henry Starr."

The man studied Henry some more. "Believe I've heard of you," he said. "You that bank robber?"

Henry's smile broadened. "Hell, my reputation has spread all the way out here to the boondocks. Mind if I get down?"

"Yeah, I 'spect that'd be awright." The man laid his rifle barrel in the crook of his left arm, keeping his right hand near the trigger. "You said something about some salt pork?"

"It's in my saddlebag," Henry said. "Okay if I get it out?"

The man nodded, but tightened his grip on his rifle, finger back on the trigger. Henry opened the bag and pulled out the pork wrapped in butcher paper. He brought it toward the fire and his new companion. "I could sure go for some of that coffee," He said.

"Help yourself," said the camper as he grabbed the offered package of meat. "Have to provide your own cup, though. I only got the one."

"Back in my gear," Henry motioned with his thumb. "I'd like to unsaddle my horse, if it's okay with you. He's been rode hard today. Need to get him fed, too.

"Why, hell yeah," the man said. "Man's gotta mind his horse first."

Loosening the saddle's cinch, Henry asked, "What name do you go by, Pard?"

"Last name's Hart," he answered. "Most folks just call me Stumpy."

"Why Stumpy?" Henry asked as he dropped his saddle, and settled in next to the fire. He grabbed the coffee pot and poured into a tin cup he'd brought out, too.

The man removed the left-handed leather glove he wore and held up his hand, extending index finger and thumb. The other three fingers, down to the second joint, were missing. Before Henry could ask, Stumpy said, "Comanche named Bad Neck took 'em back in eighty-five. We got in a disagreement about an Indin woman; well, half Indin. We was both drunk at the time, so when I passed out, he whacked 'em off. Took the woman, too."

Henry shook his head and sipped from his cup. "I've known a few Comanche. Mean bastards, most of 'em."

Stumpy stirred the fire with a stick he held in his good hand. "Well, I figure he got the worst of it. That was a rightly contentious woman; promiscuous, too."

"You headed somewheres, Stumpy?" Henry asked.

"Nowheres in particular. Left a cowhand job down near Anadarko. Foreman was getting on my nerves. Figured on maybe going up to Colorado. Heard there might be some opportunities up there."

"Colorado, now there's a nice place," said Henry.

"What about you, Starr? What I hear, you must be running from the law."

Henry drank some more coffee and looked up through the sparse oak branches at the stars. "I'd be curious to know what you heard," he said.

Stumpy had cut off a piece of the salt pork, and holding the chunk to his knife blade with his thumb, took a bite from it. "Heard there's a string of hold-ups out east, up around Tulsa, stores and such. Papers say you're probably the one who done 'em."

Henry reached for the salt pork to cut off a bite for himself. "Well, first of all, you can't believe everything you read. Most of them papers just make things up. And, second, I ain't done none of them robberies. I don't rob candy stores; I'm a bank robber. Anyway, I was. Ain't robbed a bank in fifteen years. But that's why I'm on the scout. State of Arkansas ain't forgot the last one I jacked up over there. They're trying to come and get me for that one."

Stumpy cut off some more pork. "I reckon every man has got a cross to bear."

"What's yours, Stumpy?"

Henry's campmate dunked the blade of his pocket knife into the boiling pot of coffee sitting in the coals of the fire, then wiped it on his pants leg. He looked the blade over carefully before folding it and putting the knife in his shirt pocket. "Well, except for letting Bad Neck take that woman, which was a considerable wrong on my part, I don't recall too much I done to invoke the wrath of God or man. Maybe stole a chicken or two, some beeves, a few ponies when I ran with the Comanche and Kiowa. Never held up a bank, though . . . or shot a man."

"That's commendable," Henry said.

Stumpy looked steadily into the fire, remained quiet. Henry leaned back on his saddle, lowered his hat brim to cover his eyes. It'd been a long day, and he was feeling a sleep coming on.

"Of course," Stumpy suddenly continued. "There was that time up on the Washita when I was with the 7th Cavalry."

Henry pushed up the brim of his hat, and looked intently at his companion. "You rode with Custer at the Washita?" Every Indian in Oklahoma knew about the massacre of Black Kettle and his camp on the Washita River. On a cold, snowy morning in November of sixty-eight, Custer and his troop rode down on the peaceful Cheyenne village, shooting everything in sight; not just warriors and dogs and cattle, but women and children as well. Custer took prisoners, mostly women and children, along with what horses they hadn't shot, used them as human shields while he made his retreat.

"Hell, I was just sixteen," Stumpy answered. "Joined up with the Army the summer of that year in Hays, Kansas. Figured Army life would be better than life on a dirt farm with my old man. He was as mean as any Comanch I ever met."

Henry looked hard at Stumpy, unable to hide his contempt, nor did he much want to. Stumpy could tell that.

"I know you're Indin, Starr, but I didn't shoot nobody, not even one of the dogs. I seen enough that day, though, without doing nothing to stop it, that'll surely send me to hell. Saw my sergeant shoot a small boy in the back running from him."

Stumpy fell silent. Watching him, Henry saw the man close his eyes tight and bow his head, his lips tight and twitching. Then he raised his head and poked the fire some more, sniffing and wiping his nose with his mangled left hand. "What the hell?" he said in a husky voice. Henry could tell he was embarrassed and kind of surprised at his display of emotion. "This ain't something I talk about much, especially not to no stranger. But seeing that little boy shot down ain't never left me. Usually comes up nights in a bad dream.

"Anyways, I left the Army right then and there. That night, as we was marching all them prisoners back to Fort Cobb . . . women with babies, little kids, old men . . . all on foot and in the dark, snow on the ground . . . I left the column. Reined my horse away and just rode off into the darkness.

"I expect I'd uh been hung for desertion if they'd ever caught up with me, but no one ever did. I been wandering around here in the Territory ever since. Lived with various Indin tribes; did a lot of cowboyin' over the years."

Still staring into the fire, Stumpy shook his head. "Hard to believe that day was forty years ago."

The crackling of the fire and the night sounds outside the camp were all that could be heard for several minutes. Presently, Henry rolled onto his left side, pulling his blanket up to his shoulders. "Believe I'll get some shut-eye," he said. "I got some friends up north I'd like to see. Mebbe we could ride together on your way to Colorado.

Chapter Thirteen

After a week of riding, the land had turned red and sandy. High rusty mesas, layered in ocher and beige and black, stretched north and south on either side of the two men as they rode through the valley. Henry said he knew a guy somewhere up in this area; said they'd stop and ask where to find him, next home place they saw. They'd stayed away from towns, as much as they could, preferring to ride up to farm and ranch homes to seek shelter and food and hospitality. Most times that worked.

Their second morning out, they'd come across an old Boomer northwest of a town called Watonga. Nice big painted house, big barn, lots of livestock, acres of rolling farmland. The evening before, they'd spied the farm house some miles off, a strand of smoke curling from its rock chimney. "Let's camp here," Henry said when they rode atop the knoll where they'd first seen the house. "We'll get up early tomorrow and see if those folks won't feed us some breakfast."

As they approached the house in the pre-dawn light the next morning, a portly man in bib overalls and a much-faded red flannel shirt, walked out onto his back porch to watch them. A sweat-stained droopy-brimmed hat covered his head, and the pant legs of his overalls were stuffed into the tops of ornately sewn cowboots. An untrimmed and graying mustache sagged from his upper lip, covering most of his mouth. His round face was wind-creased and sun-worn.

The two riders reined up ten feet from the farmer. Henry leaned forward with his forearms on the saddle horn. "Morning, mister" he said.

"Mornin' to you," the farmer responded in an amicable tone. "What's got you boys out riding so early on this fine spring morning?"

"We seen your place last night from where we camped. Wanted to come on down here to see if we could buy some eggs and bacon to cook up for our breakfast; maybe get some oats for our horses, too."

Without hesitation the man yelled over his shoulder, "Mother, two more for breakfast. They look to be hungry, so pile on the biscuits and bacon." A woman's face appeared in the kitchen' window, looking Henry and Stumpy over curiously. The farmer turned back to the riders. "Cain't take your money when our larder is so bounteous. You follow me on out to the barn. We'll get your animals fed and watered, too."

Walking to the barn, he asked them, "Where'd you boys camp last night?"

"Out east of here, up on that little hill yonder," Henry answered, pointing back over his shoulder.

"That'd be some of my land," the man said. "I own almost all the land far as you can see; almost four hunnert acres. Got it back in eighty-nine at the Land Run. Finest farm land on the Strip."

"Well, it sure looks it, Mister, uh . . ."

"Sweeney," the farmer said. "I'll answer to Ben, though."

"Pleased to meet you, Ben. I'm Ned Christie, up from around Durant." After shaking hands with Sweeney, Henry glanced to Stumpy to let him introduce himself.

Stumpy took Sweeney's hand. "Stumpy Hart," he said with no further elaboration.

"Nice to meet you boys," Sweeney said. "Don't get many folks stop by way out here. 'Spect my daughters will be pleased you did, too."

"Oh, you got daughters?" Henry asked, not trying to appear too overly interested.

"Yeah, I got daughters," Sweeney said a little wistfully. "Three of 'em. Youngest is seventeen."

"Must be tough having three daughters on a place as big as this," Stumpy offered. He grinned at the farmer, indicating his lack of tact was to be taken as a friendly jest.

"Damn tough," Sweeney said. He shook his head and frowned, with no apparent recognition of any humor. Then he seemed to brighten.

"They do cook good, though. Let's head to the house and see what they've whomped up."

After breakfast, Sweeney stuffed his corncob pipe with tobacco and lit it. He'd pushed back a bit from the kitchen table, puffing big blue clouds of smoke into the room and slurping his coffee. Henry leaned back in his chair equally sated from the meal. Stumpy still sopped white sausage gravy with a fluffy golden biscuit.

One of the cow-eyed daughters—the middle one, Henry thought—hovered near him, pouring coffee into his half-full cup, smiling at him a lot. He smiled back. She wasn't exactly homely, Henry decided, but she wasn't what you'd call looksome, neither. Not like the other two, to whom "homely" would be a generous description. But they were friendly, jolly girls. The oldest—a big girl, but not what you'd call fat, just tall and stout—had a beau, though, as she kept mentioning it. It so happened he was coming out that very night for supper to which Henry thought Ben looked pleased . . . and hopeful.

Sweeney had introduced his girls as Irma May, Ester June, and Bitsy, in descending order of age. Henry couldn't remember who was which with the older two, nor which middle name went with what first, but he could remember Bitsy as she seemed to be considerably younger than the others. But Bitsy appeared a misnomer, as the girl was anything but that. Probably a holdover from her toddler days, Henry thought.

"If you boys ain't in a hurry to head off," Sweeney said. "I'd like to invite you to stay on for supper tonight. You'd be welcome to bed down in the barn." Before Henry could politely beg off, the farmer continued. "Truth is, I sure could use some help today. You see, my hired man had to ride off to Edmond for a few days to be with his dying ma, and I got fencing needs done out on the edge of some of my wheat fields."

Henry and Stumpy looked at one another. Planting fence posts and stringing wire hadn't been part of their plans. "Well, Ben, we'd sure like to but—"

"Oh, it wouldn't be no trouble," Sweeney cut in. "You can see the kind of meal these girls can put together. Wasn't that a fine breakfast?" He turned to his wife and daughters who were well into clearing the table and dumping the dishes into a big pot of water on the stove. "Mother, that was a dang fine breakfast." He then looked back at Henry with a wry smile.

Henry caught Ben's allusion—there ain't no free breakfast. "'Sides," he said. "It'd sure be nice to have some men around to talk to for a spell." There was no mistaking the pleading look in his eyes, or the desperation in his voice. "I don't get a lot of that," he added.

"Well sure, Ben," Henry said, having a sudden change of heart. "We'd be glad to help you out." He looked over at Stumpy who gave him a "Sure, why not" shrug as he devoured another butter-laden biscuit. Besides, an evening with the farmer's daughters might prove amusing.

* * *

It turned out the beau either Ester May or Irma June mentioned so often at breakfast—"My beau this" and "My beau that"—was a proper name as well as a description. Henry found the thirty-something Beau Grimley, who worked at the grain elevator in town, to be a very likeable fella in a hulking, dim-witted sort of way, seemed to be a good match for Ester/Irma May/June . . . if she could nab him. He also happened to be a fiddle player of sorts, so after the ample dinner of fried chicken, smashed taters and gravy, collard greens and corn, the dinner party retired to the parlor for a round of musical entertainment—Beau playing his fiddle, accompanied by Irma/Ester on the piano.

Beau was affable enough, but his fiddle playing was excruciating. And the middle girl and Bitsy had started to become bolder toward Henry. In fact, it had all the looks of a predatory competition. Middle had taken a seat next to Henry on the settee, pushing her thigh up next to his, and encircling his arm with hers. Bitsy stood behind them, leaning her forearms and elbows onto the back of the settee, breathing hotly onto Henry's neck and occasionally whispering something into his ear, which he couldn't decipher over the piano and fiddle squall. But it had a very seductive tone.

He looked to Stumpy for rescue, but his pard, totally aware of what was going on, only looked back at him with an amused grin. Satisfied no help would come from that quarter, Henry looked to his host and wife; however, both would only glance toward him out of the corner of their eyes, pretending not to notice the unseemly and brazen advances of their two youngest daughters.

Presently, during an interlude for Beau to adjust his fiddle, Henry yawned big and stretched. "My goodness," he said, standing and dislodging himself from Middle's grasp. "That larrupin' supper on top of all that fresh air and work today, has got me wanting to bed down.

He turned to the hostess. "Miz Sweeney, I sure do appreciate all the cooking you and your daughters done for me and my pard today. I've never et finer meals. Now, if y'all will excuse me, I believe I'll turn in."

Looking at his partner, Henry added, "Of course, just because I'm leaving the party don't mean you have to, Stumpy."

"Well, I could go for another slice of that fine apple pie, Miz Sweeney. If it wouldn't be too much trouble."

"No trouble at all, Mister Hart," the woman said, standing from her chair. "I'll fetch it for you."

Stumpy smiled and nodded. There was no mistaking the annoyance in the woman's voice.

Ben Sweeney stood, too. "Ned, if you and your friend could see staying on for a couple more days to help me, I'd pay you wages . . . plus meals, of course," he said.

"That's a mighty tempting proposition, Ben," Henry said. "Me and Stumpy will talk it over, and I'll let you know in the morning."

"Fine, fine," Sweeney said. "Say, would you like some of that apple pie, too? You know, for a bedtime snack."

"No, I couldn't eat another bite, Ben. G'night." Henry hurried out the front door.

Outside on the porch, the dark silhouette of Middle rushed up to him, grabbing him around the waist. She nuzzled her lips up against his cheek, her hot breath in his ear.

"I'd like to help you bed down," she whispered. "Soon as ma and pa go to bed, I'll come out to the barn."

Henry pried her arms from his waist. "Well, gosh, uh, I don't . . . uh, you just make sure they're good and asleep," he said. "Don't want any run-in with your pa. I'd give it a good hour and a half before you come out."

Middle giggled and brushed her hand across his crotch. "See you then," she sighed.

Henry headed around the house, almost at a trot. Near the back door, he was assaulted again. This time it was Bitsy, jumping on his back, wrapping her legs around his waist. She bit his ear, then wallowed her tongue in it.

"Hey!" Henry said, more in surprise than pain. He spun around trying to get the young minx off his back. "Bitsy, damn! What're you doing?"

The girl laughed, jumping off him and spinning him to face her. "Thought we could do a little sportin' tonight."

Henry rubbed his ear trying to wipe off the saliva. "No. I don't think there'll be none of that. You're just a kid."

"A kid?" she said. "Well then, I'll just go tell my pa you made improper advances toward me. 'Spect he'll have something to say about that," she added coyly.

"No, now, hold on," Henry scratched the back of his head. "Okay, but we got to wait until your folks are asleep. I'll meet you out at the barn in, say, an hour and a half."

Bitsy reached up and kissed Henry hard, square on the mouth. Once she broke loose, she said "I'll be there."

Henry watched the girl run back in the house. Then he gave out a shuddering sigh. "Oh crap," he said.

Back in the barn, Henry packed up his stuff and saddled his horse. He went to the barn door and peeked through the cracks toward the house. If Stumpy didn't come out in the next ten minutes, he'd take off without him. It was every man for himself.

For the next eight minutes, Henry paced, taking frequent looks out the cracks. Finally, he could see the shape of Stumpy meandering toward the barn.

Henry grabbed his partner when he entered the barn. "Stumpy, we gotta get out of here." He had panic in his voice. "Sweeney's the devil, and his daughters are sirens. They're trying to trap us."

Stumpy gave out a hearty laugh. "You maybe. I don't think they're much interested in me. They think I eat too much. Anyway, that's what I tried to make them think. That's also why I told 'em I was a socialist during supper when the missus started going on about Roosevelt, and what a strong Republican she was because of him. Figured that'd sour 'em on my prospects."

Henry looked stunned. "You knew what they were doing?"

"Oh, hell, yeah. I got suspicious when Sweeney first told us he had three daughters. Daughters ain't much good on a spread like this. They're like beef cows; they get to a certain age, you got to get rid of them, or you ain't going to get back what you put into them."

Henry watched nervously through the cracks in the barn door. "Them girls scare me," he said.

"Yep," Stumpy said. "Looks like they got their own ideas, too. Healthy young females like them probably get real anxious living out here in the middle of nowheres. I suspect Sweeney's hired man didn't ride off to see his sick ma. He probably rode off in the middle of the night, too. In fact, I'd be willing to bet Sweeney has a hard time keeping a hired man." He shook his head, his expression one of sad and certain knowledge. "I seen this kind of thing happen before."

As soon as Stumpy got his gear together and saddled up, the two men led their horses quietly out of the barn. They walked them for a quarter mile before mounting, rode like the wind toward the northwest.

* * *

The sun had dipped behind the high mesa on their left. Even though it wouldn't truly set for three-quarters of an hour, darkness began to fill the shadowed valley. They'd ridden steady since noon without spotting so much as an outhouse. This was a dry and uninhabited land. Their prospects for an evening meal at a farmhouse seemed as dim as the daylight.

"We better find a campsite before it gets too dark," Stumpy said.

"Let's get on back down toward that river," Henry said. "Find some grass so the horses can eat."

They'd been following an old wagon trail which wandered away from the shallow run of a narrow river. About a mile to the west, a line of cottonwoods and willows hulked along the river's banks in the gathering gloom. They reined the horses left, trotted toward them.

Stumpy stirred the half empty can of cold beans with his spoon. "Wish we could've provisioned up before we left Sweeney's," he said.

"Don't know how we could've done that," Henry said. "We'd stayed any longer, I'd uh had to tussle with one or both of them heifers. Didn't much want to do that."

"Wull, why in a hell not?"

"It'd been dangerous on a couple counts. I figure they would've told their daddy, or maybe that was all a part of their grand scheme. I don't know. Anyway, there would've been a trumped up wedding with a shotgun aimed at my ass. Second, even without all that, the way them girls was built, and considering their eagerness, I could've been seriously injured."

Stumpy snorted out a mouthful of beans, and fell into a coughing fit alternating with gales of laughter. He grabbed his canteen and tried to wet the choke, but his whooping only made it worse.

Henry looked at his partner in sober puzzlement. "Well, it ain't funny, Stumpy. You seen the size of them girls."

Stumpy began to recover little by little. "Yeah, I expect what you said is true enough. It just struck me as funny." He threw another stick on the fire.

"You married, Henry?'

"Yes, sir, I am. A good woman. Give me a fine boy, too. Only I doubt we'll stay that way."

"You ain't going back for her?"

"Don't reckon. We never did seem to have that . . . Oh, I guess I had a fondness for her, in a way. But there was another I knew who was someone really special. Don't believe I'll ever forget about her."

"She die on ya?"

"Naw, just her love. While I was in prison up in Ohio, she found another."

"Hmmph, too bad," Stumpy said. The fire crackled and the call of a hoot owl out in the night was all that could be heard for a while.

"I sure hope we come across a farm tomorrow," Stumpy said at last. "Don't believe I can take another can of beans."

* * *

They rode up to the shack at about nine in the morning. It looked to have originally been a one room affair to which a small edition had later been tacked to one side. A tendril of white smoke rose from a tin flue on the roof. No barn, only an open stable of sorts with wooden hay and feed troughs on the back wall. The livestock, a plow horse, a milk cow, and a dozen chickens, wandered freely in the yard between the house and stable. Beginnings of a good sized garden stood off to the right of those structures.

"Anyone home?" Henry yelled. The two men remained in their saddles.

The door of the shack opened outward a crack, and a double shotgun barrel came out.

"You vant vhat?" came the inquiry of a young boy.

Henry spoke for the duo. "We was looking to get some breakfast. We'd be willing to pay."

There was a pause. "Yust a minute," the boy voice hollered out. Another pause. Henry and Stumpy could hear muffled talking inside the shack, not in English. After a minute of this, the disembodied voice said, "Vhat you pay?"

"I figured a dollar a piece for us," Henry answered.

More discussion inside the shack, then, "My pa, he say two dollar piece."

Henry and Stumpy looked at each other. "You tell your pa," Henry said. "We'll pay a buck fifty, and that will include feed for our horses. If he don't agree to that, we'll head on out."

Another brief exchange between the boy and his unseen pa. "Yah, dat be okay. You comen ze. Mudder fix you brakfust."

Inside the dark shack a heavyset man sat at a wooden table in the center of the room. A graying beard with no mustache covered his face. Brown suspenders striped grimy red flannel long handles covering his round belly and chest. The homemade table and its three chairs appeared to be the only pieces of furniture in the room, unless you counted the small cast iron stove at the back wall. The floor was dirt. A large woman, her grayish blonde hair pulled into a greasy bun, stood at the stove already frying up their eggs. The boy they'd dealt with, a gangly young teen, scrawny compared to his parents, sat on a small barrel over in one dark corner, still pointing the ancient shotgun in their general direction. The dusky room was heavy with the smell of wood smoke and unwashed bodies.

Henry smiled and tipped his hat to the man and woman. "Much obliged on your hospitality. We been powerful hungry for some home-cooked eggs. What's y'alls names?"

The man at the table gave Henry a stony stare, holding out his hand and gesturing with his fingers to indicate he wanted payment in advance. The woman continued to tend to her cooking without looking back.

"Dey don't sprechen no Anglich," the boy said.

Henry paid the man. The woman turned with the skillet and slid the smallish fried eggs into wooden bowls sitting on the table. The man grabbed the half loaf of rye bread next to him and sliced off two one-inch thick pieces. He tossed them across the table to his guests. The woman returned with a jar of corn syrup, then poured up two cups of coffee.

Henry and Stumpy sat opposite their host, and began to eat with no further conversation. It didn't take either man long to consume the fare, sopping up the egg yolk and corn syrup with the rye bread. The German family looked on in sullen silence.

After he finished, Henry reached into his pants pocket and pulled out two silver dollars which he slapped onto the tabletop. Pointing at the bowl of brown and speckled eggs sitting at the end of the table, he said, "Boy, tell your ma to cook us up six more eggs apiece. We ain't et near enough to fill us."

The boy relayed the message, which made the woman say "Ach!" with annoyance, but she grabbed the bowl of eggs and took them to the stove to fill the order.

After the meal, Henry and Stumpy stood. "Appreciate the vittles," Henry said to the fat pa, who remained sitting. He tipped his hat to the ma, and smiling warmly to her said, "Much obliged, ma'am."

"Ach," she replied with an air of disgust.

The boy stood from his barrel seat, keeping the shotgun at the ready. Henry and Stumpy left the shack, mounted up, and rode off, still heading north and west.

Chapter Fourteen

Henry remembered his friend, John Goforth, lived near the town of Hooker, but he didn't know exactly where. One inquiry in that little wind-blown Panhandle town, had sent them right to the man's door. As boyhood friends, he and Henry had roamed the woods, creeks and rivers around Fort Gibson. Now his friend had a small farm five miles west of that dusty settlement of Hooker. He'd been glad to see Henry, allowed him and his companion to stay for a week. It would've been longer, had Henry wanted, but he could tell the man's missus was interested in doing more than cooking meals for him and his friend. The Panhandle of Oklahoma could become a wearisome and dull place with its flat, sun-bleached land, its incessant wind. Could make a person desperate. That especially seemed true for the women folk; seemed specifically true for the wife of John Goforth.

The temptation was there, for the woman was not altogether uncomely, Henry could taste his desire, but in the end he couldn't betray a friend's trust. So he and Stumpy moved on north before things got out of hand; first across the southwest corner of Kansas riding through small, insignificant towns— Hugoton, Johnson City, Syracuse—where no one knew them, just two more drifting cowboys riding in with the wind and dust. They followed something of a road westward into Colorado, and by mid-afternoon came to the nothing town of Amity.

Looking into a bare sun, they let their horses walk down the middle of a flat street scarred by worn ruts. A small funnel of dirt swirled past them, a reminder that rain had come there none too recent. Clapboard buildings sat scattered along each side of the street—a saloon with a small two story hotel next to it, a general mercantile across from those, a hardware and feed store next to the mercantile. A wooden water tower rose above a well house next to the hotel. Segregated about an eighth of a mile west of the gathered buildings, a small grain elevator stood alone. No one was visible on the street. One horse stood forlornly at a hitching rail outside the saloon. A slumbering dog on the boardwalk in front of the hardware store raised his head as they approached, gave them a perfunctory bark. One other building, a squat red brick building, sat twenty paces off the end of the boardwalk that ran in front of the mercantile.

Like the towns they'd passed through in Kansas and Oklahoma, there wasn't much to look at in this one. But the small burg did have something Henry couldn't ignore—that red brick building. Amity had a bank.

As they rode by, Henry looked back at it. He turned to look at the other structures along the street. Tried to locate one other establishment: a lawman's office, but couldn't see one.

"Stumpy," he said quietly. "You say you've never robbed a bank?"

"Nope. Nary a one."

"Well, how would you like to get one under your belt?"

Stumpy turned in his saddle, looked back at the brick bank. Faced forward again and looked at Henry. "You mean that bank?" he asked.

"Only one I see. Don't look like there'd be much to it. No lawman in town that I can spot. Even if there is one, I doubt he could catch us."

Stumpy remained quiet, thoughtful. Henry looked over at him, a little puzzled.

"Whadda you say, Stump?"

"Well, you know, I done some wrong things in my life, but I ain't never took another man's money. My pa was a mean sumbitch, but one thing he taught me was that stealing was a powerful sin."

Henry snorted at Stumpy's hypocrisy. "Hell, Stumpy, how's stealing money any different than stealing beeves or horses?"

"Yeah, I done some of that, and I always carried some guilt about those. It was mainly the boys I run with, Indin boys. And the beeves and horses we stole, was two or three cut out of big herds from men with lots of money. What was stole was used to feed hungry women and kids. 'Sides, if I didn't join 'em, they'd uh scourged me, driven me from their gang, maybe worser. Guilt aside, it was more a matter of my survival. But I drawed the line on money. Stealing money just seems to me unforgivable."

He looked up and down the street some more. "It looks to me like this is a farm town. It don't look much different than the place I come from as a boy. Farmers got a tough life. What little money they do have is hard to come by. So, no sir, I don't want to be no part of stealing it from them."

"Well, seems to me stealing is stealing." Henry said. "Law don't draw a line on it neither. Robbing banks just cuts out the middle man," Spurred his horse into a trot, they rode on out of town, well past the grain elevator. They had no further conversation, all seemed to have been said. At a spot where a small wooden bridge crossed a rocky creek, Henry reined his horse down to the water, stopped to let him drink. Despite the dry land around them, the creek ran swift with clear gurgling water.

Stumpy brought his horse next to Henry's. While the animals drank, Stumpy said, "Must be snow melt from off them mountains yonder."

Henry looked to the west. Mountains Stumpy spoke of appeared as a distant blue outline on the horizon. "Doubt snow melt would travel this far. Crik must be spring-fed up around that butte." Henry indicated the geologic feature some mile or two north of them.

Nothing more was said as they let their horses drink. Presently, Henry spoke. "Believe I'll camp here tonight. I'm going back to that town tomorrow."

Stumpy didn't respond for a few seconds. "You aim to rob that bank, don't you?"

"Reckon I do, Stumpy. It's too easy to pass up. Figure there's at least a thousand in there. I'll do it with or without you, it's your choice."

"I already told you how I feel about that, Henry," Stumpy said. "I'll camp with you tonight, then in the morning I believe I'll move on."

They didn't talk much that evening at their campfire, both preferring to turn in early. Henry wanted to say something, to have a parting talk of some kind. Stumpy had been a good partner to ride with, Henry had grown quite fond of him. But it all went unsaid. The next morning, as they packed their separate gear, Henry finally said, "What's your plans from here?" It was all he could think to say.

Stumpy paused at strapping on his saddlebags, gazed out to the west. "Going to make my way to them mountains. Comanches I used to run with told me about their Shoshone cousins up there. Always thought that'd be a good place to live. I'd like to try to meet up with some of them, see if they'll let me settle in with 'em. Getting too old to roam. I'd like to find me a nice fat Shoshone woman to live out my time with. Man oughta have heat in the winter and shade in the summer."

"That sounds like a good plan, awright," Henry said as he tightened his saddle cinch. "Only be sure you get a woman you won't lose no fingers over."

That brought a hearty laugh out of Stumpy. He turned to face his riding partner, offering his hand in a shake. "Henry, you're a thievin' sumbitch, but I truly do like you. I hope you don't get your redskin ass shot off."

They shook hands, Stumpy embraced him, Henry embraced back. They broke apart, a little embarrassed.

"Well, so long, Stumpy," Henry said as he mounted up.

"So long, Henry Starr," Stumpy returned.

Henry spurred his horse and rode into the rising sun.

* * *

The town looked pretty much the way Henry had left it the day before. A horse stood hitched outside the saloon, and the old dog still lounged on the boardwalk, scratching an ear. A wagon now sat in front of the hardware store with a boy of about ten standing beside it throwing dirt clods back up the street. The boy stopped to watch Starr as he rode by.

Henry dismounted in front of the brick bank, loosely hitched his horse. No other horses or wagons were about. Looked up and down the street, adjusted his gun belt and holster. The boy at the wagon still watched him. Henry entered the bank, deciding he would size up the situation before drawing his pistol.

Inside, a middle-aged woman stood at the one teller's window as the teller counted out some money. When the door opened, the woman, with a pleasant smile on her face, turned to see who had come in, no doubt expecting an acquaintance. At seeing Henry, her smile faded some and froze. Henry touched his hat brim and said genially, "Mornin', ma'am." She nodded back, kept her frozen smile. The teller didn't even glance up, continued his counting. The woman turned her attention back to the teller to watch him count.

Bank was a one room affair with a six-foot-tall safe at the back in one corner, directly behind the teller. Safe's door stood open into the room. An empty desk sat off to one side opposite the teller's cage. So far as Henry could tell, the teller and the woman were the only people in the building. He drew out his pistol, and pointed it above the teller's head.

"Mister," Henry said, again in an amicable tone. "I'd like for you to stop counting and just hand all that money over to me."

The woman turned to look again at Henry. Gasping, put her hand to her mouth, eyes wide as saucers. The teller, a short man with thinning hair and a large mustache, froze for an instant, moved his right hand below the counter.

"I wouldn't do that, pard," Henry said calmly, lowering the pistol barrel, cocking back the hammer, and sighting it to the man's nose. "I'd put a hole through your head before you could cock and fire."

The teller froze again, but kept his hand below the counter.

"Now bring your hand slowly up where I can see it and raise both of them over your head," Henry instructed. The man complied. Henry walked to the window.

"Ma'am, would you be so kind as to move over to that corner?" He said to the woman indicating an area where the cage met the outside wall. "I'd be obliged if you'd raise your hands, too."

"Certainly," the woman said, promptly obeying the orders.

"Take all that money you been counting and put it in that bag behind you," Henry told the teller. "Then all the money in your cash drawer."

After the teller finished, Henry asked him, "Got any money in that safe?"

The teller hesitated a few seconds until Henry pushed the gun barrel onto the man's forehead. He nodded once.

"Then let's fetch it," Henry said.

After all the money had been bagged up and handed to Henry, he gave them one last order. "You folks have been real cooperative," he said. "And I want you to know I appreciate it. Less people get hurt that way. Now, before I go, I want both of you to lie face down on the floor over there by that desk."

After they were in place on the floor, Henry added, "You two stay right there until you hear me ride away, so's I won't have to come back in and shoot you."

At the door, Henry turned back to them and said. "Someday when you're telling your grandchildren about the time you was robbed, you can mention that it was done by the outlaw Henry Starr."

Outside Henry looked up and down the street, nothing had changed. The boy at the wagon still throwing clods and looking at him. Henry holstered his gun and mounted up. Before he spurred his horse, he reached inside the money bag and pulled out a silver dollar. He urged his horse into a gallop toward the western end of the street. When he rode past the boy, he tossed him the silver dollar.

* * *

There'd been no pursuit so far as Henry could tell, so he slowed his horse to an easy gait. He traveled on west, crossing the

Arkansas River. Four hours along, he passed a sign by the road which read:

Welcome to La Junta
Elev. 4,078 ft.

Welcome, yessir, Henry thought. If this town, which looked to be a fair-sized place, had a hotel and a bath he was going to stop and partake for a night. Maybe get re-outfitted a little, and decide where he wanted to go next. He seriously doubted there'd be any posse trailing him.

Earlier, still in the saddle trotting along, Henry had done a preliminary count, and it looked like he done pretty much as he'd expected; a little better, in fact. First count was over eleven hundred dollars. That'd be enough to get him some new clothes, a shave and haircut, get his horse re-shod and fed good, take a few days to relax and recreate. There was bound to be a poker game in La Junta, maybe a girl or two.

Henry rode slowly down the main street, looking over the storefronts. Saw two hotels on opposite sides of the street, decided on the one which had a sign out front which read, "Hot Baths 25 cents." He also spied a barber pole on the end of one building, the window of a haberdashery, millinery, two general stores, and three saloons. At the end of the street heading out of town, he found a livery stable and dismounted. A Mexican kid of about twelve or thirteen came out to take the reins of his horse. "Got a smithy here, boy?" Henry asked. Untied his saddlebags and threw them over his shoulder.

The boy nodded, smiling. "Si, senor." He waited.

"You rub this horse down good, and feed him," Henry said. "Then get him to that smithy, tell him he needs t'be re-shod."

The kid nodded again and turned to lead the horse into the livery stable. "Hold on, son," Henry said. He reached into his pants pocket, pulled out a silver dollar. "This here's for you." A broad white grin broke across the kid's brown face, catching the coin tossed to him. "Tell your boss I'll be around later to settle up."

"What is your name, senor, so I can tell him?"

"Ned Christie. You tell him that horse belongs to Ned Christie," Henry yelled over his shoulder as he walked away.

* * *

"Bill, it looks like our boy, Henry Starr, is at it again."

Deputy U.S. Marshal William Tilghman, sitting at his desk in Guthrie, Oklahoma said, "Hell, Chris, when did he ever stop?" He took the telegram held out to him by his colleague and read it.

"Colorado?" he asked. "What's he doing up there?"

"Robbing banks, it appears," Deputy Madsen responded.

Tilghman laid the telegram down onto the desktop and put his finger under two words. "Need help," he read aloud. Looking up at Madsen, he asked, "Ain't they got any marshals in Colorado? Why they need our help?"

"Don't know," Madsen answered. "Guess him being from the Territory and all, they figured we'd know Starr, that we might could help in tracking him down. Don't know how they know it was him, though."

Tilghman looked at the telegram again, re-read it. "Knowing Henry, I expect he probably announced himself. I'm of the opinion that he thinks folks will be as much impressed with who's robbing them as he is himself."

The deputy sat for a few seconds more studying the telegram. "Amity," he said flatly. "Hmmph. Never heard of it."

"Believe it's straight west of Garden City," Madsen said. "Near the Kansas border."

Tilghman got up from his desk, lifting his broad-brimmed hat off the rack behind him. "Well, there ain't much going on around here. I believe a trip to Colorado would be a nice change. You want to come along?"

"Don't believe I can right now, Bill. You know, I got all that stuff going on down in Oklahoma City." Madsen looked down at the floor a little sheepish.

Tilghman nodded, agreeing with Madsen that he sure enough did know, tried not to show disapproval in his expression. For the past several months his old partner had started to become more of a politician than a lawman. Still, he understood. Now that Oklahoma had gone from territory to state, things had tamed down. He and Madsen had been a big part of that taming in the wild and wooly days before and after the Land Run. Politics had already seduced the other part of the trio, their partner Heck Thomas, who'd been lured down to Lawton to be chief of police.

Towns didn't have marshals or sheriffs anymore; they had policemen and police chiefs. No, the old days were dying out, that much was clear. It was a new day, a new century. But it was a good thing, Bill thought somewhat grudgingly. Hell, that's why they'd signed on to do all the man-hunting and head-knocking and hip-shooting. They'd wanted to make the new land a better place to live; a place where a man could raise a family, make a living and go to church without the threat of any of them being robbed or molested or killed. Him and Heck and Chris had done a damn fine job at that. Still . . .

It was becoming harder to bring in desperados, but not because there weren't any. That element would always be around. It was just that . . . well, with the new law and order, they just weren't as plentiful as they once were. Like that great vanishing prairie beast, the bison, you had to range farther to find them than you once did. And like the old buffalo hunters he'd known—Cody, Comstock, Hickok—he'd done his share to thin them out, the outlaws *and* the buffalo. That's what Henry Starr was, an old buffalo. And Bill Tilghman, Deputy U.S. Marshal, would make the wide hunt to collect his hide. Still what he did best.

Chapter Fifteen

Henry looked at his five cards and tried not to frown. Mazie, the dark-skinned girl who'd befriended him the first night he'd showed up at the saloon, sat on the arm of his chair with her arm around his shoulders looking at the hand dealt him, too. He held the four, five, seven, and eight of clubs along with the Jack of hearts. Reason told him not to do it, but he'd lost so much in the past three days, desperation egged him on.

"Check," the man to his right said.

"Bet two dollars," Henry said, throwing the chips onto the pot.

"See your two and raise it a dollar," the man on his left said.

"Call," said the next man, matching the bets to him. The dealer—a man having curly hair and a well-trimmed Van Dyke beard, a string bowtie and fancy shirt—and Henry's right hand man did the same.

"I'll see your one and raise it two more," Henry said. Everyone around the table called his raise.

"Three," the man to Henry's right said, throwing out his discards.

"Take one," Henry said as he tossed his Jack onto the loose stack of discards.

The left-side man took one, the next guy took two, and the dealer took one.

He took his new card, adding it to the back of the other four. He then held them close to his chest and started spreading them. Mazie bent forward slightly to watch. Behind the four of clubs appeared the five, then the seven, then the eight. Henry rubbed the tips of his right fingers with the thumb before he revealed his new card. It was black, it was a six; but it was a spade. That's okay, Henry told himself. Got the straight. Drew to an inside straight. Damn! Maybe his luck was changing. He tried not to look too excited.

"Check," said the right man.

Henry had to take it slow, not scare anybody off. "Bet two dollars," he said matter-of-fact.

"See that, and raise five," lefty said.

The bets went around the table two more times, getting higher with each round. One player threw in. Henry was into the pot for forty dollars, and down about three hundred for the night. Adding that to the four hundred from the previous two nights, he couldn't quit on his straight now.

When all bets were in, Henry had beaten two pair, three kings and one fold, but he couldn't beat a flush the dealer had somehow materialized. Unfortunately, second place counts for nothing in poker. He slumped with dejection in his chair. "That does it for me, boys," he said. "I'm tapped out."

The dealer tried not to smile as he scooped in the pot. Mazie removed her arm from around Henry's shoulders and stood. He watched her move to the bar where she took up conversation with a dusty cowboy.

* * *

Tilghman stepped off the train in Garden City, Kansas, and headed along the station platform toward the animal car. Didn't have luggage; only change of clothes he'd put in his saddlebags, still with his tack in the horse car. Didn't carry much money, either. Most things he could sign for, the bills then sent on to the U.S. Marshal's Office in Washington, D.C.

He saddled up his horse, led him down the ramp before mounting. The sun was high and hot in the chalky summer sky. Tilghman squinted up at it, pulling his watch from his pocket: One fifteen.

At the side of the station, an old black man with white hair loaded big mail sacks from a station cart onto a wagon bed. "'Scuse me, uncle," Tilghman addressed him. The old man glanced up at him, but kept working. "Wonder if you can tell me how far it is to Amity, Colorado, and point me in that direction?"

The old man stopped his work, pulled a blue bandana from his hip pocket, mopped his face and neck with it. He paused to think.

"Yesuh. Well, it be 'bout haf a day rides," he said. He looked up at the sun, too. "I 'spect you could make it afoe sundown, if you was to go now." He pointed down the street running next to the station. "That street yonder where all them buildin's is, that be Main Street. You turn west there, that be yo left, and take it on outta town. Just stay on that road. It take you all the way on into Amity."

"Much obliged," the lawman said, and reined his horse toward Main Street. Garden City was a bustling town, much bigger than the last time he'd been there, almost three decades past in his buffalo days. Then it was nothing but another dusty little cow and farm town on the prairie. Now trees, big trees, lined both sides of the street, and telephone poles and phone lines ran smack down the middle of it. It appeared numerous sorts of commerce took place there, with many citizens moving to and fro.

Tilghman had gotten off the train in Wichita to send a telegram to the deputy in Pueblo, the one who'd contacted him asking for help. The telegram read:

In Wichita this morning 6/15/08. Will reach Garden City at noon by rail and proceed on horseback to Amity. Desire you meet me there. Bill Tilghman, Deputy U.S. Marshal.

It would be nice to stop and rest in Garden City, explore its new horizons, but the Colorado deputy would be waiting for him in Amity. Best to press on before Starr's trail got too cold.

* * *

Henry figured he'd stayed long enough in La Junta; too long, maybe. What was going to be a one or two night refresher from the trail, turned into almost a week of gambling and whoring. The hotel rules said you paid in advance for each night's stay. After the first night, Henry had paid for three more nights. That had taken him through the previous night. After his poker losses, hotel bill, meals, livery bill, shopping spree . . . and other expenses, he found he had a little over twenty dollars left in his pocket.

"You going to stay another night with us, Mister Christie?" the desk clerk asked him as he came through the lobby on his way back from the all-night poker game. It was six in the morning.

"Don't believe so, Mister Blythe. Going to get a little sleep, then I figure I'll head on out."

"Check out time is noon," the clerk said.

Henry looked at him and nodded. "You send that boy of yours up to wake me at eleven-thirty, and I'll clear out."

When Henry dropped the key off, the clerk warmly thanked him. "Where you headed, Mister Christie," he asked.

"I'm going to head down to New Mexico. Know some people down there. Never been there."

"Well, if you're ever back up this way, I hope you'll come and stay with us again."

"I surely will, Fred. I surely will," Henry said.

* * *

Jubal Smoak, the Deputy U.S. Marshal in Pueblo, received Bill Tilghman's telegram at nine o'clock in the morning, immediately struck out for Amity. A little past midday, he arrived at La Junta and decided he and his stiff left leg needed a short rest from the trail. Hobbled up to the bar in The Buffalo Head Saloon, ordered a beer and a ham sandwich. A week ago he'd gotten the telegram from the sheriff in Amity telling him about the Henry Starr robbery. He didn't quite know where to start, but figured something had to be done.

Twenty-three-year-old Deputy Smoak didn't have much experience in any direction. Only been appointed to the position a couple months back. Before that he'd been a second lieutenant in the Army, but only for eight months, a staffer at the Adjutant General's office in Denver. After graduating last in his class from West Point, he had high expectations of becoming a cavalry officer out west; horsemanship being his one redeeming skill. The Army did send him west, but only as a personnel assistant.

His boss, an avid polo enthusiast from New York, always on the lookout for skilled horsemen, requested Smoak's assignment before his rivals at Fort Collins got wind of the new officer's ability. Ironically, in a match with Fort Collins, the young lieutenant destroyed his left knee and severely broke his lower leg bones when his pony fell and rolled up on him. The injury rendered him disabled in the military's eyes, even after a year's rehabilitation, and he was given a discharge. His military boss, feeling a bit guilty about the boy's lost commission, pulled some strings, got him the U.S. Deputy Marshal's job.

So there he was, sent to Pueblo, Colorado with a pronounced limp to quell the lawless, owning no real idea or experience how to go about the job of marshaling. Even the least academically inclined graduate of the U.S. Military Academy was smart enough to recognize that, so he immediately contacted the legendary Bill Tilghman requesting help.

"What brings you around here, Deputy?" the barkeep asked. Smoak always wore the badge on his shirt, partially concealed by his open leather vest.

"Been a bank robbery over in Amity. Headed over there to investigate," he answered around a bite of the ham sandwich.

"Amity, huh?" the bartender responded as he wiped some beer mugs dry. "Hadn't heard about that. When?"

"'Bout a week ago. Fella rode in and cleaned them out.

"Any idea who done it?

"He told the people in the bank he was Henry Starr."

"Henry Starr," the bartender said, looking up at the ceiling trying to recall the name. Shook his head. "Never heard of him."

"Said to be an Indian fella out of Oklahoma. Known outlaw back there."

"You know, there has been an Indian-looking boy in here this past week spreading some money around. Lost a lot of it at the card table."

Smoak perked up, set his beer glass down. "When did you last see him?"

"He left the card game yesterday morning about six. Ain't seen him today, though, or last night. Doesn't seem like the outlaw sort, though. Kind of a likable fella."

"Where's he staying?"

"One of the hotels, I reckon. There's one next door and one across the street up near the north end."

Smoak washed down the bite of sandwich in his mouth with the rest of his beer, fished a half dollar out of his pants pocket, tossing it on the bar. "Much obliged," he said and turned to leave.

"You might check with our girl Mazie, too," the bartender said. "Believe they got well acquainted."

Smoak figured the sheriff in Amity would know when Tilghman got to town and where to find him, so he sent a telegram in care of the sheriff:

In La Junta. Discovered suspect H. Starr left on horseback for N.M. yesterday a.m. Will await your arrival here at Buffalo Head Saloon.

* * *

It took Henry the best part of three days to go eighty miles, as his horse, Jeff, had come up lame. Lead the horse the last two miles into Trinidad some ten miles or so from the border with New Mexico. His money was short, didn't think he'd be doing any horse trading; besides, he'd become too fond of the bay gelding to get rid of him. On the advice of the livery man in Trinidad, he laid up for a couple of days to give Jeff a rest and some liniment treatments to his foreleg. Henry didn't want to spend what little money he did have on a boarding room, so worked a deal with the stable man to stay in Jeff's stall. The liniment smell hung strong in that small area, but the price was right.

Worse than the smell of manure, Henry found the liniment made his nose burn and eyes water, so in the middle of the night moved up to the loft, settling into the hay by the open loft door. He awoke an hour into daylight, stood and stretched, looked out onto the main street of Trinidad. Scratching his side and pulling hay straws from his hair, he watched a couple riders trot into town. Something looked familiar with one of them, a tall, straight-backed man, broad at the shoulders, sporting a big moustache. The morning sun glinted off a spot on the other man's chest, freezing Henry in sudden realization. Those were lawmen riding in, the familiar one looked a lot like Bill Tilghman.

Reflexively, Henry ducked to the side of the open loft door, out of view from the street. He'd met the famous lawman once, but knew and feared him more for his reputation. Peeked around the edge to get another look. Yep, Tilghman, alright; didn't recognize the other man. Shorter than Tilghman, but huskier; his left leg stuck out in the stirrup, away from the horse's side. *What the hell is Tilghman doing all the way out here in Colorado?* Henry asked himself. *Surely, has no interest in that little bank I robbed . . . does he?* He tried to reassure himself; but didn't think he'd wait around to find out.

"Epperly, I gotta ride," Henry said to the livery man as he approached Jeff's stall.

The man stood at the horse's trough giving him oats. He glanced up at Henry, noticing his agitation. "Don't believe this horse is ready to ride, Mister Christie. He's gonna need a couple more days treatment."

"I ain't got a couple more days. Tell you what. I'll trade Jeff here, plus ten dollars. What can you give me?"

Epperly rubbed his chin in thought. "Well, I got a ten-year-old mare I could let you have for that. She ain't so young, but she's stout."

Henry pulled out the folded bills from the front pocket of his denims, started counting. Epperly held out his hand to accept them. "And it'll be another three dollars for the stall and feed . . . and the liniment," he said.

Henry looked at him with annoyance, counted out the extra three.

Epperly shoved the money into his shirt pocket. "Mare's out in the corral," he said. "I'll go fetch her."

As Henry finished saddling up his new horse, Epperly asked him, "Where you so all het up about getting off to?"

"Denver," Henry said. "Man up there wants to see me about some land." He finished tying on his saddlebags and mounted up. Looking down at the livery man, he said, "You take care of old Jeff, Epperly. He's a damn fine horse." Henry trotted the mare out of the barn, turned her south, and spurred the animal into a gallop.

Epperly watched a couple seconds, cupped his hands around his mouth. "Denver's t'other way!" he shouted.

* * *

"Yeah, there was a man in here like you're talking about," Epperly told the two lawmen. "Called hisself Ned Christie. He lit outta here early this morning in a real hurry. Said he was going to Denver, but I don't think so. Took off at a full gallop, headed south. Musta had something to do with you two fellas."

Epperly was right about the mare, she was sure enough sturdy. Kept up a strong pace through the high, dry land heading into New Mexico. After coming through the mountains, Henry stopped in the little town of Raton to find them some water, moved on quickly after the horse had her fill. He'd paused atop a ridge a few miles back to give the mare a breather; looking back, saw a dust cloud rising from the valley he'd just ridden. It was maybe ten, twelve miles back, told Henry whoever stirred the dust rode hard. No way of knowing from that distance if it were the lawmen, but Henry believed it was.

The terrain got flatter and hotter south of Raton, Henry kept pushing. By the time he got to a place called Abbott, the sun was almost down and the mare spent. As strong as she was, he knew she wouldn't be able to keep up the pace for another day. He stood at a water trough letting the horse drink, looking around at the town. Not much of a place, but had a fair amount of horse traffic coming in and out. Had the usual saloon and general store, a small livery, one or two other businesses. Even a little eating establishment busy with customers. Henry looked at the western mountains where the last tip of the sun slipped behind them. In another hour or so it'd be totally dark. He looked over at the front of the saloon again eyeing the horses tied there. Later on, after dark, he'd have to do some horse trading, Looked like he'd have a fairly good lot to pick from.

"C'mon, big lady," Henry said to the horse, patting her on the neck. "Let's go see if we can find us something to eat."

Henry got some feed at the livery. Asked the man there to rub her down, he stripped off the saddle and bridle. Paying the man the six bits required, said he'd be back for his horse and gear later, walked over to the eatery. Reached in his pocket to feel for what money he had left, hoping he had enough to get a big steak and some potatoes. Hadn't eaten all day and was damn hungry, bone tired. Had no detection of anyone following him for several hours, but had to assume the two lawmen still rode after him. There'd be no lingering over his meal; he'd have to eat up and get out.

Near nine o'clock, Henry saddled the mare loosely and led her up next to the string of horses outside the saloon. Piano music issued from the building, twining through loud and boisterous voices; it appeared those within were well occupied. Quickly scanning the animals, Henry chose a sorrel gelding which looked strong and fast. He untied the sorrel from the rail, led the two horses into the alleyway between the buildings to hide from the glare of the saloon door and windows. He unsaddled the sorrel, tossing the gear to the ground beside the mare, re-saddled the gelding with his own. He threw the grounded saddle on the mare, loosely strapping the cinch, led her back to the saloon hitching rail, tied her to it.

He scratched the mare's forehead, and she snuffled back at him. "You been a fine ride, old girl. Thanks for carrying me like you done. I'd say you're a fair trade for that sorrel. Hope your new boss gets to feel the same way, too." Henry mounted the sorrel and walked him down the middle of the street in the midst of all the other tracks so no one would know which were his mount's. He took the road heading east out of town, hoping his trackers would think he'd continued south.

* * *

Hard to call Perrytown a town; more like a settlement. Had a trading post, an old way station for a now defunct stage line, a rail siding for cattle and such. Didn't look like there'd been many trains coming through of late. Weeds, sprung up in the brief spring rains, stood shaggy at a few spots between the tracks. The tufts of weeds a small model, a little metaphor of Perrytown: dry and gray and sun-baked; on the verge of being blown into oblivion by the hot desert winds.

Only four houses in the village; shacks, really. Henry figured he'd go to the one in the least stage of disrepair to find his friend, Amos Perry. A town's namesake ought to have the nicest house there, he reasoned. Henry couldn't be sure Perry would remember him. Amos, once a Principal Chief of the Cherokees when Henry was a boy, had helped him when he got in trouble. That'd been a few years back, before Perry picked up and moved all the way out here to New Mexico for reasons Henry didn't know.

"Mister Perry?" Henry stood holding his hat in an attitude of humility and respect when the old man opened the door. He thought he recognized the old chief. He looked a lot older, much older than his years.

"Yes," the man responded.

"I'm Henry Starr from the Nations. Don't know if you remember me, but you knew my uncle . . . and my dad. You helped me get out of jail when I got in a scrape as a boy."

The old man's eyes brightened and he smiled. "Ah, yes. Young Henry, the son of George." He got quiet for a few seconds, then reached out with both hands grabbing Henry at the shoulders. "I knew your grandfather, too," he said softly. "He was a great warrior."

Henry nodded. He'd only known Tom Starr through the stories he'd heard. Perry released his grip on Henry and pulled him by one arm into the house. "Come in and eat," he said. He spoke Cherokee to a young boy sitting on the floor. "My grandson will take care of your horse," Amos said to Henry. "Sit here and have some venison stew." He indicated a place at the table across from him, and then spoke softly to a woman at the fireplace, also in Cherokee. The woman silently ladled up a bowl of the stew and set it before their guest.

"So, young Starr, how are things back in the Nations?"

Henry dug into the stew, shoveling spoonsful before responding. "Well," he started, taking two more hurried bites. He chewed a chunk of venison, and swallowed. "I reckon it's about the same as you last saw it. 'Course, the Cherokee Nation is part of the State of Oklahoma now, as are all the nations."

"Yes, I knew that was coming," said Perry.

"How'd you know that?" Henry asked. He spooned in a couple more bites of stew.

"The White Man has never been honest," Perry said. He leaned forward putting his forearms on the table, talking into the tabletop. "When he told us to come out to the Territory, he said the land would always be ours; it would be our nation forever. We already had a nation in the land he called Georgia and in the mountains of the Carolinas and Tennessee; it had been there long before the white man came. We didn't want to come out here, but their leader Jackson forced us. I was just a boy when we walked across The Trail. I saw my mother die and my baby sister, many cousins. Then those after Jackson told us we couldn't have our government; they said our children could not speak Cherokee and must go to white schools."

Perry fell silent watching his guest scrape the last of his stew from his bowl. Henry noticed the old chief watching him. He licked the spoon and set it down in the bowl. "Is that why you left the Territory?" he asked.

Perry spoke Cherokee again to the woman and motioned with his hand toward Henry's bowl. She came to the table with the pot of stew and ladled more into Henry's bowl. He didn't protest, and resumed his eager eating.

"If you are Indian," the old chief said. "You cannot escape the whites. It does no good to run from them. No, it was the Ross men who drove me from the Territory."

Henry nodded and continued eating, keeping his eyes on the bowl of food. Perry continued. "Much of the time we Cherokee treat each other worse than do the white men."

There was consent with Henry, more nodding.

"And you, young Starr, why did you leave the Nations?"

Henry finished the stew and set the bowl aside. He looked at the man opposite him, then at the woman by the stove. "I, uh . . . there was some confusion on something I once done in Arkansas. New governor was going to let them haul me back there."

The old man's face creased with sad amusement. "Still running from the law, are you?"

"Two lawmen," Henry said with a grin, then added with braggadocio, "One of them is Bill Tilghman."

"Tilghman, huh?" Perry said. He arched an eyebrow. "Remarkable. He doesn't come after just anyone."

"I stopped at a bank in Colorado to make a withdrawal. Apparently, they didn't take kindly to it."

Perry shook his head in bewilderment. "It's a mystery," he said. "Never understood why white people place so much importance on their paper. How does it have value? A deerskin has value. A good pair of moccasins has value. A shank of hog has value. A log house has value. The value of the white man's paper comes and goes. After his Civil War, the only value his paper had was to start cook fires. Then, as now, you'd be better off having squirrel meat in hand than white man's money."

The boy came back into the house, the old man turned to look at him.

"My son died in the Nations," he continued. "My wife a year ago. I now have only my grandson, and my daughter-in-law. They are of great value to me."

Perry ended his quiet lecture, sat looking at his guest. Henry avoided his host's gaze, shifting nervously in his chair. He could feel the query in the old chief's silence, didn't know how to respond. Judging that, Perry moved on.

"Are you bringing Bill Tilghman to my door, then?"

"Naw, naw," Henry said, shifting around some more and coughing into his hand. "I lost them in the town of Abbott west of here. I saw no sign all day they'd found my trail."

Perry shook his head and grunted. "I doubt the great Tilghman lost your trail. He has the mind of a stalking bear. Sooner or later he will find you."

Henry said nothing, only stared at the fire.

At length, Perry said, "You will have to leave tomorrow. I will give you provisions for a few days ride."

Chapter Sixteen

Henry rode east. It was high summer where dust devils and rattlers ruled the sun-baked Texas Panhandle. Through the long endless miles, his mind replayed the voice of Amos Perry. There was no missing the admonition: he should return to his family. When he'd left Perrytown two days ago, he'd meant to head southwest to Albuquerque, but the old man grabbed the reins of his horse and said, "You will not find what you seek by running away. Return to your son, return to your young wife."

So, out of respect for the old man, he turned and rode east. He intended to ride out of sight, then circle wide to head back west. He'd kept riding east, thought about his son.

Slouched in the saddle, his head drooped as did the sorrel's. Henry dozed in the afternoon heat, the rocking rhythm of the horse's slow gait. A shotgun blast brought him fully awake, and he reined the horse to a stop. From the volume of sound, the gunshot appeared to be some distance away in front of him. Despite the near flatness of the land, he saw no shooter through the hazy air. Rode ahead another two hundred yards at a lope, scanning the land. A second boom sounded; this time louder coming from his right front. He pulled the horse to a stop, stood in the stirrups. Could see, maybe a half-mile off, the rippling lump of a figure sitting on the ground. Another discharge, he saw the muzzle flash. Henry could not distinguish a target, though. It appeared the shooter aimed at the ground, as big clouds of dirt would explode some thirty or so yards out.

Henry angled the horse to approach the gunner from the rear, coming at him at a fast walk. At about fifty yards—a fairly safe distance from the gun's blast, he judged—Henry stopped the horse. Loosened the holster strap over the hammer of his Colt, resting his hand on the handle. "Hey!" he yelled.

The man turned, not quite pointing the shotgun at Henry. Placed his hand on the ground and pushed himself to his feet, looking back at Henry. A big man, round at the middle, wearing overalls and a brimmed straw hat bent at many angles.

"Whatcha shootin' at?" Henry shouted.

"Dogs," the man hollered back.

Henry stood again in the stirrups and squinted to look. "What dogs?" he asked. "I don't see no dogs."

"See, that's my problem," the man said. "It be prairie dogs. Ever time I get a bead on one, damn critter ducks back down in his hole."

"You wouldn't shoot me, would ya?" Henry asked.

"Naw, come on in."

The man waited while Henry rode up to him. Leaning with his forearms on the saddle horn, Henry looked down and asked, "Why you shooting at prairie dogs?"

"Why, f'supper, uh course" the man answered. Turned to look back at the prairie dog town thirty paces off, cracked open the breach of the shotgun to put in two new shells— a big double-barrel piece. Two of the fat rodents stuck up from the mounds of their burrow holes, looking back at the two men; then another joined them. One chittered insolently.

"Damn varmits," the man said. He leveled the shotgun, winged off another shot. A cloud of yellow-gray dirt blossomed, when it cleared there was no sign of the prairie dogs.

"Mind if I take a shot?" Henry asked the man.

"Hell, be my guest." Handed Henry the shotgun, looked toward the town. "They damn varmits," he muttered.

"You keep that coon gun," Henry said. "Believe I'll try my Colt."

He sat on the ground, crossing his ankles, keeping his left knee high. Pulled the pistol from its holster and laid the barrel across his knee to steady it. He sighted along its length toward the mound where they'd last seen one of the foolhardy dogs, waited.

After thirty seconds, the top of a furry little head to the level of its eyes popped above the crest of the mound. It waited another cautious few seconds, then emerged up to its waist.

"There he is," whispered the fat man. "You got a shot. Take him! Take him!"

"Hold on," Henry said quietly and calmly.

In five seconds the second dog stood from his mound, the first one brazenly started his taunting chatter at the men. Henry shot him in the mouth, flipping him once over backwards. Before the sound of the first shot faded, he swiveled the pistol barrel slightly, took out the first one's surprised partner.

"Hot damn!" the fat man said. "That's some fine shootin'."

Still sitting, Henry asked, "How many you going to need for supper?"

"You stayin'?"

"I ain't never et prairie dog, but I reckon so."

"Then one more ought'n do it, if he's fair size."

Henry parked the pistol barrel on his knee again, and waited.

* * *

"What be your name, mister?" the fat man asked. He'd tied the hind feet of the six supper prairie dogs to either end of a length of twine, slung them over his shoulder. Walked alongside Henry, who sat astride his horse. Some of the younger varmints, curious to what was going on above ground, had stuck their heads up, too. Henry nailed them. The fat man assured Henry they'd all be cooked.

"Name's Zeke Proctor," Henry replied.

"What brings you out'n t'here, Mister Proctor? Ain't country we see a lot of folks travelin'."

"Up from Lubbock to sell a man some horses over in Tucumcari."

"Know some folks in Lubbock. You know Burt Dooley?"

"Can't say's I do."

"Huh. Kinda funny you wouldn't, as he's in the horse bidness, too."

"Just had a short stay in Lubbock. Actually live in Fort Worth," Henry added. Figured he'd better do some asking, before his story got too complicated. "Who might you be?"

"Proper name's Reverend Blakey, but most just call me Jake."

"You're a preacher, then?"

"Damn sure am."

Henry scanned the horizon. "Don't see no sign of a town nearby. You got a church? Or you just preach to prairie dogs?"

Blakey laughed a little. "Naw, we got us a church, awright. But it ain't a town church. We built it out here on the land. Kindy next to m'house. Sort of in the middle for all my congregants— my two brothers and they families, my oldest boy's wife and they kids, then there's my wife and daughters. They's an old hog farmer some miles off with a passel shows up. All told, with they kids and all, we got about thirty gathers up at most meetin's."

"Seems like a pretty fair-sized congregation, considering the population around here," Henry said.

"Well, we stir up a pretty good shoutin' to the Lord. Fact is, we're havin' a meetin' tonight. You eatin' supper with us, I expect you'd want to come along."

As they approached the house, a wind-gouged clapboard structure which appeared to lean slightly in the direction the prevailing winds blew, a mongrel dog came out from under the porch and stood barking at the men. A large stern-faced woman appeared at the open front door and stood, hands on her stout hips. Two somber young girls, who Henry judged to be about eight and ten, hung behind the woman on either side.

Jake stopped ten feet in front of the group, picked a small rock from the ground, threw it at the dog. "Shaddup, Roy!" The dog cowered at the rock strike on the ground beside him, trotted tail-tucked back to the underside of the porch.

Jake offered introductions. "This here's my wife Beulah and my daughters Lovely and Dandy." Jake made a gesture in their general direction, leaving it to Henry to figure out who was who. Jake yanked a thumb toward Henry. "This here's Zeke Proctor, a horse trader from Lubbock. He'll be stayin' f'supper." With that he held up the string of prairie dogs for his wife's inspection.

Frowning, Missus Blakey studied Henry and the prairie dogs, said to Jake, "You git them dogs gutted and skint, 'n bring 'em to me, I'll fry 'em up."

"Yes'm," Jake said, headed toward the grinding wheel next to the barn.

Henry, still sitting astride his horse, watched Jake walk toward the barn, and looked back at Beulah. They stared at one another, each sizing the other up. After a bit, Henry tipped his hat, she nodded back. He turned the horse and trotted him to where Jake sat at the grinding wheel sharpening a knife.

Henry dismounted and looked around. What he thought to be the church sat a hundred yards off from the house, ruts of a dirt road winding off away from it. Except for the cupola with a small cross atop it, it didn't look much different than the house or barn.

"How'd you get to be a reverend all the way out here in the middle of nowhere?" Henry asked.

"My daddy's the one built that church yonder, me and my brothers helpin'. Took us better part of ten years, hauling lumber out here from Amarillo a little at a time. Daddy was part of Hood's Texas boys at Sharpsburg. Told me the night after the battle, he set in a ditch cryin'. Couldn't stop hisself, he said. Around midnight, a voice come to him clear as day, said he needed to build a church. Daddy believed it were God, so he took it as a sign. Said he just got up and walked off from that place; walked all the way back to Texas. Decided he'd saw all the fightin' and dyin' he wanted to in his life, so he'd build that church God wanted. T'other thing was, after warrin', he wanted to git t'hell away from folks, so he hauled us—it was just my ma and me then—all the way up here from Fort Worth. I was jist a boy. House and barn was already here. Were his uncle's, he said, who'd died and give it to him.

"Daddy weren't a real reverend; jist called hisself that. Figgered God hisself had ordained him. After I got big enough to suit him, he laid hands on me and declared me a reverend, too. So I went along with it. I brung Beulah out here after the folks passed on. She were a pie-anna playin' whore in Amarillo, but she seen the light and repented. She be a hard woman, though."

* * *

"Now, which one are you, Lovely or Dandy?" Henry asked the solemn little girl looking up at him as they sat at the table. Judged her to be the youngest. A sickly looking little thing, her big eyes dark and sunken in their boney sockets.

"Dandy," she answered, un-smiling.

"Well, how'd you come by such a pretty name as that?"

"I 'ont know," she said. Scrunched her brow and looked annoyed.

"I give her that name," Jake said looking at her and smiling. "One spring day Beulah was off down by the crik gatherin' wild onions. I was in the field plowin', when I heared her start to screech like a chicken hawk. First thing I thought was she'd been bit by a cotton mouth, so I took off to git to her. I tell ya, runnin's hard across a plowed field, but stumblin' and fallin' I eventually got there. When I did, there was Beulah layin' in a field of dandelions holding that little baby girl on her lap. She come out almost as yaller as them flowers, so I named her Dandelion. We mostly just call her Dandy."

Henry smiled at frail little Dandy, she looked back at him impassively. Turned to Lovely and said, "Then I guess you must've been born in a bed of rose petals."

Lovely smiled and started to giggle, but after looking at her mother, lowered her head and returned her gaze to the plate of fried prairie dog and collard greens in front of her.

"You's comin' to the meetin', ain'tcha?" Beulah asked Henry. Sounded more like a demand than a question.

"Reckon so, ain't like I got far to ride to get there," he said. Lovely and Jake were the only ones to laugh.

The brothers arrived first just as Jake opened the doors and windows of the church. They rolled up single-file in separate wagons. Twins Jonas and Eli pretty well matched Jake's roundness of body. Jonas had six kids; Eli eight, ranging in age from sixteen to two. Before the wagons stopped the children spilled over the sides, and converged into a loud, rambunctious mob. Jake introduced Henry; the men greeted him with hearty handshakes, the wives with polite nods. Ten minutes after that, two more wagons trundled in from opposite directions. One brought Jake's son Juney and young wife Ruth, who held an infant. A toddler of about three climbed down from the back of the wagon followed by a big wire-haired dog named Bob. In the other wagon came the hog farmer, Silas Warner, with a boy of about eighteen sitting beside him on the seat. Silas's wife, Naomi, their two teenaged daughters, and a boy of about eight sat in the wagon bed. The Warners also brought a dog—a mostly hound-looking cur with only three and a half legs who they called Shorty.

Twilight had begun, the moon rose full as all the flock filed into the little church. Things started up without much preamble. Silas Warner walked to the front—where Jake already stood, rhythmically clapping his hands—and uncased a fiddle. Silas's oldest boy Billy sidled up next to his daddy cradling a banjo. The two faced each other twisting the knobs on the necks while plunking various strings. Beulah waddled past Jake, sat on the small bench of an ancient upright piano up against one of the side walls. Others funneled into the few pews, all the time clapping along with Jake. A few began stomping a foot alternate to the claps.

Beulah launched into a badly tuned, but upbeat and pounding rendition of "Standing on the Promises." At the chorus measures the congregants joined in lustily, not missing a single clap or stomp. Sang the chorus over and over at least five or six times, as one or two individuals at each passing would give forth an impromptu shout out. "Jesus!" they would holler. "Jeee-zus! Oh, Jeeeee-zus!" When Beulah brought the hymn to an end with a hammered chord or two, a running of her fingers up and down the keyboard, the churchgoers clapped and jumped and whooped with more praises to the heavens. Several of the smaller children had started crying, along with some of the women.

Henry didn't know quite what to make of all this, but he clapped in turn, positioning himself at the back of the pack. Thinking it was time to sit, he'd bent to do that when Silas and

Billy broke into a churning hymn which roused everyone again into clapping and hollering and jumping. Jake had started dancing back and forth by this time, singing out, "The Holy Ghost is got me! The Holy Ghost is got me!" The crowd acknowledged his possession, with more shouts and moans, urging him on. Beulah joined in at the piano following Silas and Billy's lead. By then the dogs Shorty, Bob, and Roy had come into the church, running up and down the aisle barking to the Lord.

This went on for two or three minutes before one of the women joined Jake in his dancing. She hopped on one foot, then the other, head thrown back, eyes closed, arms stretched upward, skipping back and forth from one side wall to the other. Little Dandy started twirling through the room, arms held straight out. Juney's wife Ruth, still holding the baby, bounced in place, her head lolling. Just before she collapsed onto the floor, one of the other women snatched the infant from its transfixed mother's bosom.

By this time several of the others, women and children and Eli, had joined in the dancing up front. Jonas had fallen down on all fours yipping like a coyote, and the dog Roy stopped by to join in with Jonas in the howling. The other dog, Bob, had attached himself to one of Jake's legs and commenced to humping it, while Shorty ran around whacking all the jumping and whirling kids with his right front stump.

Henry stood at the back of the church clapping and whooping, taking it all in. Had to admit, it cheered him some. All the commotion stopped about as fast as it had begun. Jake kicked Bob loose from his leg and raised his arms. Silas and Billy ceased playing, Beulah followed on for about ten seconds before she stopped. The dancers and twirlers and howlers composed themselves and returned to the pews, giving occasional shout-outs. The small hot room was awash with the smell of human sweat and musky dogs.

Jake closed his eyes and bowed his head. Clamped his hands together, held them out in front of him slightly raised. He breathed hard, made weeping sounds. The group got quiet. Sweat ran in rivulets down his fat face.

"Oh, Jesus, I'zuh sinner," Jake rasped. Some moaning and wailing issued from the crowd, several acknowledged Jake's testimony with amens. "I ain't always done accordin' to your Word, I often use your name in vain. I done danced with wicked wimmin in my life, and I run with John Barleycorn. No, there ain't no doubt about it, I be a goddam sinner. But they be hope fer me, 'cause I's washed in the blood. Yes, washed in the blood, halleluiah!"

Jake paused to let the gathered interject as the Spirit moved them. He launched into an impassioned, rambling testimonial prayer, with members of the group adding their two cents. After two minutes, Henry lifted an eyelid to peek around at the congregants. All stood with arms raised, heads tilted heavenward, all eyes tightly shut, weaving, muttering. All, that is, except Dandy, who stood next to her sister in the second pew, somberly looking back at Henry. He smiled and winked at her, closed his eyes again to wait out Jake's prayer.

At ten minutes, it didn't appear Jake was anywhere near the end of his praying. He seemed to be building steam, the congregation had begun to moan and weave with increasing vigor.

Henry decided he'd had enough of the prayer meeting, moved quietly to exit out the door behind. Sliding into the aisle, Dandy still watched him. Put his right index finger to his lips, indicating that she should say nothing to alert the others. She gave no acknowledgement one way or the other, only looked back at him gravely.

Henry slipped out the church door, trotted to the barn. He quickly saddled and mounted the sorrel, trotting him by the front of the small church building. Looking in the row of windows, he could see all still swayed in a building frenzy to Jake's continuing prayer. No one had apparently seen him slip away, except Dandy. It didn't appear she'd mentioned it to anyone, or, if she had, they didn't hear it, or didn't care. He spurred the horse into a gallop, rode off into the moonlit night, heading east.

Chapter Seventeen

The land turned softer the further east he went, and started to undulate. Some places a ridge would heave to a narrow palisade eroding off into a gentle grassy slope. Trees became more plentiful—scrub oaks and hackberry stood in small huddled groups across the grasslands with one or two set apart amongst them like outlying sentries. Sycamores and willows and elms gathered along the creek banks.

Henry came upon a forlorn settlement of mud and stick huts, a few tepees covered with patched and rotting hides. Riding into the village, he slowed the sorrel to a walk along the wide muddy path that served as the hamlet's only street. Several scrawny dogs, standing close to dwellings, joined in a chorus of barking at his passage. Here and there inhabitants stuck their heads out of lodgings to see what was going on, or stopped their outside activity to turn and stare at the approaching stranger and his horse.

Cheyenne, Henry surmised, believing he'd ridden inside their territory. A sorrier lot he'd never seen; looked beaten and starved. Just as they showed no defensive aggression as he approached, no welcome came, either. They watched him with sullen eyes sunk in hollow sockets.

A thin old man with a tattered blanket wrapped around his shoulders, walked to the middle of the road, stopped to await Henry's approach. He started speaking loudly when the horse came within twenty yards, waving and gesturing wildly with his free hand, holding the edges of the blanket to his chest with the other. Seemed excited and agitated, neither friendly nor angry. Henry understood not a word he spoke. The man's nearly toothless mouth spit out sounds like one of the barking dogs. Neither did he lower the volume of his voice as Henry rode up to him. The old man reached out a boney hand to touch the horse's shoulder. Leaving it lay there, he bent, turned sideways to look toward the animal's hind quarters, all the time talking non-stop in his near shouting voice.

"Do you speak English, grandfather?" Henry asked, shouting down at him. The old man paused at Henry's question, glancing up for a moment, rheumy eyes meeting Henry's briefly. He resumed his shouting in his native tongue, his attention back to examining the horse.

A woman's voice came from behind them. She said something loudly to the old man, yet in a gentle voice. She walked up, putting her hands on the old one's shoulders, turned him to lead him away.

"What's he saying?" Henry asked.

She looked up at Henry. "His old. Not see good. Not hear good. Not think good."

"Well, what does he want?" Henry said smiling. "What was it he said?"

The woman pulled the old man closer to her. She struggled to speak in English. "Father once horse warrior. His fought many battles. Like see good horse."

Henry looked down at the old man and his daughter with pity, nodded. The old man began his loud speaking again; the woman shushed him. "Does he want to ride my horse?" Henry asked.

The woman looked at the ground, then back up at Henry, smiling. "No. His ask you to come feast tonight."

"A feast?" Henry looked around at the few gaunt faces looking back at him. "You're having a feast tonight?"

"No feast," she said. "Father want you stay so we give feast."

Henry looked at the small loosely gathered crowd again, at all the hovels and destitution. It didn't appear these people were in any position to throw a party. "Don't mean no disrespect, sister, but how is it your daddy thinks we could have a feast?"

The woman looked up at Henry, her smile still curved her lips, with a sardonic edge. "His want us cook your horse," she said.

Henry scanned the hungry faces of the people around him again. He straightened some in his saddle, suddenly a little uneasy. The sorrel moved back a step, snorting and bobbing his head as if sensing his rider's uneasiness . . . and the crowd's hunger. A soft ripple of laughter cut through them.

She said to Henry, "Peoples hungry. Game here not much. But not be scare; we not cook your horse. You stay, eat rabbit."

Henry hesitated. The little crowd started to loosen, turning back to their endeavors. He said to the woman, "I could use a bite. Thank ya kindly for the invite."

The woman nodded, continued to lead the old man toward a hut. Henry dismounted and followed them, nervously looking back a couple times. They came to a fire pit beside the hut. A small animal lay skewered on a spit over the fire, presumably the lunch rabbit. A boy of about ten sat beside the low flames, upwind, jabbing a stick into the coals. He looked up at Henry, one eye milky, the other dull and liquid. A scar near the middle of his upper lip drew it upward in a permanent, humorless grin. The woman spoke to him softly, he looked at her. He said something back, like a question. She answered him, and he looked again at the fire, poking at the coals angrily with the stick. Shot an angry glance toward Henry.

The old man went to the ground slowly, sitting cross-legged next to the boy, resumed his loud one-sided conversation. Henry sat across from the old man, the boy between them. The woman went into the hut and shortly reappeared with several small well-used wooden bowls. She removed the spit from the fire, began dismembering the cooked animal, placing pieces in the bowls. She handed Henry a bowl, one with twice as much meat as the others. The boy looked at Henry's food with longing; the old man yammered on.

Henry was famished, but didn't feel right about the portion given him. Reached out with the bowl, motioning for the boy to take some of the meat, he eagerly clutched some. The woman snapped at the boy, he pulled back his hand.

To Henry, she said quietly, "His not eat more. You eat first."

"Well, I . . ." Henry hesitated, looking at the saddened boy, the woman. Understood the woman's reprimand, her pride. Would be an insult for their guest not to eat his fill. Even with their meager meal, he must be given the largest portion. He picked up one of the legs from his bowl and bit into it. He ate all the meat off the bone, gnawing it to the greasy gristle. He threw the leg bone to the cur tied up beside the hut, and sat the bowl on one of the fire stones nearest him.

"Very good," he said. "But I et right before I come into your camp." He looked at the woman, the boy. "Don't believe I could eat another bite."

The boy looked at the woman, she nodded. He grabbed Henry's bowl and began devouring the remaining meat. The old man gnawed on his one piece of meat with his few remaining teeth, and talked on with his mouth full, spitting bits of chewed rabbit in Henry's direction as he spoke.

Henry watched the old man. "Still talking about my horse?" he asked the woman.

"Some," she answered. "His talk turns like wind. Comes, goes from many places."

She picked up a piece of leather, resumed working it. Henry he could see she was forming a moccasin. Looked at the moccasins she wore, the old man's. Noticed the boy went barefoot.

"You making moccasins for the boy?" he asked.

She shook her head. "Make for man in village. Trade for food."

Henry looked at the handiwork in her hand. "Fine work you done there. You ever sell these?"

She shook her head. "Not sell," she said. "Peoples poor. Not have money. Sometime Trader man Smith at post take, give trade."

"You got any made up?" Henry asked. "I'm headed back to see my boy, 'bout your son's age there. I'd sure like to take him a pair of those as a present. I'd pay you cash money for 'em."

The woman continued working the piece of leather, not looking at Henry. He began to figure she either didn't understand him or didn't have any to give him. "If you got a pair made, I'd give you two dollars for 'em," he said.

Still not looking at Henry, she glanced at the boy. She said something to the youngster. He sat down his bowl, rose to his feet, walked into the woods behind the hut.

Once the boy was out of sight she said, "Got moccasin. Sell you two dollar." She sat down her work, got up to go into the hut, returning with a small-sized pair. They were beautifully made. She offered them to Henry.

Henry took the moccasins and examined them. "My, my. Believe these might be worth three dollars." He pulled three silver dollars out of his vest pocket, the last of his take from the Amity bank, handed them over to the woman. She took the coins without giving a word of thanks, returning to her work on the unmade moccasin.

"What name do you go by?" Henry asked her, setting the pair of moccasins down beside him.

The woman furrowed her brow in thought. "White words say me . . . Talks to Moon," she answered.

Henry nodded. They sat in the silence of their own thoughts. After a spell she added, "Father called Hitting Snakes. Boy is Looks with One Eye." Hitting Snakes had lowered his volume to a mutter. The boy re-entered the camp, his skinny arms laden with firewood.

"Well, I best get going," Henry said. "Need to get further along before dark." Talks to Moon didn't answer or look up from her work.

Henry stood. "I sure thank ya for the meal," he said. Talks to Moon gave a nod. When Henry moved to put the moccasins in his saddlebag, the boy said something to him in a sharp tone. Henry turned to look at him, then to Talks to Moon with a questioning look. Looks with One Eye stood pointing at Henry angrily, questioning his mother. She responded to him quietly, but tersely. The boy stomped and got louder, his voice rising into hysteria. Talks to Moon reached over, batted the boy several times across the face and head, speaking harshly to him. The boy, crying, ran off.

Henry watched the scene, perplexed. The woman returned to her place by the fire, took up her moccasin work again. "What was that all about?" he asked.

"You go," she said. "Boy not like me sell you moccasins. You go."

Henry stood there for a minute trying to unravel all that. Talks to Moon looked at him with tear-brimmed eyes, said angrily, "You go!"

Henry mounted and rode away. Once clear of the village, he goaded his horse into a lope. After about two miles, he pulled the sorrel to a stop, wheeled him about and spurred the horse back toward the village. He reined up next to the fire where Talks to Moon still sat, and dismounted.

"You know, I got to thinking," he said as he took the moccasins out of his saddlebag. "I really ain't all that interested in these moccasins. Don't believe they'd fit my boy. 'Sides on second look, I don't think the work's all that good. I'll sell 'em back to you for a dollar."

Talks to Moon stared up at Henry for some time; she looked towards the woods where the boy had gone. Wiping her hands on her dress, she retrieved one of the silver dollars from a pocket, handed it to Henry. When their hands touched, she grabbed his and held it. "His thank to you," she said. Henry gave a quick nod, mounted up again, and rode off.

Chapter Eighteen

Looking down from the hilltop he could see Tulsa spread out along the river valley. It was early evening, dusk, and the lights of the town were coming on, twinkling in the still crisp air. Lines of poles strung with wires told him more electric lights shined amid a few remaining gas lights. A few oil rigs stood on the town's edge like tall dark skeletons. Believed the place looked bigger than the last time he saw it.

How long had that been? Henry had wandered the red lands after he left the Cheyenne village. He'd drifted, finding work as a hand at a farm or ranch, stayed a few weeks, a month or two, then moved on to the next. Chief Perry's words stayed in his mind. He'd pondered it, all the guilt that roiled inside him; fought his desire to take easy pickin's from a bank or a store in his path, much like a sober drunk would yearn for a bottle. Now he'd returned, clean and clear-headed. Had it been a year? More than a year? Henry realized he didn't know the current day or month. Could figure the season by the cool air and the color of the trees—it was fall. Must've been almost two years since he'd left his young wife and boy. Wondered if he'd still find them there, if he'd recognize Teddy.

"She hasn't lived here in over a year," the woman answering the door told him. She looked at Henry with suspicion, perhaps a little disdain. "Real estate man sold us this house for a song. Told us the owner's husband had left her and her child, that she needed the money bad."

Henry nodded, looking a little shamefaced. "You happen to know where she went?" he asked.

The woman squinted up her eyes, giving him an accusatory look. "You her no 'count husband?"

"Well, I . . ."

"That poor little boy's father?"

"Ma'am I just—"

168

"I don't believe I need to tell you anything else. Good night, sir!" She shut the door firmly in his face.

Reining the sorrel to a stop under a street light, Henry pulled his watch out of his vest pocket. Just past eight. He figured Bagby would still be in his office at this hour. If he wasn't drinking there, he'd most likely be across the street drinking in The Black Gold Saloon.

Sure enough, when Henry dismounted in front of Bagby Real Estate, and peered through the window, he could see Hiram sitting at his desk. An open bottle of whiskey sat atop the desk; a half-full glass of amber liquid sat next to it. Henry turned the door knob and walked in.

Bagby looked up, his expression showing surprise when he recognized Henry walking out of the shadows. He leaned back in his chair and sneered.

"Well, I'll be damned," he said, the words slurred some.

"Hello, Hiram."

"Law ain't caught up with you yet?" Bagby asked.

Henry pushed his hat back from his forehead and looked around the dark office. "I don't reckon the law knows I'm back in Oklahoma, Hiram. But either way, I ain't lettin' them send me to Arkansas."

"Arkansas? Hell, Henry, ain't nobody around here going to send you to Arkansas."

Henry shifted his stare back to Bagby. "What're you talking about?"

"Why, Governor Haskell denied your extradition. Your lawyer friend come around here almost two years ago, just after you left. Wanted to make sure you knew that. Said he told you that over the phone, but the connection was bad."

"Haskell denied it?"

"That's what the man said." Bagby started laughing. "I heard you robbed a bank in Colorado. Man come in here asking about you a few weeks back. Fella named Smoak, a deputy U.S. Marshal. They figured you'd be coming back here sooner or later.

Said he was partnered up with Bill Tilghman out of Oklahoma City. Asked me to give 'em a call if you showed up."

"Bill Tilghman," Henry repeated, nodding.

"Musta been a pretty important bank to get a man like Tilghman after you."

Henry looked squarely at Bagby. "You know where Ollie might be? And the boy?" he asked.

"Ollie don't want anything to do with you, Henry, or the boy. After you left them starving, she moved in with me. She's divorced you. Can't change a leopard's spots. You're still a low-life sumbitchin' outlaw. Best you just stay away." Bagby opened a desk drawer, and pulled out a pistol, laying it on the desktop. He grinned back at Henry, picked up the glass of whiskey and downed it.

"Guess I can understand that, Ollie not wanting to see me," Henry said. "But I want to see Teddy. Don't figure he understood why I left. Need to explain a few things to him."

"Oh, he understands plenty," Bagby said. "I told him all about you. He's a smart-assed little cuss, though. Whippings don't seem to get through to him, so I'm sending him off to a military school over in Claremore. Figure they'll pound some sense into him. He's leaving tomorrow." He moved his left hand over the handle of the pistol, rested it there.

Henry moved swiftly around the desk and grabbed Bagby by the throat with his left hand, heaving him forcefully out of his seat and up against the wall. With his left, he ripped the pistol from Bagby's grip, smacking him on the side of the face with it. Putting it in his own grip, he shoved the barrel hard up Bagby's left nostril, cocked the hammer. "You listen to me, you slimy drunk. Ollie may have thrown in with you, but I aim to see my boy.

"Now, you still live in that big house over on Archer Street?"

Bagby, sweating and visibly shaken, tried to nod.

"Then I'm going to head on over there. Don't plan on staying around with a man like Tilghman after me, but I'm going to go see my boy, just the same. I'll see Ollie, too; let her tell me what she wants to tell me. Let me tell you something about that boy. I still got friends in this town, big mean friends; Going to have them watch you, Bagby. I hear about you laying a hand my boy again, I'm gonna come straight back and kill you. But before I do, or if I can't, I'm going to have my friends break you up some before I get here. You understand that?"

Bagby, breathing hard almost to a whimper, just squeaked. Henry pushed the gun barrel harder against Bagby's nostril. "Say it out loud!" Henry demanded.

"Y-yes, yes! Understand, understand!" Bagby sobbed.

"Awright, then," Henry said, not lessening the pressure of the gun barrel against Bagby's nose. "So after I leave here, you going to call the law and tell them where I'm headed?"

Bagby coughed and gasped as Henrys grip tightened on his throat. "Naw, I won't do that," he rasped.

"Like hell you won't," Henry said, smacked Bagby across the side of the head with the pistol, knocking him cold. He yanked the phone wire from the wall, bound Bagby's feet to his hands behind him. Reaching into the man's hip pocket, he removed a handkerchief and stuffed it in Bagby's mouth. He shoved the unconscious man under the desk so he couldn't be seen from the window. Turning out all the lights, he left the office, closing the door behind him.

A middle-aged black woman answered the door at Henry's insistent knocking. She opened it a crack, peered out at him with a look of pique on her round face. She waited for Henry to speak first.

"I'm here to see Ollie," he said.

"Who you?" she asked brusquely. "What you want?"

"I told you what I want. I'm Ollie's husband. Now are you going to go get her, or am I going to have to kick this door open?" He was in no mood to be polite.

"You jist hole yo' ho'ses," the woman said, willing to give back to him what he was dishing out. "I'll go ax her do she want to see you. You bettah be nicer, now, or I go call the poe-leese. I got me a shotgun right here by da doe."

Henry backed up a step, removed his hat. "Awright," he said. "I'm sorry, ma'am."

The woman sniffed. "Thas bettah. You waits right there on the porch," she said, and closed the door.

When the door opened again, the first thing Henry noticed was that Ollie was pregnant. It occurred to him that this was the second time this had happened to him.

"Well, damn, Ollie," was all he could think to say.

"Why'd you come back, Henry?" she asked.

"That little bastard Bagby's?" he asked in return, gesturing to her protruding stomach.

Ollie moved back to slam the door, Henry put his hand out to stop it, moving across the threshold. "Wait, wait," he said in a gentler voice. "Let's talk." He could see the bulk of the black woman in the shadows of the parlor, holding a shotgun.

"What do you want to say," Ollie asked; her voice disinterested, angry.

"Didn't think you'd divorce me, Ollie."

"You didn't leave me much choice, Henry. I had a child to care for. We had no money, and Hiram took us in."

"Don't look like that's all he's done. Damn, Ollie. Bagby's a scumbag."

"I've known worse," she said, looking away from his stare, clutching her robe to her neck.

"Yeah, I reckon," Henry said. He looked back into the dark entrance of the parlor catching a glint of the shotgun's double-barrel drooping toward the floor. "Guess I can't blame you for what you done. We never had what you'd call a tight marriage. I'll head on out and leave you be, but I would like to see Teddy before I go."

"He's asleep," Ollie said.

"Wouldn't hurt to wake him, Ollie. May be the last time we get to see each other for a while. I'd like to give him a hug, tell him I love him."

The shotgun and its bearer came out of the parlor shadows. The black woman leaned the gun up against its corner by the door. "I'll fetch Teddy, Miss Ollie. It be okay. Boy ought to see his daddy afo' he go."

Ollie looked at the floor, thinking. "Alright, Maddy," she said. She opened the door wider, motioned for Henry to step the rest of the way into the entry. The black woman rustled up the stairs.

It was awkward in the entry. Henry held his hat, looked around at some of the trappings in Bagby's house. "Why don't we go into the parlor," Ollie said at length. Henry nodded and followed her.

He sat stiffly on the edge of the settee, Ollie in the chair opposite. "He treatin' you okay?" he asked her.

After a few seconds, she answered, "We live well."

"That ain't what I asked," Henry said.

Ollie examined her fingernails, looked toward the stairs. "Hiram is . . . has his ways of doing things. I can't complain," she said tersely. Henry nodded, deciding to let it go at that.

Maddy came down the stairs with her hand on the boy's shoulder, guiding him in his somnambulant walk. She turned him into the parlor, stopping him in front of his father.

Henry reached out and put his hands on the boy's shoulders. "Hello, son," he said softly, smiling at the little sleepyhead.

"Daddy?" the boy asked groggily. He rubbed his eyes with his fingers and blinked hard.

"Yeah," Henry said, pulled the boy close to him in a hug.

"Are we going back home now?" the boy asked.

Henry put his hand on the back of the boy's head and squeezed him tighter. "No, Teddy, I just wanted to come by and see you. Daddy's got to go on another trip."

"I don't want to stay here, Daddy. I want to go with you."

"I know, son, I know. And I want to take you with me, I surely do, but I can't. You got to stay here and go to school, take care of your momma. I ain't going somewhere a boy can go."

"Why not?" Teddy asked. "Please, Daddy, take me with you," he whimpered. "I don't like living here. I don't like Hiram."

Henry looked into the teary little eyes, ran his fingers through the boy's black hair. "I'm sorry, son. But don't you worry about Hiram. I had a talk with him, and he agreed not to bother you no more." He looked up sternly at Ollie, holding his stare. Her eyes flooded, she let out a quick sob, looking down.

He looked back at Teddy. "You hear me?" The boy nodded solemnly.

Henry hugged him again, kissed him on the forehead. "I love you, son. Don't you never forget that," he said. Teddy nodded again.

Standing, Henry said, "I better be going." He gently pushed the boy over to his mother. Maddy followed him to the door to see him out. Once there, he stopped and turned to her.

"Maddy, I reckon you know how rough Bagby has been treating the boy?"

"Yessuh, I does," she said shaking her head sadly side-to-side. "Break my heart seein' him whip that sweet boy."

"I had a meetin' with Bagby before I come over here. Told him if I heard anything about him mistreating Teddy, I'd see he got some of that back. Maybe even kill him." He stopped to see what the woman's reaction would be. Her eyes narrowed and she nodded.

"Hope that'll scare the coward into stopping, but if it don't, I got friends here in town who'll take care of him. Told Bagby that, too. There's a man named Feingold owns a jewelry story over on Third Street. I'd appreciate it if you'd let him know about anything that happens. He'll see that it won't happen again. I'm going to go tell him about you."

"I'll do that, Mistah Henry. You can count on it."

"Thanks," Henry said. He put on his hat and stepped out the door. Turning back to the woman before she closed the door, he said, "Bagby's tied up and stuffed under his desk in his office. I'd appreciate it if you'd give me an hour or so before you send anybody over there to fetch him."

Maddy put her hand over her mouth, and widened her eyes. "You sho nuf did that?" she asked.

Henry smiled and nodded.

"Well . . . I 'spect I better go tell Miss Ollie . . . pretty soon. First I gots to go get that boy back to bed. He gots a big day tomarrah."

Chapter Nineteen

Henry rode southwest for no particular reason. He thought maybe he'd head for Texas, maybe he'd go back to New Mexico; he hadn't decided. When Feingold asked, that's what he told him.

He drifted along, his horse at a walk. Trail weary and cold, he hunkered in the saddle bobbing in and out of sleep fits. The road was narrow, not much more than a deer trail covered with the fallen and falling leaves of hickory, oak and walnut trees that arched over it. It rose on low hills, dipped into shallow hollows as it twisted and turned through dense woods. In the cloudy gloom of the gathering November evening, the forest stretched thick and dark in every direction. The cold dank air had the feel of impending rain.

At the edge of a doze, Henry heard the snort of a horse which wasn't his own. He snapped his head up and looked about, reining hard to his left to look behind him, his right hand drawing out his Peacemaker.

Some thirty yards behind him a rider had stopped, looking back at him. The man wore dungarees and a plaid shirt under a leather vest with some sort of dark fur sticking out at the edges. On his head sat a fur hat of some kind; his feet were shod with moccasins, a large broad-shouldered man of indeterminate age. Long black braids hung down to his chest. No mistaking his facial features and dark skin were those of an Indian. He gripped a Winchester rifle at the stock waist, the butt resting on his right thigh, the barrel pointed skyward. The carcass of a small deer lay tied across his mount's rump.

The sorrel grunted nervously in Henry's tight rein, spinning in his tracks. "How long you been following me?" he shouted back to the man.

The rider gave no immediate answer, only looked back at Henry stone-faced.

"You speak English?" Henry shouted. "What do you want?" Still no response.

"Look," Henry said, pointing his gun at the man. "I ain't above shooting a brother if he means me harm."

The man laid the barrel of the rifle he held into the crook of his left arm. "Are you hungry?" he asked Henry.

"What?" Henry returned, not sure he understood what the man asked.

"Do you want to eat?"

"Well . . . yeah. I reckon I do." Henry answered, still a little confused.

"We will ride to my house, have my wives cook this deer," the big Indian said.

Henry holstered his pistol. "How far to your house?" he asked. The man rode up to him, gestured down the road with the rifle barrel, riding on past Henry at a trot without looking back. Henry spurred the sorrel, pulling up beside the rider.

They rode along in silence. After about a mile Henry said, "What's your nation, brother? I'm Cherokee myself."

"I am Quahadi. I am Comanche," his companion answered with force and pride.

"What do folks call you?"

They'd started to break out of the trees coming onto a slight downslope. Out on the flat plain of the valley stood an enormous frame house. A tall fence of pickets surrounded it, and the cones of teepees filled the grounds near it, curling ribbons of smoke coming from their peaks. Several big white stars adorned the roof of the house.

"I am Quanah Parker," the man said.

Henry had momentarily forgotten his question when he saw the house, but the man's answer gave him pause. "You're Quanah Parker?" he asked with astonishment.

"Yes," the man said. Pointed his rifle at the distant settlement with its large building. "That is my house." He rode on ahead as Henry sat still on his horse, watching him. The name Quanah Parker had reached far and wide throughout America, even parts of Europe, especially so in the Indian Nations. He was a living legend.

* * *

"Do you like tobacco?" Quanah asked Henry. He'd walked to a large cabinet set up against a wall of the dining room, pulled a box of cigars out of a drawer. Opened it to offer Henry one.

Henry hesitated. He'd never used tobacco, but he didn't want to insult his esteemed host, the last great war chief of the Comanche. The man seemed to sense Henry's reluctance. "It good American tobacco, from Virginia," he said, still with the opened box held out to his guest. Henry smiled weakly and took one of the cigars. Quanah grunted approval, passed the box to the other guests. The man called Stands in One Place helped himself to a couple.

They'd dined late, as it'd taken Quanah's wives—he had five—several hours to dress the small doe, and then to prepare and cook the venison stew. Besides Henry, three others had come to dinner. Stands in One Place was already in the dining room when Quanah and Henry entered. His host had introduced the man, adding, "He is brother of third wife." He said it almost under his breath with a tone of antipathy. Stands in One Place sat in a rocker in one corner of the room most of the time, wrapped in a blanket. He left the chair only to come to the table, returned to it once he'd eaten. He spoke not a word to Henry, uttering only a few Comanche phrases to Quanah during the course of the meal. The second man seemed cordial enough, coming in through the door from the kitchen, full of talk and warm greeting, although he eyed Henry with suspicion. He was also Comanche, Quanah called him uncle. Henry learned his name to be Mad Coyote.

"You are Tonkawa?" Mad Coyote asked Henry. It seemed more of an accusation than a friendly inquiry. He looked at Henry with narrowed eyes and raised chin. Quanah immediately spoke to the old man in Comanche using an abrupt, harsh tone. Henry would later learn being called a Tonkawa by a Comanche was the equivalent of the worst racial epithet a white man could give to a black man.

Mad Coyote looked back at Henry coolly. "Ah, Cherokee. We not see many Cherokee." Again with disdain. He then took his seat at the table. "You look Tonk," he added with no apology in his voice, and despite Quanah's disapproving glare.

The four men ate most of the meal in silence. Occasionally, one or two women—Henry supposed them Quanah's wives—came into the dining room carrying fresh bowls of food, taking others out.

At about the midpoint of the eating, the door to the outside burst open, in strode a big white man. He wore a knee-length, fur-lined buckskin coat and a tall range hat. He shed the outer coat, hanging it on the peg of a wall-mounted rack, his hat on top of that. Dressed in a brown-vested wool suit, he looked every bit like a banker, except for the pant legs stuffed inside ornate cowboots. His face, wide and weather-worn, was decked with round wire-rimmed spectacles and a bushy mustache. Henry thought he sort of looked like Teddy Roosevelt from pictures he'd seen.

"Big Boss!" Quanah said when the man came through the door. The other two men raised their greeting, too, with whoops and loud cries. The women came in from the kitchen, surrounding the man, chattering excitedly, saying "Big Boss! Big Boss!" The man grinned broadly, returning all the greetings with hugs and shoulder slaps and handshakes.

Once all the excitement over the man's arrival subsided, he settled into a chair between Quanah at the head of the table and Henry on his right. "Thought I'd been here sooner," he said to the table. "Got tied up with a dang banker in Lawton."

"You ain't a banker?" Henry asked with a grin. "You sort of look like one."

"This *Apu Numu*," Quanah said. "Big Boss. He have many cattle. Pay Comanche lots money for them cattle eat our grass in Big Pasture."

Big Boss turned to Henry on his right. Grinning, he extended his hand. "They call me that, but you don't hafta. Name's Burk Burnett." Henry took the handshake.

"Who might you be?" Burnett asked.

"Zeke Proctor," Henry said. "From over around Durant."

"You Choctaw?" Burnett asked.

"Chero-KEE," Mad Coyote interjected. Henry looked at him with a tight smile, to Burnett he said. "Moved to Durant from Arkansas. In the horse business."

"Horse bidness?" Burnett looked at the host, then around the table. "You here sellin' horses to these boys? 'Cause they loves horses, but I don't think they'll buy any. Believe they'd rather steal 'em from you."

That brought a hearty round of laughter and shouts from all at the table, even from Stands in One Place. Henry nodded and chuckled good-naturedly.

Burnett continued. "Money don't mean a whole lot to Comanches, but horses do. The number of horses they own? That's how they measure wealth." He stopped to fork a piece of deer meat from the stew, and pop it into his mouth. Around his chewing, he continued, "Now Quanah here, and I expect old Mad Coyote, too, they've gathered up a lot of horses in their day. Took 'em from white men and Indin alike. Didn't matter to them who they belonged to, as long as they could say they belonged to them in the end. The stealin' part was important, too; part of the prestige of being a Comanche warrior."

"Naw, not trying to sell horses here," Henry said. "Just passing through. Met Quanah on the trail. He invited me to supper."

Burnett nodded as he ate. "Yeah, he'll do that, especially to Indian brothers."

"Not Tonk," Mad Coyote cut in.

That started a heated discussion in Comanche between Quanah, Mad Coyote, and Stands in One Place.

"Comanch don't much like Tonkawas," Burnett said out of the side of his mouth to Henry as the argument raged across the table. "Consider them a wholly inferior race. But I do believe Quanah is defending you. Tonkawa aside, though, Comanch don't have a very high opinion of any Indin outside of themselves, Kiowas, and Cheyenne."

Once the Comanche argument ran its course, and the meal ended, Quanah had moved to fetch the cigars. Burnett stuck a kindling stick into the wood stove, put the light to his cigar. Puffed up a cloud of blue smoke, and handed the burning stick to Quanah. The lighter passed from man to man until it came to Henry. With some unease, he held the flame to his stogy and sucked in the fire, which immediately made him cough.

Quanah, Burnett, and Stands in One Place laughed. Mad Coyote muttered something, shook his head in disgust.

Henry waved the thick smoke away from his face. "I guess I ain't much of a smoker," he said in a choking voice.

Burnett slapped Henry on the back. "Don't worry about it, son. Quanah never smoked one of these neither until I brought him some. Now he just uses them to impress people. He wants you to believe he's civilized."

Henry tapped his cigar to knock off the ash. "Civilized? I don't know about that, Mister Burnett. Even among my people, Quanah Parker here is legendary. The last of the great war chiefs to fight against you invading white men." Henry shook his head sadly, looked squarely at Parker. "Wouldn't want to believe he's turned white."

Quanah looked at Henry with a scowling grin. "Do not listen my great friend Big Boss too much, Zekeproctor. He make you think Quanah Parker has become American.

"It is true I now live like American, have big house, dress like whites, but I do not always think like American. Do you think Cherokee? I think so. I think Comanche. I think about my Comanche . . . and children of Comanche . . . and their children to come.

"Americans are here. They will stay. We cannot drive them out. They will grow strong while we will not. We must learn from him so that our children will not hunger . . . so they will be warm in winter . . . so they will be strong as the Americans are strong.

"This has long been on my mind. Americans know many things. We must learn from them . . . or the sun will set on us forever. But I will always remain Comanche."

The room got quiet for a few seconds, filled with more tobacco smoke. "That was damn well spoken," Burnett said breaking the silence. "I've never underestimated my friend Quanah, Mister Proctor."

The room got quiet again; the men smoked. Three of the women came into the room to work it over on their after-meal cleanup. Several small children appeared jumping into Quanah's lap, crawling over him from around his chair. They chattered and squealed as the great chief grabbed and tickled them. He laughed with obvious delight as the children tumbled over him in their play.

Henry noticed Burnett studying him while all the child play was going on.

"Where 'bouts you headed, Mister Proctor?" Burnett asked.

"New Mexico," Henry said. "Man out near Tucumcari wants to contract with me on a few head."

"Rancher?"

Henry started to shift nervously in his chair. He didn't like being questioned. "Has a small ranch out there, I believe."

"What's his name?"

"Um . . . goes by the name Perry."

"Perry," Burnett said, rubbing his forehead with his index finger, the cigar forked between it and the middle. "Know most the ranchers over that way. Don't believe I know a Perry."

"Well, like I said, he's got a small spread."

"You ever been down around Gainesville? I swear I seen you somewheres before."

"Naw, never been there," Henry answered.

"Well, you sure do look familiar," Burnett said. He continued to scrutinize Henry intently.

Henry smiled at Burnett, stood and stretch. "I believe I'll call it a night. Mister Parker offered me a bed upstairs, so I'm going to head on up to it. Got to head out early tomorrow."

"It's sure been a pleasure meetin' you, Mister Proctor," Burnett said as he stood and extended his hand. He held onto

Henry's hand continuing to examine Henry's face. "Yessir," he said. "I believe I know you from somewhere."

"Well, when you figure it out, you let me know," Henry said as he broke the handhold. He nodded to the others. "G'night," he said and quickly left the room.

* * *

Even into the second day of riding, it bothered Henry that Burnett seemed to recognize him, but he'd put all of them at the Star House well behind him. By that evening he'd be in Perrytown, and two days after that, Albuquerque. Thought he'd see if he couldn't find an easy store or two to rob along the way. Starting to get low on funds. Hoped old Chief Perry would still welcome him, at least for a one night stop-over.

Not quite dark when he rode up to Perry's place. Could see no one out and about, but a dim light shined from the front windows. An unexplained disquiet came over him as he dismounted and tied off his horse. Walking to the door, the still evening air seemed unusually quiet. Looked about with unease before he raised his hand to knock; that's when he heard something move at the corner of the house to his left.

"Evenin' Henry," a deep voice spoke softly but firmly. He turned quickly to see a tall man pointing a six-shooter at him. His first instinct was to duck slightly, put his right hand on the butt of his own holstered Peacemaker.

Behind him, he heard the distinctive click of a Colt hammer being cocked back into the firing position. "Hold it right there, Starr!" another voice spoke sternly. He turned to look back, seeing the silhouette of a shorter stockier man at the opposite corner of the house.

"I'll take that pistol," the first man said. He'd stepped closer to Henry within an arm's length. "Put your hands up high, Henry, so I can take it out of your holster. Best not to try anything or Deputy Smoak won't hesitate to shoot you in the back."

Henry squinted in the fading light to better see the man addressing him. He wore a dark fedora and a three piece suit. A bushy mustache nearly covered his mouth, and his long lean face was lined and weather-worn. Even in the gathering dark, Henry could see the penetrating look of the steel-blue eyes.

"Well, I'll be damned," Henry said. "Ain't you Bill Tilghman?"

"That I am," the man said. "Been looking to meet up with you for some time now, Henry." He holstered his own piece, holding Henry's Colt loosely in his left hand. "Fella pointing that pistol between your shoulder blades is Deputy U.S. Marshal Jubal Smoak, out of Pueblo, Colorado."

Henry turned his torso to look back at Smoak again. Touched his raised right hand to his hat. "Marshal," he said with a nod.

The door creaked open, and Otis Perry stuck his head out. He looked at Henry with a sad expression. "I'm sorry, Henry," he said. "Why don't you come in and have something to eat?"

Later, at the table, the two lawmen drank coffee while Henry ate beans and cornbread. Perry's daughter-in-law puttered at the stove; his grandson sat on the floor in one corner watching them.

"How'd you find me?" Henry asked the deputies.

"Been chasing you almost two years now, Henry," Tilghman offered. "Almost caught up with you a couple times, but you've been very elusive. Man you roughed up in Tulsa gave us a call a week or so ago, so we knew you'd come back home. Still, we didn't know which way you'd headed out, but then we got lucky. Cattleman I know named Burk Burnett called me; said he'd had dinner with you at Quanah Parker's house. Took him a while to figure out who you were, but then he remembered seein' wanted flyers we'd put out with your picture on it. Apparently, that bank you robbed in Colorado had some of his money in it. Said you told him you were going to see a man named Perry in New Mexico, so the rest was easy. I caught a train to Tucumcari; Mister Smoak here come down from Pueblo. We both got here yesterday, and just waited."

"So what happens now?" Henry asked.

"We'll be taking you back to Colorado for trial. I expect you'll do some time at the Canon City Penitentiary."

Henry looked at the lawman, the sad-eyed old chief looking back at him, the boy sitting in the corner. "I promise you, Mister Tilghman, no matter how long they keep me in that prison, I'm through robbin' banks."

Chapter Twenty

"Henry Starr, it is the decision of this board to grant you parole."

Hearing that news wasn't something new for Henry, nor was he surprised. In all his days he'd been given sixty-five years in prison for his times found guilty of crimes. Once even sentenced to hang, but he didn't hang. He'd only served a total of fifteen of those sixty-five years in four separate prisons, if you counted his stay in Judge Parker's Fort Smith jail.

Never a model citizen, Henry had always been a model prisoner. If he led a charmed life it was because he charmed the wardens and parole boards. They'd always believed their prison systems had reformed him; that he'd go forth and never rob again. Henry always proved them wrong. After his six-year stint in the Colorado prison, despite the promise he'd made to Bill Tilghman, he'd robbed sixteen more banks in a six-month period, including the dual heist in Stroud.

This time, though, the board and the warden at the Oklahoma State Penitentiary really believed Henry no longer had it in him to rob a bank, even if he wanted to. At forty-seven, he seemed old beyond his years. The five years he'd spent in the dank, cold McAlester prison had taken its toll, as had the bullet from that butcher's boy back in Stroud, which was still lodged in his hip. He barked with a consumptive cough, stood stooped at the shoulders, walked with a pronounced limp. No longer any need to keep him in prison, the warden had said. Not only was he a contrite and exemplary prisoner, he was a broken man. Besides, all the men who'd ridden with him were either in prison themselves, or stove up worse than Henry, or dead.

Bill Tilghman was the only man not to believe Henry Starr was through robbing banks. When he read the news of Henry's parole, he shook his head and laughed. "You conned 'em again, didn't you Henry?" he said to the walls of his office. He put down the paper, picked up the phone to call someone he knew in Tulsa. The man worked in the parole office there; Tilghman figured the fella could tell him how to get in touch with Henry. Bill had a proposition for the old outlaw.

"Hello, Henry. This is Bill Tilghman."

Henry waited a few seconds before responding, listening to the static on the line.

"Henry? You there?" came the voice from the other end.

"Yeah, I'm here," Henry said at last. "Just trying to figure out why you're calling me, Bill. I paid for my crimes fair and square. Warden didn't see any reason to keep me locked away. I ain't done nothing since I been out, which is only a week now."

"I know, Henry. I know. I ain't trying to arrest you. I got a business proposition I want to talk over with you."

More silence on Henry's end. "Ain't interested in becoming a lawman, Bill," he said.

Tilghman laughed. "No, I don't expect you are, but it's not that. You ever seen a movin' picture show?"

"Yeah, I seen me a couple."

"Did you ever see the one called 'Passing of the Oklahoma Outlaws'?"

"No, can't say as I have." Henry began to wonder where this was headed.

"I made that movin' picture; wrote it, even played a part in it."

"Is that a fact?" Henry asked flatly. "Anything in the story about me?"

"Yeah, I put in a couple things. Wouldn't be much of a story about Oklahoma outlaws without you." Tilghman laughed.

"Well, thankya, Bill. I'll take that as a compliment."

"It's done pretty well. Movin' pictures seem to be the coming thing, and, see, that's why I called. I'd like you to make a picture show about those bank holdups you pulled in Stroud. I know some picture people who're looking for a story like that. Like to put them in touch with you."

"That wasn't my best work, Bill. I can think of a half a dozen other jobs that turned out better . . . for me, anyway."

"Well, that's the thing, Henry. Most of these picture shows you see about the West show the outlaws to be the heroes, the lawmen to be the villains. I'd like to put it t'other way around. That's what I done with 'Oklahoma Outlaws.' Stealing and killing just ain't the way law-abiding citizens live. Lawmen are out there to keep things upstanding, and that's what I'd like you to show with your story, Henry. It'd be a powerful message, especially coming from someone as famous as you."

"Famous, huh; is that what you call it?" Henry snorted. He held the phone to his ear, he scratched the top of his head and side of his face. Sat down on the hotel clerk's desktop. Hemmed and hawed, reaching out to shut the open office door from intruding ears, speaking softly. "I just don't know, Bill. Even though I done outlaw things most my life, I've kept a pretty good reputation amongst the common folks. Everyone knew I robbed banks and such, but no one had to fear me. 'Spect that's even true with most of you lawmen."

"No you ain't been fearsome in your criminal life," Tilghman acknowledged. "I'd say confounding and worrisome more'n anything. Tell me, when was the first time you got in trouble with the law, Henry? How old were you?"

"About sixteen, I reckon."

"You've got a boy, don't you? How old is he now?"

"He's getting' on about that age, too."

"Looking back on it, would you want that boy to have the kind of life you've had, that is, south of the law?"

"Naw, I don't suppose so."

"Well, this'd be your chance to show him and a lot of other boys like him that outlawin' ain't as glamorous as they might think."

Henry had a mental flash of Kid Wilson confronting him on the streets of Inola. "Well, s'pose what you say makes sense, Bill. But I do got a couple questions."

"What's that, Henry?"

"What's in this for you? Why you wanting me to do this?

"Ain't nothing monetary, really. Oh, the people who want to do this will give me a little something; you know, for my expertise and such. They asked me if I could get in touch with . . . guys like you. Asked me to see if you'd be interested in telling your story. But it's like I said, Henry, I want the public to see—kids, mainly—that crime don't pay."

"It don't, huh? Well, how much you figure I'll get for this venture?

"The film folks, will let you do what they call 'direct the story.' That means you can tell all the actors what to do during the filming. You can even play yourself in the movie, if you want. That's what they done with me on my picture. But it's got to be the truth, no glamorizing. After it's released for people to see, they'll probably give you around ten or fifteen percent of the receipts."

"Ten percent?" Henry scoffed. "Now who's the thief, Bill?"

* * *

He stood leaning against the brick wall of the building warming himself. The afternoon air had turned mild on that early spring day, the bright sun made the bricks radiant with their gathered heat. Something he'd come to do in the yard wall at Big Mac the last couple of years, finding warmth for his old bones at the end of winters. The basking also seemed to help him think more clearly.

Tilghman's proposition intrigued him. Acting wasn't something he knew much about, nor moving pictures. Still, it wasn't like he had a whole lot of prospects. Not many people wanted to hire a crippled-up old con. What contacts he'd had in the real estate business, those still around, were on the other side of that bridge he'd burned the night he'd beaten up Bagby. Even though Bagby was dead from putting a bullet through his own pickled brain, and never much liked amongst his peers anyway, Henry's association with him didn't serve him well, even though most secretly applauded Henry's thrashing him. His old friend Feingold was still around, but not much help in getting Henry honest work. Ollie still lived in Bagby's big house. She seemed to have done alright for herself, but he didn't have much contact with her, or Teddy.

No, his prospects were thin. He thought he could probably still rob a bank if he had to, but he just didn't think he had the energy. Besides, the thought of that meat locker of a prison at McAlester deterred him. Maybe the warden was right about him.

He'd gone out earlier in the day to find a movie house, locating one called The Circle, now stood at the west wall of that theater soaking up the afternoon sun's heat and thinking. Coincidentally, the movie house was showing something called "The Great Train Robbery." It was only about ten minutes long; Henry had paid his nickel and sat through it six times.

It was a fascinating thing to observe that picture moving like it did, like the words of a story book come to life. Magical stuff, Henry mused as he watched a Model T Ford automobile clatter past him on the cobbled brick street. The world was becoming a whole different place from his fast-riding days. Could be he didn't fit into it anymore.

He knew about train robberies, though. Had robbed one or two in his time. Those boys in that picture show didn't appear to make what they done look too real. First off, there was only three of them and they unloaded about a hundred people off the cars and proceeded to relieve them of their valuables. No sane train robber would do that. It was too likely some yahoo would draw on 'em and shoot. And another thing, he'd never seen a train with that many people on it. Most he ever saw was about thirty. Third, they unhooked the engine from the cars and took off down the tracks in it. Now why would they take the time to do a blame fool thing like that? Then they stopped and went out into the woods to count their dough, and let the posse sneak up on them to shoot 'em dead. Stupid all the way around.

No sir, he didn't think whoever made that movie had ever robbed a train, or anything else. "If I make a movie about a robbery," he said to himself, ". . . it'd damn sure be accurate." He suddenly realized he was talking to the air, looked around a little sheepishly. Seeing no one within earshot, he coughed out a short laugh. "Yep, I'll show the world how a robbin's supposed to be done."

But at that moment he had more immediate concerns, like where and how he'd get his next meal. He'd already been to Feingold asking for a loan. The old Jew had given him one, more out of sympathy than good sense. Henry had a few bucks of that left, having paid a week in advance for his flophouse room. He thought he had enough to rent a horse and saddle. His older sister lived southeast of Dewey, some thirty miles to the north. He was pretty sure he could go up there and play on her sympathies some, too. Plus, her place was on the road to Nowata, and there was someone else he wanted to check in on up there.

* * *

The house looked pretty much how he'd remembered it. Maybe a room or two added, a new porch. Painted now a pale yellow, with a picket fence around it, and a yard. Two shade trees stretched up from the sides of the house; one on the east side, one on the west. Elm, he thought. Their limbs still bare in their winter sleep.

Someone was going in and out of the barn, working the morning chores. Appeared to be a strapping young man, perhaps a teen-aged boy. Henry couldn't rightly tell at the distance from which he watched. At the back of the house, white smoke whipped and swirled away from a kitchen stove pipe in the brisk March wind.

Looking north, Henry sat and watched the scene as he once had almost twenty years past. He wondered if Meg would mind seeing him now, would even recognize him. That boy at the barn must be the one she was pregnant with the last time he saw her. He looked to be a big fella, much like his pa.

He'd asked his sister Elizabeth, "Do you know anything about some folks named McGuinness over around Nowata?"

"Of course, I do," she said. "Everybody knows of the McGuinnesses in these parts. Probably the most prominent people in the area. Good people, too. Always helping out folks struck by misfortune. Had their own hard times, though. The oldest McGuinness boy was lost in the Great War. Probably what did in Mister McGuinness. After his boy was killed, grief seemed to take over his life. Died himself not a year after his boy. Word is his heart give out. But Miz McGuinness, Megan, she still works hard in the community over at Nowata. Used to be a school teacher there, but she gave that up some time back. Heads up a lot of doin's by the church ladies. Still a handsome woman, even as a widder. Everybody thinks highly of Megan McGuinness."

Henry smiled and nodded. Elizabeth had no idea the woman she spoke of had once been his wife. Oh, she knew he'd carried off a girl from Nowata, but she never put it together that Megan McGuinness and that girl were one in the same. Elizabeth had been married and living off near Dewey, fifty miles away, when all that had taken place. Henry hadn't been real close to his sisters over the years, only making a re-acquaintance now that he needed some help.

"Why you want to know about the McGuinnesses?" Elizabeth asked.

"I had some dealings with Mister McGuinness some years back," Henry answered. "He helped me straighten some things out in my troubled youth. Like you say, he was a beneficent man."

His sister nodded, letting Henry's explanation go at that.

So there he sat, on his horse on that hill looking down at the McGuinness estate again. He had the desire to spur the animal forward, but something kept him from it. Presently, he noticed the boy at the barn had spotted him. Stood looking up at Henry, wiping his hands on a cloth, studying the outrider on the hill, their hill. The boy went into the barn, came back out carrying a shotgun, making sure Henry could see it. Started walking slowly toward the house, cradling the gun, never taking his eyes off Henry. When the boy reached the porch, Henry reined the horse, rode back out of sight heading south.

Megan had come from the kitchen to open the drapes of the big south window in the parlor. Emily was coming up from Tulsa with her children for a week's stay, and Megan was excited about their visit. Throwing back the heavy curtains, she immediately caught sight of the rider on the crest of the south hill. It startled her and she gave out a small gasp. Something about the man triggered a barrage of old memories—the way he sat on the horse, the lean body, the toss of the hat on his head. Too far away to make out distinct features, but there was something about him she knew. She put her fingers to her lips. "Henry," she whispered.

The rider turned his horse and rode out of sight down the back side of the hill. She stood watching the ridgeline for several seconds, wondering if he would re-appear, half hoping he would.

The front door opened, and Silas came in. She glanced down at the double-barreled shotgun grasped in his left hand.

"There was a rider up on the hill, Ma. Just sat there looking down here. Not sure what he wanted, so I came back to the house. He looked kind of suspicious. Reckon we should call the sheriff?"

Megan looked out the window again, at that vacant spot on the hill. "No," she said. "I believe he's moved on now. I doubt he'll be back."

There was something strange in the way she'd said that, sort of a sadness, Silas thought. He looked at his mother curiously, but didn't say anything.

Chapter Twenty-One

"Henry, old chap, why don't you brandish two revolvers?" DuMer asked.

The man was small and slight, kind of frail looking, despite his well-tanned face and neck. Had delicate hands with long, thin fingers unaccustomed to manual labor. His small green eyes were set over a sharp nose, above a pencil moustache, atop a nearly lipless mouth. Straight red hair was lacquered to his head like a coat of paint, most of the time hidden under a strange looking little cap he called a beret. Always wore a tan linen coat with strange-looking pants. "Riding pants," he called 'em; puffed out at the side of the thighs and tight at the calves. Talked with an accent that wasn't quite British, wasn't quite Yankee. Whatever it was, even Henry could tell it was fake and snobbish. You got the feeling the little man felt he superior to everyone around him, even though he spoke in a friendly manner. Name was DuMer; first and last, only DuMer. Said he was from Los Angeles, California, as was the film crew who'd come with him. Henry took a dislike to him the minute they met.

Called himself The Producer/Director, whatever that was. DuMer informed Henry at their first pre-production meeting that he, Henry, would play the lead role in the film and would be the Story Consultant. Henry, not exactly sure what that job entailed, just shrugged.

"It's not what I done," Henry answered.

"Yes, but it would make you look much more forceful, more menacing."

"Mebbe so, but the fact is I never belted on two guns. Always wanted one hand free to do other things. Like I said, holding two guns ain't what I done."

Looking down, DuMer touched his forehead with a skinny index finger, closed his eyes. He sighed. As if talking to an unruly child, he looked at Henry, "It doesn't really matter what you . . . *done* or *didn't done*. What matters is what the movie audience perceives. And they must perceive you as a ruthless, deadly criminal."

"Why?" Henry asked.

"Because that's what puts their butts in theater seats, my good man."

"But it ain't the truth. I never carried two pistols; never was a deadly criminal, just a bank robber. This's supposed to be a true story, ain't it?" Henry argued.

"And so it shall be, Henry," DuMer said in a patronizing tone. "But it's our job to make the truth more entertaining. To be entertaining, we need to make you a dark villain. This is a tale about classic good versus evil. You're to be the Evil; young Curry over there is to be the Good."

So it had gone their first day on the set. DuMer had earlier scouted the streets of Stroud and decided the location would fit the scene of the actual crime. Not much had changed there in the five years since the Starr Gang's dual robberies.

A week before, when they'd first met in Tulsa, DuMer said he wanted to go to Stroud to see if the location would fit the story, or look for someplace else. Henry was perplexed. "Why wouldn't you film the story in Stroud? That's where it happened," he queried DuMer.

"Well, *mon ami*, actual historic locations in movie-making don't often work for the lens. We need to make sure these two banks are situated in such a way that our filming can make your story seem convincing."

Days later, DuMer decided the streets of Stroud would indeed work for the filming. "Yes, I believe we can make this film believable here," he said. He patted Henry on the shoulder and walked toward the film crew setting up on Third Avenue between the two banks.

Henry, speechless at DuMer's remarks, watched the little dandy walk away. He'd gone forty paces before Henry could gather himself to speak. "Believable?! Hell, You can damn well believe it's believable!" he yelled. "I got a bullet in my ass to prove it!"

Paul Curry, the boy who'd put that bullet in Henry's ass, walked up beside him, looking toward the film crew and the receding DuMer.

"I don't like that little bastard," Henry said to Curry.

"Naw, he don't much lend himself to likeable," Curry concurred.

The day Henry and DuMer had come into town, they started looking around for cast members. Henry would play himself, but DuMer thought they could get some locals to fill in the other spots. When Henry suggested it, DuMer conceded that using actual Stroud citizens would lend some authenticity, more importantly, they would be cheaper to hire. Some of the film actors back in California were starting to think themselves more valuable than they actually were, so DuMer brought none with him. Nor would he send for any.

That first day in Stroud, the two men stood in the street and looked up at the store sign. Big white letters on a red background read, "Curry Meat & Grocery."

"This's the store that boy shot me from," Henry said. "Believe his name was Curry, Paul Curry."

"Well, let's go see if he's still around," DuMer said.

Inside, back at the meat counter, a burly man greeted them. "What can I do for you gents?" he inquired.

"You Curry?" Henry asked him.

"That I am," he answered, wiping his meat greasy hands on the drape of his blood-soiled apron. He smiled back at them genially.

"Looking for a young fella named Paul Curry."

"That'd be my son," Curry answered, the smile fading some as mild concern invaded his expression. "What's this about?"

"Well, sir, I'm Henry Starr, and this here is Mister DuMer. We—"

"Henry Starr . . . the outlaw?" Curry cut in. He moved to his right a step, picking up a meat cleaver.

"Well, not anymore," Henry answered. He smiled nervously as he eyed the cleaver in Curry's hand.

Curry's look had become hard, intimidating. "If you're here to get even, Mister Starr, think again." To emphasize his statement, Curry whacked the edge of the cleaver onto the butcher block counter. "My boy only done what any citizen in this town woulda done . . . were trying to do. Just so happened Paul was a better shot."

Henry put his hands up to his chest, palms out, continuing to smile. "Naw, naw, you got it all wrong, Mister Curry. It ain't nothing like that. I got no hard feelings against your son. I'm out of the outlawin' business. We're here to offer him a job."

Curry still looked suspicious. "What kind of job?"

"A actin' job. Mister DuMer here is a moving picture producer from California. We're making a moving picture about my bank robberies here and how bad an outlaw I was. Mister DuMer here tells me it'll be titled A Debtor to the Law."

"A actin' job?" came Curry's incredulous question. "What kind of actin' job?"

"Why, sir," DuMer chimed in. "All your son has to do is play himself. Shoot Henry here in the ass like he did before; figuratively speaking, of course. Not in the literal sense. We'll pay him fifty dollars."

"Fifty dollars?" Curry tapped the point of the cleaver several times on the counter, thinking over the ridiculous offer. "That's a heluva lot of money for pretending to shoot an outlaw in the ass."

"We pay top dollar for our talent," DuMer said. He flicked an eyebrow with a long middle finger, and smiled haughtily at Curry.

"What's going on, Pa?" The voice came from behind the two men standing at the meat counter display. They turned to see a tall slender young man. Looked somewhat gaunt and sickly, which made DuMer frown.

"Well now, are you Paul?" DuMer asked.

"Yes, I'm Paul Curry." As he looked at the two men, recognition hardened his expression. "You're Henry Starr," he said.

Henry nodded and smiled, but made no advancement toward the young man, sensing his discomfort. "Yes, son, I am. But there ain't no need to be alarmed. Me and Mister DuMer here want to offer you a job."

"What kind of job?"

Henry and DuMer looked at each other, and DuMer gave Paul the whole spiel they'd given his father. Paul looked questioningly at his dad.

The elder Curry shrugged. "Sounds like easy money to me. I think you should take it."

* * *

It turned out the same tellers were still working in both banks, as was Sam Patrick, the bank officer Henry had used as a human shield. None were thrilled to see the old outlaw again, but quickly warmed up to the idea of being in a motion picture and getting paid for it. DuMer also had no trouble holding auditions for the gang member parts, garnering a plethora of extras. Henry had some problems with some of those picked as gang members, but, as usual, had no say in the matter.

Lorrie Hughes, the little girl Henry had made an accomplice buying her silence with a handful of stolen quarters, had turned thirteen, didn't want anything to do with the filmed re-enactment. It didn't really matter, though, as DuMer elected not to have that part portrayed in the film. He felt it showed too soft a side to Starr. Henry started to protest, but Lorrie rushed up to him, pulling on his sleeve so he'd bend down to hear her whisper.

She cupped her hand next to his ear. "I didn't give back those quarters you gave me," she said softly.

Henry stood upright and looked at her, smiled and winked. "Yeah, I don't see that we need to get the girl involved if she don't want to," he said to DuMer. The director nodded, went on to other matters.

As time went on, Henry and Paul Curry got to be pretty good friends. They could even joke about their past encounter.

"You was a pretty good shot with that twenty-two," Henry said to him.

"Nah, not too, I reckon. I was aimin' for your head, not your ass."

"Well, it was an honest mistake," Henry said. Got a good laugh from the crew and extras gathered around them.

"I recollect you was a bigger feller four years ago," Henry said to Curry. "You get hurt in the war?"

"I joined up with the Army last summer. Never made it to France, though. Never made it any further than Fort Dix in New Jersey. Come down with the Spanish Flu. It liked to killed me. Did kill a lot of fellas I knew, fellas I went in with. Seemed like they was burying them by the hundreds every day."

"I read about that epidemic in prison," Henry said. "Looked like it was coming this way, but seemed to die out before it got this far west."

"I ain't totally got over it, I don't think. Not sick anymore, but weak as a kitten, lost a lot of weight."

"You ain't so weak you'd miss and shoot me in the head, are ya?"

"Lucky for you, I'll be shooting blanks."

* * *

"And Action!" DuMer shouted into the megaphone he held from his perch next to the camera. He and the cameraman were on a boom raised ten feet above the street, filming the actors below. Guns drawn, Henry and three of his "gang" skulked along the walk in front of the bank, until Bill Woodard behind Henry— the man playing the part of Lige Higgins—stubbed his toe on a warped board and lurched forward, accidentally firing his pistol into Henry's back. Henry yelped and jumped forward. DuMer hollered, "Cut!'

Henry turned in circles leaving a spiral of smoke swirling upward before a grip ran up, tamped out the small flames on the back of Henry's leather vest. Starr removed the vest and looked at it, which still smoldered some.

After all were comfortable that Henry wouldn't go up in flames, the director spoke. "Are you okay, Henry?"

"Yeah, I think so," Henry answered. He rubbed the spot in the small of his back. "That close, even blanks can punch a hole in ya." He gave his assailant an irate look.

DuMer sighed and shook his head. "Mister Woodard, please watch your step, try not to shoot Mister Starr in the back. He appears to be combustible."

The crowd laughed.

"Soary, Mister DuMer," Woodard said, grinning; then to Henry more soberly, "Soary, Henry."

Henry nodded and put his vest back on. "Second time I been shot in this town," he said.

"Alright then, if everybody is sorry and all apologies accepted, let's try it again," DuMer said.

They stopped at the double wooden doors to look about furtively, then disappeared inside.

"Cut!" DuMer said.

Later, during lunch, Henry sat on a barrel outside The Stroud Five and Dime eating a ham sandwich. Paul Curry and Woodard occupied the bench in front of the store window, eating the same.

"Do you boys realize you are the onliest ones who ever shot Henry Starr?" Henry asked around his mouthful of sandwich. "And both times it was in the back." He grinned at them.

"Don't believe I shot you in the back, Henry," Curry said. "Mine was more from the side,"

"Well, now I could drop my pants right here and prove it," Henry said.

"No, no, don't do that," Woodard waved his hand and looked away. "Leastwise, not during lunch."

Henry laughed. "Aw right, Bill. I won't. But keep that piece pointed away from me. Next time I might shoot back."

They all chuckled, went back to their eating. Presently, Samuel Patrick, who'd joined the group for lunch, had a question.

"How come you come back here to make a movie of your crime, Henry?" Sam, the bank officer Henry had used as a shield during the robbery, still held his position at the bank, also hired to play himself.

Henry chewed and thought about it. "That's a durn good question, Sam," he said. He took a drink from his mug of coffee. "Thinking back over my life, I believe I seen the error of my ways. Ya know, I've got a boy. Ain't seen him much lately with being in prison and all, but I'd like for him, 'n other boys like him, to see how being an outlaw ain't the smartest thing to do in life. Hope the message gets through to them, if they see the picture show, not to go the way I've gone."

The small group considered in silence what Henry had just said, giving a nod or two.

"Course," Henry continued after half a minute. "The money I'm making off this re-enactment will be at least twice what I got in the actual holdup. Actually, didn't get none of it, as Paul here shot me in the ass, and I went straight to prison. I don't think they'll send me to prison for acting, 'though I do believe it's a form of highway robbery."

"So it's still about the money," Sam said.

Henry grinned. "Yeah, most of it," he said.

* * *

"Okay, that's a wrap," DuMer said to the cast and crew. "Thank you all. You can see Miss Sweeney at the hotel to pick up your compensation."

Miss Sweeney was a tall woman with a homely face and a lithe body whom DuMer had only introduced as his assistant. Carried a steno pad to which she constantly affixed notes from comments DuMer spoke to her, and she barked orders to the crew for things that needed doing, which they carried out unflinchingly. Always wore leather trousers with a leather vest over a dark tight blouse. Had a severe look, and rarely smiled; when she did, it had more of a sneer quality than cordiality. Everyone was afraid of her, including, apparently, DuMer.

Henry walked over to where DuMer stood talking to Miss Sweeney who towered over him, his back to Henry's approach. "What happens now?" Henry asked.

DuMer stopped his conversation with Miss Sweeney, and turned slowly toward Henry. Miss Sweeney glared at Henry through slit eyelids.

Regarding him coolly, DuMer spoke after a few seconds. "Ah, Henry, my good man . . . Yes, well, we'll pack all this up and take it back to California. The film will be edited, marketed. I expect it'll be released in about six months or so."

"Six months?" Henry asked, a little distressed. His deal was a percentage of the proceeds the movie would produce.

"More or less," DuMer said. "These things take a little time."

"You mentioned something about an advance when we started all this," Henry said. "I'm going to need something to live off of 'til I start getting my piece of the action."

DuMer looked up at Miss Sweeney; they traded an annoyed look. "Well, of course, we'll pay you a per diem for your meals and lodging you charged here on location." He tapped his chin with a long finger while he thought.

"I think we can advance you . . . three hundred dollars?" The last part came out a question as he glanced up at Miss Sweeney for confirmation. With an icy look of disdain at Henry, she gave a slight nod of assent.

DuMer smiled condescendingly at Henry. "That should keep the wolves away until your royalties start coming in," he said.

Henry did some quick ciphering in his head. If it took six months before he started getting his percentage, that'd be fifty dollars a month he'd have to live off of. He figured he could live off fifty dollars a month. "What if the movie ain't out in six months?" He asked.

"No chance of that, Henry," DuMer said. "It'll most likely be out sooner, than later."

"Awright, then," Henry said.

"Fine. Miss Sweeney will pay you this afternoon," DuMer said, and both he and the tall woman turned and walked away.

The next morning when Henry went to settle up with the hotel for his room and meals, he found he came up eighteen dollars short with his per diem allotment, so he had to pay the difference out of his advance money. When he went to find DuMer to complain, he was told the little bastard, his tall daunting assistant, and their motley film crew had cleared out the night before.

Chapter Twenty-Two

No doubt about it, Hulda was a pretty girl. Henry couldn't take his eyes off her.

His friend E.D. Standingfox had suggested they go down to Tahlequah. It was past mid-summer, time of the Green Corn Festival. E.D. promised there'd be a lot of celebrating, dancing, and beautiful women. About a two-hour automobile trip in E.D.'s new Model T Ford to the Cherokee capital. The reveling would go on for several days.

He first spotted Hulda in the Corn Dance, although he didn't know her name, or the fact that they were second cousins. She moved with the second circle of dancers, the inside circle, the women dancers, holding baskets. They danced in a shuffling step to the beat of the drums and wail of the drummers. It was a solemn, reverential procession. She looked the part of a Cherokee princess in the long buckskin dress she wore, dyed snowy white, festooned with feathers and bright beads. Henry moved through the crowd, stepping to the front edge. He had a certain celebrity among the Cherokees, they all greeted him and talked to him as he moved into the gathering. A Debtor to the Law had come out about a month past, and most of them had seen the movie or heard about it. The film notwithstanding, the deeds of Henry Starr had rippled through the Nation for over twenty years. Not a fabled warrior among the people, far from it; but any action which gave the white man grief, even those unlawful, gained him regard and gave him a certain hero status.

He smiled, shook the hands, acknowledged the greetings of those who pressed around him, but his eyes always returned to her. Several dancers looked up at the commotion going on near the inner edge of the crowd; if Hulda noticed him, she gave no indication.

He walked toward her when the dance ended with every intention of engaging her in conversation. She glanced at his approach, gliding swiftly into the midst of a group of clucking women; deliberately, it seemed. Henry stopped and watched her with a look of dismay as she submerged securely into the whirlpool of older females who swept her away.

His friend E.D. came up behind him laughing, slapped him on the shoulder. "Now that's one fine looking woman," he said. "Don't get your feelings hurt, though. Every stud here has or is trying to get on her dance card, but ain't none of 'em done it yet. She treats all of us the same way she just treated you."

"Who is she?" Henry asked.

"Name's Hulda Starr."

"Hulda Starr," Henry repeated. Both men watched the girl's head, all of her they could see, floating away from them. At one point Henry thought he saw her look back in his direction.

"Maybe you're related," E.D. said.

"Could be," Henry said. "But I know she ain't my sister."

E.D. laughed and threw his arm over his buddy's shoulders. "Let's go get some of that fried chicken," he said.

* * *

"I hear we might be related."

The girl jumped, looked back over her shoulder at Henry. She sat at a picnic table eating her supper. Across the table a large woman in her fifties, also dressed in buckskins, gave him a disapproving glare.

"You scared me," the girl said, turning back to her plate of food, not smiling.

"I'm sorry," he said. "I sure didn't mean to do that." He sat down on the table bench, his back to the girl's dinner mate. Smiling his most charming smile, Henry said to her, "You're Hulda Starr."

The girl looked at him and frowned. Looking down at her plate, she moved some of her potato salad around with a fork, "How do you know my name?"

Henry laughed. "Didn't have to go far to find that out. Just about everybody here knows your name, especially the men."

The girl blushed and looked at him. "Oh, I doubt that."

Henry thought he saw a smile for a second.

"No, it's true," he said. "I'm Henry Starr. Thought we might be related." He reached up and gave his hat a gentlemanly tip.

"Lots of Starrs here," the girl said. "It's a big clan. All of us are probably related in some way or another."

Henry nodded. "Yeah. I guess I just wanted to make sure we ain't first cousins." He grinned at her.

"This is my mother," Hulda said, indicating the woman at the table, behind him.

Henry turned, tipped his hat to her, also. "Pleased to meet you, ma'am." He realized Hulda's mother wasn't that much older than him.

"Your father was Hop Starr?" the woman asked without acknowledging Henry's greeting. Nor did it appear the woman held any admiration for his notoriety.

"Yes'm. That's right."

"My husband, Ellis, and your father were cousins."

"First cousins?" Henry asked.

The woman shook her head. "I don't think so. I'm not sure of the distance of the relation between them." Looking at Henry looking at her daughter, she scowled. "Nor between you and Hulda," she added.

Henry glanced back at the woman, then to Hulda, looking her straight in her beautiful brown eyes for several long seconds. She held her look back at him, too, with perhaps a faint smile. "Well, it's pretty easy to see she came from the good looking side of the family," he said.

Hulda looked down and giggled. Her mother uttered an unimpressed "Hmmph."

"I made a moving picture." Henry hoped that would impress Hulda . . . and her mother. "Have you seen it?"

"No," Hulda's mother stated for the both of them. The girl looked at Henry again and gave him an apologetic smile. Yes, that time she definitely smiled at him.

After a bit, Henry removed his hat. "Miss Hulda, I wonder if you'd do me the honor of partnering up with me at the Friendship Dance this evening?"

Hulda looked at her mother, who frowned and shook her head emphatically "No."

"Yes," she said, looking back at Henry. "I believe I'd be delighted."

* * *

It surprised Henry to learn Hulda's age. She'd just turned twenty-three; he thought her more like eighteen. Didn't matter to him, as long as it didn't matter to her. However, it did matter to her mother, Martha; she considered him a scoundrel, as much as told him so. Henry didn't care about that either.

Hulda's father Ellis, on the other hand, seemed quite pleased his daughter chose to step out with such a man, any man for that matter. Her mother kept such a tight rein on her, he was beginning to think she would never leave home. He thought his wife was probably the main reason young men shied away from Hulda. Having Hulda interested in such an important man as Henry Starr made him very proud. Plus, Henry didn't seem the least bit intimidated by the girl's mother. That pleased Ellis, too, and impressed him. He'd cowed from Martha's lashing tongue for over thirty years. The fact that Henry didn't seem to fear his wife helped Ellis overlook the fact that Henry was almost his own age, and an outlaw and ex-con.

The couple courted for about six months before she agreed to marry him. He took her off to live in Tulsa, which pleased Ellis and made Martha cry.

Henry still had trouble finding honest work. The war ending soured the economy, all those boys flooding back into an already tough job market made slim pickin's for an old ex-con, even one with his notoriety. He ventured back into real estate some, but without much success. Nobody was buying much at the time. Hulda had gone to work at a downtown department store selling women's foundation garments, but her income didn't make enough to hardly keep body and soul together.

Henry had hoped to be living off his movie royalties by then, but that wasn't happening, either. From all indications the film was doing quite well; he'd not received a penny from DuMer and company. He tried to call the little twit a time or two, but never got through to him. He'd talked to Miss Sweeney once, who just gave him some hateful and condescending double-talk about expenses versus profits or some such. Henry threatened to come out to California, kick some bull-ridin' girl and French weasel butt until he got his money, but Miss Sweeney mentioned the State of Arkansas still had an outstanding warrant for his arrest and extradition.Should he leave the protection of Oklahoma, she'd let the authorities know. Even a call to Tilghman didn't do any good.

"Did you sign a contract with DuMer?" Tilghman had asked.

"I didn't want to sign nothing with that little weasel," Henry said. "It was a gentleman's agreement, but I should've known better. DuMer ain't no gentleman."

Tilghman sighed. "I'll give 'em a call, Henry. But without nothing in writing, I doubt I can talk them into anything."

Henry was trapped, jobless, and cheated out of his promised money. The hard times put a strain on the newly wedded couple's relationship.

"Mother told me I was making a mistake," Hulda said tearfully. "You are worthless!" They'd just gone fifteen angry shouting minutes over Henry's late night return from a poker game where he'd lost their rent and a week's grocery money.

"Yeah, no surprise your mother would say something like that," he said. "She had her way, you'd be under a glass jar for everybody to look at, but not touch. You want to go on back to your momma, you go on. I ain't gonna stop ya."

That brought an "Oh, I hate you!" from Hulda followed by her running off to the bedroom, slamming the door behind her, flinging herself on the bed to cry for a spell.

Disgusted, Henry left the house to wander the early morning streets trying to walk off his anger and frustration. He found himself back at the saloon where he'd played poker earlier, but it was closed. Stood there looking around, not sure where else to go. Sure as hell wasn't going back to that house with that whimpering child. He pulled out his watch and looked at it.

Maybe his friend E.D. Standingfox would take him in. Figured E.D. owed him; after all, had it not been for E.D. he'd likely never have met up with Hulda.

Henry's pounding the door, started two neighbor dogs barking. E.D., his hair sleep-tangled, eyelids heavy, opened the door. He looked confused . . . and annoyed. "What the hell do you want, Henry?" Looked around at his wall clock. "Good God, man. It's three in the morning."

"Me and Hulda had a fight," Henry answered. "Didn't want to hang around listening to her cry and moan and groan about leaving her momma. Figured I'd come here."

E.D. rubbed his face, stood back from the door entry. "Well, come on in," he said with a sigh.

"I don't know, E.D., it ain't really Hulda's fault," Henry said. Standingfox had made a pot of coffee, they sat at the kitchen table discussing Henry's situation. "Poor kid, she really didn't know what to expect when she took up with me. I think she thought I'd be rich and famous. Guess I did, too. Anyway, that's probably what I led her to believe."

E.D. didn't say anything, just sat drinking his coffee and nodding groggily.

"I'm starting to think she and her momma are right," Henry continued. "I'm starting to feel pretty worthless, that's for sure."

E.D. took his cue to speak up. "Aw hell, Henry, you ain't worthless. You're just going through some bad times right now. Lotta guys in your shoes nowadays. Times're tough. I'm damn lucky to have my own job. Don't know how much longer that's gonna last, though. Me and the foreman don't see eye to eye on most things."

"Well, I don't know what to do. Things is getting kind of desperate," Henry said.

E.D. reached back and grabbed the coffee pot off the stove, refilling their cups. "Man once told me we should do the things we're best at, do the things we like, and success was sure to follow."

Henry nodded, took a sip of the fresh coffee, looked at the kitchen wall. A half-minute passed before he spoke. "You know, E.D., I believe that man was right." He fell silent again, sipping his coffee. Two full minutes passed. "Yes sir," he said. "What you just said makes a whole lot of sense."

* * *

They patched things up . . . to a certain degree. Told Hulda he was sorry for the way he'd been acting; that she was right, he had been worthless. But he was going to change that. Told her he had a lead on a job in Arkansas, needed to go over there to see about it. Be back in a few days.

"But aren't you afraid you'll get arrested?" she asked. "I thought the law was still after you in Arkansas."

"Well, it's been a long time. Don't figure anybody over there'll recognize me. 'Sides, ain't going to use my real name."

Henry went to the closet, reached up to the shelf above the rod of clothes. Felt towards the back corner for something he'd put there months back, a small box. Finding it, he pulled it down and removed the top, being careful not to let Hulda see. Inside was a roll of bills, a hundred dollars; money he'd carefully rat-holed for when the day came. The day had come. It could've been used to pay the rent and buy groceries, maybe even save his marriage. But the smoldering coals had burst into flame. The recovering drunk had opened the bottle and downed a shot. No turning back. He slipped the bills into his pants pocket, put the box back on the closet shelf.

"Well, how will you get the job if you don't use your real name?" Hulda asked.

Henry fiddled with his bag, trying to decide what to put in it, how to deflect his young wife's questions. "It's a cash-only job, a temporary thing. They won't need my real name."

Hulda watched him, looking at him uncertainly. "Henry, what is this job? What're you doing?"

He buttoned up the valise and turned to her. "Hulda, you don't need to know any more than what I've already told you.

Now I'll be back in a couple days, and all our money problems will be solved."

She sat on the bed and folded her hands in her lap. "Oh, Henry," she said sadly. He continued gathering his things, not looking at her, not saying any more. She watched him.

"If you do this, Henry, I won't be here when you get back. I'm going back home."

"This is your home, Hulda."

"No it's not, Henry. Not anymore."

"Well, I reckon I expected as much." He moved close to her, put his fingers under her chin, lifting her face until their eyes met. "It's probably best." He kissed her gently on the lips. "You take care of yourself, darlin'. I expect we'll see each other at a better time and place."

"Henry . . . don't," she cried softly.

Chapter Twenty-Three

When E.D. rolled up in a big green Buick touring car, Henry stepped off the curb and opened the backseat door, throwing his bag onto the seat. He slid onto the front passenger side, rubbed his hand across the smooth supple surface of the front seat looking around at the interior. Rolled brown leather, smelled brand new.

"Nice car," he said. "Did you steal it?"

"Sorta," E.D said. He mashed the car into gear, rolled off down the street.

E.D. looked over at Henry and grinned. "Told the guy selling it I needed to show it to my business partner, that you lived out of town and it'd take a couple days. Told him we was in the oil business, and we needed a good car to travel around to our well sites. Said I wanted something fast, too."

"He let you take it without checking on you?"

"Well, he was pretty eager to sell this car, I convinced him I was a high roller. Told him I'd bring him the cash in a couple days. Left my Model T with him as a deposit. He shook my hand, told me I looked like an honest man."

Henry rolled his head back and laughed heartily, as did E.D.

"So where's this guy you wanted me to meet?" Henry asked. "The one has this big job in Arkansas."

"Taking you to him right now," E.D. said. He glanced back at Henry's suitcase. "Movin' out?" he asked.

"Maybe, I guess. This thing checks out with your guy, figured we'd head on over there, get the show on the road. Don't expect Hulda'll be here when we get back."

E.D. nodded. "Figured as much, on both counts. That's why I picked up this car."

Lars Soderholm, and a boy who looked to be about eighteen or nineteen, sat at a table in the back corner of Gundersen's Bar and Grill. A rare steak, half eaten, sat on the plate before Soderholm. He raised a tankard of beer to his lips as the two men walked toward him, eyeing their approach. A wide and thick man with a flat face and blond hair in a high-sided cut, Soderholm's arms had the size of small tree trunks. Thick reddish-blonde hair curled atop the massive forearms. Close-set, deep blue eyes gave him a piercing, ominous stare. The boy was skinny, had dark hair, dark eyes, an acne-pocked face baring a dark scowl. His hand curled through the handle of a mug of beer on the table.

"Howdy, Lars," E.D. said. He gestured toward his companion. "This here's Henry Starr."

Soderholm set the stein on the table, wiping the beer foam off his upper lip. "Yah, I haf hert of you," he said looking at Henry without smiling. "Sit down. I vill haf Astrid bring you a steak and some beer."

"Who's the kid?" Henry asked.

Soderholm belched. "Dis is Yimmy. My cousin. He vurks vit me."

Henry looked at the boy, but said nothing. "It's Jim, not Yimmy," the boy said with hostility. "Lars still talks like a stupid Swede. I ain't no kid."

Henry raised his eyebrows, looked at Lars. E.D. whistled and scratched the back of his neck. Lars looked at Jim and grinned, shaking his head. "Yimmy iss always pissed about sumtin," he said to the two men. He motioned to the empty chairs. "Haf a sit down." Grabbed up a knife and fork, went back to work on the steak.

The two men sat. E.D. looked around to make sure they were out of earshot of the others in the place. He leaned toward Lars and spoke in a low voice. "Tell Henry what you told me about that bank in Arkansas."

Lars sawed off another bloody chunk of steak and shoved it into his mouth. He looked at E.D., then Henry, as he chewed. "Dis bank is in a town called Harrison. It is ripe fer da pickin'."

Henry was skeptical. "Any money in this here bank?" he asked Soderholm.

"Yah. Day got a shoe factory in dat town vhat does all dare business in dat bank. I used to vurk dare in dat factory. It's da only bank in dat area. Lotsa people from all around use dat bank."

Henry drummed his fingers on the tabletop, thinking. "What about its location in the town. Is there a lot of traffic?"

"No, it's off da main street. Near to da road outta town. Ve could be in und out uh dare quick, across da state line to Missouri in a couple hours." Lars looked at E.D. "Dat is, if you got dat fast car I told you to."

E.D. grinned back at him. "Oh, I got a fast car."

"It sounds good to me," Henry said. "I think we ought to drive over there and take a look, see if it's as promising as you say."

Soderholm nodded and smiled crookedly back at the two men. "Let's finish our steak first before ve go. Yah? It's a long drive to over dare. I tink ve could get hungry before ve get dare."

"You boys go ahead and eat your steaks," Henry said, rising from his chair. "I saw a haberdasher down the street. I want to get outfitted with a new suit for this job; if I'm getting back in the bidness, want to look my best. I'll be back directly."

* * *

The four story brick building was called a department store. It was nothing like the single-story frame buildings called "mercantiles" Henry had known as a boy, the kind he'd robbed when he needed guns or food or clothes. The kind of place you could ride up to, take what you wanted, empty the till, out the door riding away in less than five minutes. No, it was a modern thing, a city store; always full of people, scads of people. Sat on the corner of First and Main Streets; a twenty-foot-tall sign, extending from the corner of the building, displayed "Moore's Department Store" vertically in bold black letters. At night the sign was lit by dozens of electric lights. Each floors held an abundance of merchandise, each different, departmentalized. First floor displayed and sold clothing for men, women, and children. A sign by the contraption called an elevator informed the shoppers the second floor held sheets and towels and dishes and such; the third, furniture. The fourth floor wasn't accessible to the public, maybe a warehouse and offices, Henry guessed. Another sign invited customers to visit The Tea Room for refreshment and lunch. An arrow on the sign pointed down a wide aisle toward the café's entrance thirty yards away.

"That suit looks like it was made for you, sir," the sales clerk said. He was a round, balding man in a tweed vest and bow tie. He had a pin cushion strapped to his forearm sleeve, a cloth tape measure draped around his neck. Henry faced the mirror, admiring himself; the man fussed around him, brushing his shoulders and back. "I don't see that we'll need to make any alterations at all."

The suit was soft wool, navy in color with light blue pinstripes. "Does seem to fit well," Henry said. Turned sideways to the mirror.

The clerk stood back. "Very handsome, sir. Very handsome."

"How much?" Henry asked.

"That is from one of our finest suit makers in Chicago," the clerk said. "Normally, it retails for eighty dollars, but we have it on sale right now for fifty-nine, ninety-five."

"What's your name, partner? Henry asked.

"It's Ernest. But I go by Ernie," the clerk said.

"Well, Ernie, how about I give you forty dollars for this suit."

"No, no, I couldn't do that, sir. It's against store policy to—"

"Be a damn shame not to sell me this suit, Ernie. You said yourself it wouldn't take no extra work."

"Well, I . . ." the clerk said. "I'll have to check with my supervisor."

"You do that," Henry said, returning his gaze to his reflection.

Ernie came bustling back five minutes later. Henry waited for him, wallet in hand. "Well, sir," Ernie said. "My boss said we could sell you that suit for no less than forty-five dollars."

Henry opened his billfold and took out some bills. "Tell you what, Ernie. Here's fifty. Why don't you tell your boss you got the forty-five and you keep the other five."

The clerk hesitated slightly, then took the money. "Why thank you, sir, that's most generous. If you'll remove the suit, I'll put it in a box for you."

"Ain't necessary, Ernie. Believe I'll wear it outta here. You could get me a box for my old clothes, though."

With his Moore's box under one arm and wearing his new navy blue suit, Henry walked toward the store exit. The sign directing him to refreshment in The Tea Room caught his eye and he stopped to read it again. The day's special was a chicken salad sandwich with something called French fried potatoes. He'd missed out on his steak back at Gundersen's, now he was getting hungry. Thought he'd give the chicken salad a shot, and he liked fried taters no matter what their nationality.

At the café's entrance Henry looked over the dining room. Filled mostly with women, he doubted he'd be able to get a big bloody steak there like he could've at Gundersen's, he didn't think he could eat a steak, anyway. The prospect of his coming endeavor had him too excited and nervous to have a big appetite. The food in this dainty little place would suit him just fine.

He took a table at one of the big windows overlooking the street. Main Street, on that afternoon, teemed with folks and their conveyances. After ordering his lunch, he sat watching the flow of people on the walk outside the window. A trolley trundled by in the center of the street, automobiles and trucks chugged up and down. The window glass barely muffled the noise of it all.

Henry thought about the first time he'd seen Tulsa, this street. Been a boy, his dad was still alive and had come here to do some trading, bringing him along. The place was little more than a settlement on the Arkansas River then, mostly dispossessed Indians. The street, the one they called Main now, was a multi-rutted odorous road of sticky mud and horse manure. The town was a wild place, almost lawless. Sitting on the wagon bench waiting for his dad, he'd witnessed a shooting—a cowboy blown backwards through the doors of a saloon and into the muddy street by a .44 slug from the close range blast of a Colt revolver. First time he'd seen a man shot.

He shook his head at the memory, and laughed softly. A whole different world back then, but a world he understood. This one now was probably a better world, at least a cleaner one. But he wasn't sure it smelled any better. The stench of horse manure had been replaced by something more noxious coming from the ass-end of all those gasoline engines. And safer? He couldn't say. People still got shot in the streets. Naw, the old times weren't easy times in a lot of ways, but Henry knew how to live by the rules of the times then, what to expect. Now he wasn't so sure. He felt increasingly out of step and off-balance. If he was going to survive, he'd have to adapt, and quickly. Used to be you and a gang of boys would ride up on horses, rob your bank, thunder off, shooting up the place as you rode away Now, he and his gang would use an automobile for their get-away. Faster, probably, but with all of you in one car, you couldn't split up if a posse come after you. Yep, it would take some getting used to, this new way of robbing banks. The job in Harrison would be his new start, he decided. He would succeed or die trying.

The last thought gave him pause. He suddenly felt a sharp sadness, at the same time a great peace. He couldn't dwell on it, because someone came into the dining room who drew his immediate and full attention.

Outfitted to the nines, she moved with grace, leading a girl of about twelve. They sat at a table at the opposite end of the dining room from him, about forty or fifty feet away. Megan.

She looked a little lined about the eyes and mouth; older, yes, but still beautiful. No longer a strikingly pretty girl, but a stylish elegant woman, a handsome matron with a distinguished bearing. Henry couldn't stop looking at her, half-fearing she might look over and recognize him, too. She seemed oblivious to anyone around her, though; giving her full attention to the young girl with her, talking earnestly to her and laughing easily. Presently, he stood and walked toward their table.

"Howdy, Megan," Henry said. He smiled shyly, looking uncertain.

Megan looked up at Henry, the smile she'd been giving the girl in their conversation still there. She furrowed her brow, changing her expression to one of genteel cordiality. "Forgive me, sir. Do I know you?" she asked.

Henry laughed a little and rubbed his forehead. "Well, I reckon it has been a long time. It's Henry, Megan. I'm Henry."

Megan's eyes widened, and her hand went to her mouth as she audibly drew in breath. "Oh my, Henry," she said. "Why you've . . . it's . . . Oh, I'm so sorry, Henry. It's such a surprise to see you; I'm at a loss for words."

"Aw, it's okay, Megan. I can understand your surprise. I shouldn't uh snuck up on you like that. I don't reckon I look anything like . . . well, like I did the last time we seen each other."

Flustered, he turned to the young girl who looked up at him in great puzzlement. "And who's this attractive young lady?"

"Forgive my manners," Megan said, recovering some of her composure. "This is my granddaughter, Evelyn. Evelyn this is Henry Starr. He and I were once, um . . ."

"We was close friends back when we was kids," Henry said, coming to Megan's rescue. "You might even say we was best friends." He looked again at Megan. "The very best friends."

The girl smiled warmly at Henry, extended her right hand, fingers and palm down. "It's a pleasure to make your acquaintance, Mister Starr."

"Why, thank you, Missy, but I believe the pleasure is all mine." He took her hand lightly in his, gave her a quick bow. She giggled.

"Won't you join us for lunch, Mister Starr?" the girl asked.

Henry and Megan exchanged awkward glances. "Why, yes, Henry," Megan said. "Please join us."

"You know, I can't think of nothing I'd enjoy more than dining with two beautiful ladies, but I'm afraid I have a bidness appointment to keep."

He turned to look Megan. "I just wanted to step over and say hello. It's been a mighty long time since we last seen each other."

He held her gaze intently for several long seconds. "Lord knows when we'll be seeing each other again."

Henry waited. He could see tears welling in her eyes. "Yes," she said. "It's so good to see you again, Henry."

He nodded to them both. "Well, goodbye to ya," he said, turned and walked away. He heard the girl say, "Is something wrong, Nanna?" He heard Megan respond, "No, it's nothing, dear."

At his table he found his sandwich and French fried potatoes waiting for him. He picked up two of the potato strips, stuffed them into his mouth, munching them. Taking two dollar bills out of his wallet, he laid them on the table. Picked up his box of old clothes, and left the café, summoning all the strength he could not to look back at Megan.

* * *

February 18, 1921

The morning, gray and cold, had an icy fog sitting on the winter hills around Harrison, Arkansas. The road they drove took them right by the front of their objective—the People's National Bank. The building didn't look like a particularly inviting place. Dark-bricked and flat-roofed, it squatted in the cold fog of that early February morning like a jailhouse, plain and devoid of ornamentation.

"Let's find somevere to get some breakfast," Lars said from the backseat where he and Jim rode. "I don't vant to vurk on uh empty stomach."

Henry took out his watch and looked at it. Just past eight-thirty. "Yeah, we got some time," he said. "Don't reckon the bank will open for an hour or so."

They'd driven since midnight, coming down from Springfield, Missouri where they'd laid over Wednesday night and most of Thursday. Henry had suggested they take a northern route as he didn't want to cross Benton County in Arkansas. That would've been a more direct route, but no use tempting fate, he decided.

Henry felt alive, euphoric. "You know," he said, sipping from his cup of coffee. "I don't believe you can get any better meal than a good breakfast of fried eggs and bacon. If I's a condemned man, that's what I'd want for my last meal." He grabbed the napkin next to his plate, wiped his mouth. "Now if you'll excuse me, I need to go change." He picked up the Moore's box he'd sat beside his chair and stood up. "It's almost time, boys," he said to the table.

Henry had changed back into his old suit for the road trip, not wanting to get his new suit dirty or mussed. Wanted to look his best when he entered that bank and announced himself. Fifteen minutes later, he came out the café washroom looking every bit the dashing gentleman in his navy blue wool suit with the lighter blue pinstripes. Even turned a few ladies' heads as he passed back through the café, which pleased him.

E.D., however, was not pleased. "Not too damn smart, you getting people to take notice of you, Henry."

Henry just grinned.

* * *

The plan: Henry would enter the bank first and go to one of the standing tables, pretending to write up a deposit slip. This would give him the opportunity to check things out—how many people in the bank, their location, where the safe was, if it was open. He'd act like he'd forgotten something and leave the bank to pass on the details to Jim and Lars. He'd reenter the bank, take up his position at the table to continue his pretense. He carried no gun. His cohorts would bring in the hardware and announce their intent two minutes after Henry had reentered the bank. E.D. would wait in the car as the get-away driver. Henry would assume the lead roll and orchestrate the rest of the hold-up, using his calm charm to reassure the victims, so there'd be no panic during the robbery.

Henry closed the door behind him, looked around as he walked to the farthest standing table. Four customers stood about in the bank, one at each of the two teller windows, one in line, one at the writing table nearest the door—a right handsome woman, he couldn't help but notice. She had a child in tow, a little girl of about seven or eight who stood silently beside the woman. The girl watched Henry, staring solemnly at him. A uniformed bank guard stood by the door, wearing a pistol. Looked to be a man in his sixties, somewhat portly, not much of a deterrent. Two tellers, one at each window; a bank officer sat at a desk in the open area to the left of the teller windows, another man worked at a desk in an enclosed office in the back corner. He sat in plain view through the windows along the inner walls of his office. At the back wall was a door to a walk-in vault; it stood open, slightly.

Henry took a deposit slip from one of the pigeonholes on the table top and started writing; looking around as he did so, taking in the details of the setup. Satisfied with his surveillance, he started patting his coat and looking through the pockets. "Fiddlesticks!" he said aloud, started walking to the door. The woman at the other table looked up at him as he passed, and Henry touched the brim of his hat. "Mornin' ma'am," he said. She smiled and nodded. The little girl remained silent, looking at Henry like a forlorn owl. "Forgot something," Henry said to the guard as he approached the door, the man reached over and opened it for him. "I'll be right back," he added. The guard bobbed his head.

In the car, Henry gave his instructions. "So everyone knows what to do?" The three men nodded. "Okay, just stay calm and let me do all the talking. Wait two minutes after I go back inside before you come in."

Henry reentered the bank; looked at the guard, patted his side coat pocket. "Got what I need now," he said. Went to the table where the woman and little girl still stood. The woman glanced up at his approached. Henry offered her another smile, which she returned. Felt his dapper appearance impressed her. "Sure is foggy this morning,'" he said.

"Oh my, yes," she said.

"How you doing this morning, darlin'?" Henry asked the girl.

"Fine." He thought of little Lorrie that day back in Stroud.

Henry took another slip of paper from a pigeonhole and started writing on it. Every few seconds he glanced up to check the whereabouts of everyone in the bank. All remained pretty much in the same places as before. The woman finished her writing, picked up her things, grabbed the girl's hand, and went to stand in line. The Regulator clock on the wall next to the teller windows ticked unwaveringly in the relative quiet of the room. The only voice sound came from the near-whispered talk of the tellers. Feet shuffled on the wooden floor; someone coughed.

The bank doors crashed open, and in charged Lars and Jim. Lars swung to his left leveling a shotgun at the bank guard's nose, who looked back at him startled and afraid.

"This here's a hold-up!" Jim yelled. "Ever'body put your hands up!"

Gasps and exclamations exhaled in the room; the woman gave out a feeble shriek, pulled the child close to her. The man at the desk rose quickly, his chair screeching backward. The man in the office stood halfway, leaned sideways to get a better look out one of his office windows.

"Do it NOW!" Jim demanded. All complied. The man in the office came to his doorway, putting one hand on the doorframe, his jaw clenched.

Henry moved to the guard's side and removed his pistol. He told him to go over to where the customers stood along the wall, their hands raised high. Lars walked over to one side of the teller windows, now pointing his shotgun at them.

"Folks, you all need to just stay calm," Henry said in a relaxed and pleasant voice. "As long as you do everything we say, won't nobody get hurt.

"I'm Henry Starr." He paused to let that sink in a bit. Looked around at the faces to see if any expressions registered recognition. "For those of you who ain't heard of me, you'd best know I don't normally shoot nobody during the course of my hold-ups, unless I absolutely have to.

"Just take it easy and let us do what we come to do, we'll be out of here in no time."

He paused again to let his words take effect. Everyone looked stunned, yet willing to comply. Satisfied, Henry turned his attention to the two bank officers. "You two come on over here," he said motioning them in his direction with his free hand, pointing the guard's pistol with the other. The two men advanced.

"I know you fellers got some money bags back there," he said to the two tellers. "I want you to start filling them up with what you got and hand them to my men."

He turned to the two men now standing in front of him. "What's your name, mister?" he asked the man who'd come out of the office.

"Meyers."

"You some kind of big shot in this bank, Mister Meyers?"

"I'm the president."

"President? Hell, this ain't going to look good on your record then, is it?" Henry grinned. Meyers looked at him stone-faced.

"Well, while your boys over there are gathering up that money, why don't we go into your safe and have you get what's in there for us, too," Henry said.

Meyers and the other man looked at each other, turned to walk toward the walk-in safe. The door to it stood ajar about a foot.

Henry felt elated and on an adrenaline high. Things were going better than expected. He figured they'd be out of there speeding away in that big touring car in no more than five minutes. Good to be back doing what he did best, being at the top of his game. My luck's changing, Henry thought to himself.

Meyers' man grabbed the safe door and pulled it open, using his weight to swing it back so he was behind it, his back to the wall. Meyers entered the safe in front of Henry. The little girl was crying hysterically now, clinging to the woman, saying, "Mommy, mommy," so Henry thought he needed to give her and the hostages some more reassurance. He turned to speak to them.

"Honey, you don't need to worry about nothing, now. Won't be long and we—"

A gun blast roared from inside the safe, a sledge hammer blow hit Henry in the small of the back, knocking him skidding forward to his knees, slamming face-forward onto the wooden floor. The pistol flew from his hand clattering away. Henry tried to rise, but couldn't.

Lars and Jim, stunned by the sound, looked in the direction of the safe. The woman screamed and put her arms around the girl, crouching protectively. The others at the wall went immediately to the floor. The guard, his arm across the terrified woman's back, drug her and the child to the floor with him.

Meyers, standing in the safe entrance, levered another round into the firing chamber of the Winchester he held, and without hesitation fired at Lars. The round went wide, snapping between the heads of Lars and Jim, slapping into the wall behind them. Meyers levered another round.

Jim and Lars bolted out the bank door, flying down the few front steps as another shot rang out behind them, the bullet whanging off the doorframe. They dove into the backseat of the car.

"Get the hell outta here!" Jim yelled.

"Where's Henry?" E.D. asked.

"Just go, go! Git going!" Jim responded.

E.D. looked up at the bank door just as a man came out of it holding a rifle. He was trying to lever it, but was having trouble. E.D. revved the Buick's big engine and popped the clutch. The powerful touring car lurched, roared off down the street. They heard another gunshot, a slug popped through the back window and out the center of the windshield.

The Winchester's loading mechanism jammed again, and Meyers swore at it. He stood and watched the green touring car recede, careening across the Willow Street bridge. The robbers had gotten away, at least they didn't make off with any of the bank's funds. Well, one of them didn't get away. Meyers turned and went back into the bank.

Everyone but the woman with her child and the guard were crowded around the wounded gang leader sprawled on the floor.

The woman and the girl still sat on the floor, sobbing; the bank guard knelt beside them trying to give comfort. Meyers walked up to the circle of standing men, and parted them. "Is he dead?" he asked.

"Naw, he ain't dead yet. But I think his back's broke," one of the men said. "Looks like you shot him right in the backbone.

"John, go fetch Doc Lauder. Edgar, call the police," Meyers ordered. He knelt beside Henry, bringing his face close to the robber. Henry, his eyes open, breathed rapidly, sweat glistened his forehead and face.

Meyers began to speak softly to Henry. "Sorry I had to shoot you, Mister Starr, but I couldn't let you rob us. I keep this Winchester inside the safe in case the likes of you come along. Last bank I was in up in Illinois, a bunch uh guys like you busted in and robbed us. I was caught flat-footed. One of them shot my teller. Like you said, it looked bad on my record. Swore then I'd never let it happen again."

Henry tried to smile, speaking with effort. "Hell, it's okay, Meyers. I s'pose I been pretty lucky up 'til today." Henry coughed weakly and grimaced. "You reckon you've killed me?" he asked.

Meyers raised his head up, looked at the bullet hole in the back of Henry's coat where a red splotch of blood slowly spread. "I won't lie to ya, Starr. It don't look too good. You just take it easy. We got a doc coming," Meyers said.

The people in the room got quiet. The only sounds were the ticking of the Regulator clock, the continued sobs of the woman and little girl. After a bit Henry spoke again. "You know, I just bought this suit," he said. "One of the nicest suits I ever owned."

He lay quiet for a few seconds. Then he added, "Got married once in a suit just like this . . . long time ago. Colorado."

Meyers said nothing.

Henry spoke again. "If it ain't too tore up and the blood don't show, I'd like to be buried in this suit.

"You tell the undertaker that for me, Mister Meyers? He's a man named Morton in Tulsa. Abe Morton. You call him."

Meyers looked up at the men around him who all looked solemn and uncomfortable.

Henry coughed some more. "Will you?" he asked again.

"Sure, Mister Starr, I'll do that," Meyers said.

Epilogue

Abe Morton leafed through the newspaper, his habit every day, looking for the newly deceased. Opened the paper to the obituaries first, reading those, then backtracked toward the front pages, scanning the headlines. On page three, one headline caught his eye, along with the picture beside it. "Long Career as Outlaw Ended by Death; Shot in Arkansas Raid," it read. The photograph was a portrait of his old friend and client, Henry Starr.

The story went on to say that Henry had lingered for four days after receiving his wound in an attempted bank holdup, was attended at his death in a jail cell at the Boone County Sheriff's office by his young wife of one year, Hulda Starr; his seventeen-year-old son, Teddy; and his sister, Elizabeth.

The phone sitting on the desk in front of him rang. Morton picked up the receiver. "Morton's Funeral Parlor."

"Long distance calling for Mister Abe Morton," a tinny female voice said on the other end.

"This is Abe Morton."

"One moment, please," she said. After about a minute the operator returned. "I have your party on the line, sir. Please go ahead."

"Hello?" Abe said into the phone.

"Mister Morton, this is Sheriff Johnson in Boone County, Arkansas," a gruff man's voice responded.

"Yes, sir. Do you still have the remains of Henry Starr?"

"Why, yes, we do. He's in the county morgue. Before he died, he said he'd worked out his burial arrangements with you. Told us to call you. So this is all correct?"

"Yes, it is, Sheriff. Mister Starr prearranged his burial through our establishment. I'd like to arrange for the body's shipment back to Tulsa. Are his wife or sister still there in Harrison?"

"Yes, they are. I believe you can reach them at the Sturtevant Hotel."

* * *

They brought him back to Dewey, Oklahoma. His sister's wish, who lived there. Morton fixed him up good, even managed to dress him in the blue pinstripe suit Henry was so proud of. Morton had the suit cleaned as best he could, and arranged it on Henry so that none of the blood stains showed too much.

They set up the funeral service in a little church in Dewey, the one his old mother had attended on occasion before her death. The place was packed the day of the service, more by the curious than the mournful. There was a small organ at the front of the church, over near one wall, from which a large middle-aged woman warbled out a slow medley of hymns as the folks filed into the church. Some went up to the open casket to pay respects, shook their heads or wept a little.

Preacher James would give the eulogy, such as it was; comfort the survivors, offer a prayer. It would be brief. Miz Treacher, who sang in the church choir, would sing a couple hymns about "the sweet by and by" and "when we all get to heaven, what a day of rejoicing it will be." Then they would haul Henry out of there to the cemetery, and put him in the ground.

Most had been seated when the stately woman came in. Dressed in black from hat to shoe with a thick black veil obscuring her face, she walked up the center aisle of the church, stopped at the head of the casket. She stood there looking at Henry for a long time. Some thought they saw her shoulders quiver some, although no one could hear any weeping. She bent forward slightly, whispered something. Those in the first few pews later said they heard her, although no one could make out her words. Some of those same people said it appeared she placed something in with Henry. She had turned, walked back up the aisle and out the church door. No one recalled seeing her later at the cemetery.

As the last notes of Miz Treacher's final hymn died out in the rafters of the quiet church, Morton moved to the front of the congregated.

"This concludes the funeral service," he said solemnly.

The church cleared quickly. The few family members lingered a bit by Henry's remains, but none too long. Once alone with his assistant, Morton moved to close the coffin. He noticed it lying at the tip of Henry's left third finger—a diamond ring. Appeared to be the one Henry had given him many years prior and told him to deliver to a Missus Megan McGuinness of Nowata in the event of his death.

Morton reached in and slid the ring as far as it would go up onto the deceased's left ring finger, closed the casket lid on the outlaw Henry Starr; his earthly debts all paid in full.

A Personal Note from the Author

Thank you for taking time to read *Red Lands Outlaw* If you enjoyed it, please consider telling your friends or posting a short review on Amazon. Word of mouth is an author's best friend and much appreciated.

Would you consider being in my Readers Group? As a member you'll receive periodic emails from me (no spam) about new releases, promotions, giveaways, blog posts, etc. No more than about twice a month. I would love to have you in the group. Go to my website to sign-up and receive a free ebook: http://www.philtrumanink.com

Thanks again – Phil Truman

About the Author

Phil Truman is a native Oklahoman, born in the small town of Miami in the northeastern part of the state. A former teacher, coach, businessman, and Vietnam Era veteran, he and his wife have lived in the Tulsa suburban city of Broken Arrow for more than 30 years. Phil's website is at www.PhilTrumanInk.com. He can be contacted at Phil@PhilTrumanInk.com.

Other Novels by Phil Truman

West of the Dead Line, Tales of an Indian Territory Lawman

The Dead Line, as it came to be called, was a railroad, the Missouri, Kansas, and Texas, cutting across the middle of Indian Territory down through Cheyenne and Comanche and Kiowa lands. It was a line on the map, a demarcation. West of it there was no law, only outlaws. On trails out there, notes would be put up on trees and posts letting lawmen know they'd be killed if they continued their pursuits west of the Dead Line.

In the storied history of the American West, no place comes close to matching the dangers and mortality federal officers faced doing their jobs. Their courage, resolve, and dedication to duty were beyond reproach . . . for the most part. Those who survived became titans in the legends of the West, particularly one man called Bass Reeves. These stories are fiction, but the encounters this lawman faced, and The Dead Line, were not.

GAME: an American Novel

Year in and year out the football powerhouse Hert City Trojans import a ringer to fuel their championship charge, but their luck is about to change. In the small backwater town of Tsalagee, first-year coach Donny Doyle knows the only way he can fulfill his promise to unseat the Hert City juggernaut, is to beat them at their own *GAME*. But in his own recruit, the mammoth and powerful, yet troubled and ominous Leotis McKinley, Doyle finds more than he bargained for. Truman's character-rich novel *GAME* spins an energetic tale around the intensity of small-town high school football in America. And yet, amid the fast-paced drive of the story, lies an account of the human spirit struggling through adversity and finding victory. Readers of any age or gender will feel the triumph, honor, and glory that comes from the... *GAME*.

TREASURE KILLS: Legends of Tsalagee Book 1
Legends from a small town come in many forms. Near Tsalagee, Oklahoma a monster lurks and an infamous 19th Century outlaw's booty lays hidden. When two renegade bikers ride into town looking to find the Lost Treasure of Belle Starr, local legends Hayward Yost and Socrates Ninekiller suspect the ruffians' involvement in the murder of a local farmer; a man rumored to have knowledge of the lost treasure's location. . . and its curse. As events unfold, others in the community are drawn into the hunt – a Wiccan who moves to town to pursue her New Age lifestyle; her bumbling, socially inept boyfriend women can't seem to resist; a young Iraqi War veteran home to heal his physical and emotional wounds; and a mysterious creature known in Native American lore as a forest demon whom they call "Hill Man who screams at night." Mystery, romance, comedy, and adventure await in *Legends of Tsalagee.*

Made in the USA
Monee, IL
23 March 2020